INFLUENCE

First edition. June 1, 2020.

Written by Daniel Hurst

INFLUENCE

DANIEL HURST

www.danielhurstbooks.com

To mum and dad, the best influencers I could have asked for

Influence *(noun):* the capacity to have an effect on the character, development, or behaviour of someone or something

Bad-Influence *(noun)*: something or someone that teaches others to do wrong

PhoGlo Trending To Be Most Powerful Platform On The Planet

PhoGlo is the social media website taking the world by storm.

In just three years, *PhoGlo,* short for Photo Glow, has already become the online sharing platform of choice for almost a billion people who use the popular app each day to send photos to their followers, or 'glowers' as some in the community like to call them.

While it is still relatively early days for the company, it has already taken its place alongside more established social media platforms and is a big part of the 'Influencing' culture that exists online.

The most popular influencer on *PhoGlo* is currently Mason Manor, a thirty-year-old British woman who has 200 million followers and is paid to promote and advertise to her huge following on a daily basis.

But as the platform continues to grow at a rapid rate, there are several other influencers coming hot on her heels and with the influencing industry as a whole predicted to be worth over $50billion by 2025 you can be sure there will be many other people out there who are aspiring to be a *PhoGlo* phenomenon.

#GetYourOwnBeach

Ivy Lane

My finger hovers over the *Share* button - inches from the screen. But I'm having second thoughts. I know in these situations that it's best to trust my gut instinct. With that in mind, I retreat back through the post I was about to publish to my *PhoGlo* page and give it another pass.

The photo itself is perfect; I have no doubts about that. Then again, it's hard to go wrong with a photo of a beach in the Maldives.

White sand. Turquoise ocean. Deep blue sky. No one could fuck that up. But the photo is only the beginning. Without the filters, it's nothing. Just a mannequin in a shop window without any clothes on. It might still look pretty, but it isn't going to sell anything.

It's all about the filters. My current choice is Siesta, but I have a nagging feeling I should go with Clairvoyant. The former really highlights the glare of the sun on the water, but then the palm tree in the corner looks bomb with the latter.

It's all a question of what will draw the eye in more. I think the green is stronger. I think we have a winner.

As I make the necessary changes and internally breathe a sigh of relief that I didn't commit too soon to my previous choice I feel a gentle breeze brushing over me. I look up from the screen for a moment and see the lush foliage that surrounds my accommodation swaying hypnotically in the tropical wind. It really is beautiful here.

I instantly look back down at the screen. I need to get this post up.

The filter is set, but I spend a couple of moments in the Edit section, tweaking the Lighting, Colour, Heat and Shade. This is what I call 'working under the hood'. It's no good choosing the perfect filter if you haven't got the levels right beneath it. But like a highly skilled mechanic, my fingers know what to do almost before my brain has sent the instruction and within seconds, I have done the necessary.

The photo is banging. This could even be one of my best.

Of course, the colours of this little island in the Indian Ocean are so rich and true that I could potentially get away with not filtering the image at all. But then I would need to qualify it by writing #NoFilter underneath it, and I hate to do that.

One, it's pretentious and two, it always makes me think that if a person has gone to the effort of saying they haven't filtered it then maybe they actually have and are just trying to pretend they haven't.

Urgh. Cringe. Always use a filter. You'll only regret it if you don't.

Trust me.

I often think about the person that came up with the word 'filter'. Whoever it was surely had no idea the trouble they were going to cause in the future. They probably just thought the word would be used to describe a part of a machine or something a plumber would one day need to fix.

But it's used for something much more important than those things. It has become a key tool in how people display themselves to the world.

It has become *the* vital part of social media.

And it's no exaggeration to say it has become my life.

I copy and paste the caption and hashtags that I had prepared earlier, right before my change of heart had caused me to backtrack and lose it the first time. Now I'm almost ready. All that is left to do is share my location. But it's not as simple as hitting the 'Add Location' line. Oh no. It might work for you, but I won't get away with that.

I press 'Advanced Settings' and search for the hotel I'm currently a privileged guest of. I find the name easily and with them now tagged I'm finally ready to go.

My finger is once again poised over the *Share* button. Even though I know the post is ready, I still experience the familiar wave of anxiety that I always do at this point.

I have been known to spend over an hour at this stage in the past, questioning if I am really ready to go through with it or whether there is a better image to be taken or something more that I could do with the editing. I even threw up once before sharing a post although in my defence that one was a big deal.

But I push any lingering doubts firmly to the side now. My mind is made up. This is the post I will publish.

My thumb touches the *Share* button and just like that the message I have been working on physically and mentally for god knows how long is finally on its way to the mobile phones of my 1.3m followers.

I feel sick. But that's normal. You would too if you had that much power at your fingertips.

I quickly check the post is up and confirm the caption has come out as I intended it. Everything seems okay until...

OHMYGOD.

My heart almost leaps out of my chest when I think I spot a spelling mistake with one of my HashTags.

No wait. False alarm. I was seeing things. The spelling is fine. Thank god.

I take a deep breath and wait for the avalanche of affirmations to start rolling in. The comments will follow in good time, but we all know it's really just about how many people will press the little yellow Glow button to indicate that they are a fan of my post. That's what I will judge myself on and more importantly, what the people paying me will judge me on.

But I feel good about this one. You can never be too sure when it comes to social media, but this particular post has all the ingredients to be a big success.

The photo is the most important thing, and just as I suspected, my choice of filter has the beach I'm standing on looking A-MA-ZING.

My caption is on point, a perfect blend of personality and humour:

Waking up to this view. Not bad for a girl from Grimsby.

And the Hashtags are solid, every single one of them fulfilling their role and ensuring this post reaches its maximum audience.

#OceanView #Maldives #WinterSun #LovingLife #GirlDoneGood

But it's the single line above the image that is the driving force behind all of this and the reason I'm standing on this beach in the first place.

In Paid Partnership with OceanView Resorts.

It was annoying that we now had to say when we were explicitly advertising something, but those were the rules in this new age of social media influencing and let's face it; it's a small price to pay when you are literally getting free things.

I get free food, free clothes, free travel and free holidays, which is the reason I'm here in paradise today.

In exchange for all these freebies, I must use my extensive platform to promote these generous companies and hopefully encourage my followers to spend some of their hard-earned cash on purchasing these things I get for free, which boosts my client's profits and reinforces my status as a powerful influencer.

Getting paid to experience the finer things in life is the dream of many, and I am living proof that it is attainable. If a girl like me, from a humble council estate in Grimsby, can become a well-paid and well-travelled online celebrity, then there's no reason other people can't do it too.

And many others do.

Influencing is big business. It's competitive, it's stressful, it's a lot of work, but it is lucrative. And most of all, it's powerful. Companies are paying big money to have people like me send direct messages to the phones of millions of people instantly.

It's advertising on crack.

But what's the saying? *With great power comes great responsibility*.

For every good and genuine company out there, there are a dozen others who want to use you to send more unscrupulous messages. Where one man sees the chance to sell, another man sees the chance to brainwash. There can certainly be more sinister things advertised on your social media timeline than just holiday locations and designer dresses.

The tropical breeze blows stronger around me this time, and I'm reminded of what I had to do to get to this position.

And what I'm still expected to do to remain here.

Except I'm not going to do it. Not anymore. Now I'm only going to use my platform for good and not the things they want me to.

But just like the breeze that is swaying the palm trees on this idyllic island, things aren't always this smooth. One day a hurricane will barrel through here and snap those palm trees. It's happened before, and it will happen again.

Just like I'm not the first person to rise to fame and fortune by doing ungodly things to other people. Just because the public don't know about those things, it doesn't mean they didn't happen.

But I've decided I'm not going to do those things anymore. I can't change my past, but I can change my future. I have told the people that helped get me my platform that I am done working for them. From now on, I will go it alone, without their advice or instruction.

I just hope they respect my wishes...

#MondayBlues

Emily Bennett

Sometimes I wonder what life would be like if we all knew what the future had in store for us.

Like today, for instance. Here I am sitting on a crowded train, surrounded by glum faces all staring out at a sky that's as dark as the mood in here. Presumably, the only reason we all got out of bed this morning and boarded the 07:10 service that runs from Billericay to London Liverpool Street is because we believe somehow that better things are ahead for us all.

One day I won't have to do this anymore. One day I'll be rich. One day I'll be happy.

But what if we could see into our future and what if we saw that those things were never going to happen for us? Would we still be able to get out of bed and ride that train to the job we hate?

Maybe.

Or maybe it would just be anarchy.

With my daily bout of deep reflection and morbid thoughts over and done with for now, I go back to the other thing that passes the time on my commute. My mobile phone.

Thank god for phones. What the hell did people do on journeys like this before them?

Read the paper? How exciting. People watch? Meh. Talk to the stranger next to them? No thanks, especially not the stranger sitting next to me today. He looks like a cross between Donald Trump and that guy from *Tiger King*.

I use facial recognition to unlock my screen, and my finger instinctively finds the app for *PhoGlo.*

I know it's been less than five minutes since I last checked it, but as I said, I'm bored.

I see that I have new notifications and so that's the first thing I check on. I have two new followers which is cool until I see who they are.

Two dweeby looking teen boys, neither of them older than fifteen and neither of them in any way influential on this platform. They probably saw one of my bikini pics and just about managed to hit the *Follow* button amongst the tidal wave of hormones and desires surging through their bodies at that moment.

But it's another two to my total, which now makes that 4,732. It's good to have them on board. But I won't be following them back. And I definitely don't want to think about what they'll be doing the next time I upload a photo of myself in a figure-hugging dress.

Moving on, I see that my post from last night now has 381 likes. Not too shabby for a picture of a vegan burger without the bun. There's also a new comment from @play_er07 which is to be expected considering he's commented on every single photo that I've published since he began following me a couple of months ago.

That's a lot of comments. This particular one says **"mmmm looks tasty"** which would be fine if it wasn't the exact same comment that he left on my last selfie.

I like it to be kind. He's harmless, and we all need our fans. Even ones that call themselves play_er.

I do a quick once over of my profile page, just to make sure everything is in order which of course it is because why wouldn't it be? But best to make sure.

My current profile picture is one of me smiling on a boat during my holiday in Greece last year. My blonde hair looks great in the sun, and my face is tanned and clear. It's a far cry from what I look like right now but it's nothing a good filter can't sort out.

My bio description underneath the photo is short and clean:

Emily Bennett
Public Figure
Ahead of my time
London

I guess my names okay. I thought about changing it, or at least making one up to use online, but in the end, I decided it it's better to be authentic in the long run.

I also used to have my age, which is twenty-three, besides my name, but then I removed it. I might put it back in the future. I'm experimenting.

When you switch your *PhoGlo* account from a Personal one to a Business one, there are a number of different features you gain access to, and one of those is the ability to select your profession.

As an influencer, or wannabe influencer to be exact, the best one to use is Public Figure. There is no option to list your profession as Influencer. Not yet, anyway.

Okay, so strictly speaking describing myself as a public figure is a bit of a stretch. I'm not famous. Nobody on this train knows who I am, never mind anybody in places like America, Australia or Asia. But it's all about the perception. I also believe in the law of attraction, which states that if you want something, you first have to visualise it and imagine that you already have it.

Believe and achieve. I want to be a famous and successful social media influencer, and even though I'm not quite there yet, it doesn't mean I can't fake it until I make it.

I chose to write 'Ahead of my time' in my bio for two reasons. Firstly, it's bold and sassy and that's something every wannabe influencer must be. But it's also what my father used to say whenever he made one of his bad jokes.

You know the ones. They're called 'Dad jokes' because they're so bad. One of his favourite ones was:

"I slept like a log last night. I woke up in the fireplace."

Terrible, right? As everyone would be cringing and sarcastically laughing at his latest attempt at humour, he would give that cheeky smile of his and say, "I'm ahead of my time."

God, I miss that smile.

He was called Dave, and it's been eight months since he died. Bowel Cancer. He was only 51. When I eventually have the large platform I desire, I will use my fame and power to raise money for other sufferers of the disease. I might even be able to start my own charity. He'd be so proud of me. But he'd have been proud of me no matter what because he was great like that.

He was the best.

The last piece of information in my bio is my location. London, one of the greatest and most iconic cities in the world. Having that on there definitely elevates my account to the next level. And let's face it, it's way better than putting on where I actually live, which is a town called Billericay in Essex.

There's nothing particularly wrong with the town itself. It's a standard suburban hub surrounded by green fields and farms. But there are already a few popular influencers from Billericay, and they like to portray the place in a certain way. Let's call it the 'Essex' way.

You know, where the tans are so fake that they look like gravy stains and the nightclubs are so trashy you almost feel sticky just from looking at the photos.

I made the decision early on that I wanted a different tone for my profile and London fit the bill perfectly. It has connotations of elegance, prestige and class, as well as more modern ideals like wealth, power and excess.

It's important that my photos fit the description, and I ensure that they do. There are no photos of dark brown legs and bottles of Lambrini here. Just stunning shots of some of the capitals most famous landmarks mixed in with me drinking cocktails in high-end bars and clothes shopping in West End stores.

I love London, and I'm lucky I live so close to a city that can help me grow my brand. That's the goal, after all.

To grow.

The more followers you have, the more power you have, and with power comes influence. That's why people with large followings are known as 'influencers.'

One well-edited post of a certain product sent out to thousands or even millions of fans can boost sales exponentially. A photo of an influencer eating at a certain restaurant or wearing a certain handbag can expose it to massive numbers of potential customers.

But it's not just businesses or products that influencers can sell. They can sell something bigger. Something just as unattainable but nevertheless just as desirable.

They can sell a lifestyle.

The holidays. The parties. The celebrity friends. It might not seem like much but in a world where we all want the best for ourselves, seeing people who already seem to have it all is impossibly alluring. Not only that, it's aspirational. It's motivational. It's everything. And the best thing of all?

You can get paid to sell this lifestyle.

The train passes through Havering, a place where nobody aspires to be, and so I look back to the phone in my hand and at *PhoGlo*, in the search for a better view.

I find one quickly.

It's a picture-perfect scene straight out of a holiday brochure. The sand is white and pure. The ocean clear and true. And the sky, cloudless and comforting. It looks a million miles away from where I am right now, both literally and metaphorically.

The post belongs to Ivy Lane, a full-time influencer and one of my favourites to follow. I love her because she started out as a normal English girl with a big dream. I love her because like me she's from a small town, although hers is in the north while mine is in the south.

But most of all I love her because despite all the money, fame and success she has experienced since she made it big on *PhoGlo* she has never changed. She's still the funny, charming, down to earth person she was in her early posts.

It's no exaggeration to say she is my role model. I look up to her and aspire to be just like her. And there's no reason I can't be just like her. All it takes is a talent for selling 'the lifestyle'. And if you don't have it yet then remember the golden rule:

Fake it until you make it.

Which is exactly what I plan to do today.

I don't usually catch the early train into work, but I woke up at 4 am this morning with an idea for my next post, and if I'm going to make it happen, I need to be the first one in the office.

Yes, I'm tired, and yes, I really could have used the extra time in bed, but if I want to be like Ivy Lane one day, then I have to make sacrifices. I have to be willing to do anything.

Even something that could cause me to lose my job.

#StartYourDayRight

Ivy Lane

It's breakfast time and I'm hungry. I'd kill for a bacon sandwich right now. Preferably one smothered in brown sauce. But that wasn't on the menu, and it definitely isn't what's on the plate that was just delivered to my room by a smiling Maldivian man in a ghost-white uniform.

Instead of the bacon sandwich and the brown sauce I have a tiny portion of sliced avocado and red berries. Healthy? Yes. Well presented? Sure. But satisfying?

Hell no.

Of course, I knew this is what I would receive when I heard the knock on the door of my $3000/night room two minutes ago. After all, I was the one who ordered it. Still, that doesn't make it any less disappointing now it's actually here.

I ignore the rumbling in my stomach and resist the urge to devour what few calories are on the plate in front of me because I have a job to do first. I hold my phone above the plate and check the screen to see what the photo looks like. The food is so well presented that it would be almost impossible to make it look bad, but I'm not just looking for a good shot.

I need a great one.

I'm not keen on the bird's eye view photo of the breakfast, so I drop down to my knees to get a different perspective. Taking a photo from this angle allows for me to get something else in the background, and I initially think the view between my open terrace doors is an ideal one.

I could caption it #BreakfastWithAView or something like that.

But that wouldn't be very original and is no different to what all the thousands of wannabe influencers out there who are desperate to take my place would do. So I have no choice but to look around the swanky suite for further ideas.

I see the king size bed across the room, where I spent last night trying to sleep off the jet lag that came after an eleven-hour flight from the UK. As comfy as it was, it didn't really work. I struggled to sleep, a combination of too much caffeine on the journey and too much anxiety about the message I received just before take-off.

But I don't want to dwell on that now. Everything feels better in the sunlight, and I'm sure I'll sleep better this evening before I head back to the airport and board my flight to Dubai tomorrow morning.

Maybe I could put the plate on top of the duvet and come up with some caption about breakfast in bed. The green and red colours of the food might look great against the pure white duvet, but then again, the colour of the plate on the duvet would mean its white on white, and that is a serious no-no.

I dismiss the bed and seek inspiration elsewhere.

I see the door leading to the bathroom, which is a marble and gold-infused area where I experienced the best bath of my life last night before falling into bed. I do plan to take a photo in there before I leave to show off its decadence, but the bathroom isn't the most hygienic place to display my breakfast, so I dismiss that from my list of options too.

I could always go outside onto the terrace and capture a photo of my breakfast with the stunning view of the sea in the background. But that would be too similar to the post I put up earlier this morning on the beach.

Think Ivy, think.

I shake my head at my lack of imagination. I'm usually better than this. The jet lag must be worse than I thought. Or maybe it's the nagging anxiety that I haven't been able to shake recently, and made so much worse by that message I received before take-off...

I break off from my search for the perfect photo for a moment and go to the part of the *PhoGlo* app that displays my Direct Messages. Scrolling down through all the new ones I've recently received after my photo on the beach this morning, I eventually find the message that I'm looking for.

It's from Sebastian, and it was received at 10 am UK time, which was when I had been sitting in the first-class departures lounge at Leeds/Bradford Airport killing time before my flight took off.

Just reading it again gives me the same chills that went through me when I read it the first time.

This is your final warning. Failure to comply with the rules of our agreement will result in swift action.

If that message was read by an outsider, which is somebody with no prior knowledge of the agreement in place between me and the person who sent it, then it wouldn't seem too bad.

A little mysterious perhaps. Maybe a little ominous. They might even think it was a joke.

But I know exactly what it means, and it certainly isn't a joke. Surely they wouldn't kill me for failing to comply with their rules? I've done so much for them. I've made them profits. I've proved myself time and time again.

But now enough is enough. I know it's time to draw a line under this and move on if I am to stand on my own two feet. I don't need them anymore, and there are a million other girls out there just like me that they could use to do their dirty work.

Of course, I've told them this already, only a couple of hours before I received this message. Which means they have taken it about as well as I had expected.

But what can they really do to me? It's not as if they can call the police. I've got more on them than they have on me.

Hurt me? It's possible, but when and how?

Kill me?

I shiver as the thought crosses my mind. As ridiculous as it sounds, it's the same thought that kept me from sleeping on the plane all the way from England to this beautiful island in the middle of paradise. It's the same thought that kept me from drifting off in the most comfortable bed in the world when I landed here last night.

And it's the same thought that I cannot shake, no matter how much I try to distract myself with filters and edits and glances at the tropical paradise on the other side of my bedroom door.

Because as crazy as it sounds, I know it's possible. Why wouldn't they kill me? I know they've killed other people before. Hell, even I've killed someone before...

'Enough' I say and snap myself out of it. That train of thought doesn't lead to anywhere good.

I look down at the pathetic yet photogenic breakfast in front of me and will myself to get the right shot of it so I can eat what little of it there is and get outside in the sunshine, where everything seems a lot better, and my dark thoughts fade away into the background of my cluttered mind.

I notice the swan sitting on my bedside table, in the same place where I left it when I moved it off the bed after checking in last night. Of course, it isn't a real swan. It's one of those clever designs where the maid has turned the crisp white towel into a beautiful creature, and it's meant to impress the guest when they arrive and make them realise how lucky they are to be here.

To be fair, it worked. I love swans.

I walk across to the table and carefully pick up the linen bird before carrying it back to my breakfast and setting it down beside the plate, where with a little manipulation I am able to make it appear as if the swan is bowing its head towards my food in an attempt to gobble it up before I do.

Cute.

I take the photo, and it looks as good as I had anticipated, causing a small wave of relief to come over me. This is what I'm known for - my creativity. Even with the jet lag, and the hunger, and the worrying message on my phone, I'm glad that part of my brain is still working properly.

I race through the filters and edits and type in my caption:

Healthy breakfast with my new friend Mr Swan!

I quickly copy and paste the series of hashtags that I'd already prepared for this post beneath the caption, set my location and remember to tag my generous hosts then finally I'm ready to share it.

Done.

Without wasting another second, I set my phone down and devour the contents of the plate, which doesn't take long. The avocado had started to get mushy, and the berries had gone warm, so it didn't even taste that great. But it will do until the next meal.

Standing up from the table, I head to the suitcase lying on the floor in the corner of the suite. Barely a minute has passed since I posted that last update to my followers and my mind is already on the contents of my next one.

A shot of me in the sea in my bikini.

This one will be a paid advert for MyStyle, the high street retail chain who have kindly offered to clothe me during my trip this weekend in exchange for two posts promoting their latest summer swimwear line.

As I unzip the suitcase, I wonder for a moment what I would be doing if I was still an innocent and unrecognisable girl in Grimsby. But I already know the answer. I'd be trying to get the perfect shot because that's what I've been trying to do my whole life.

And it's what I'll probably be doing until I die.

#EarlyBirdCatchesTheWorm

Emily Bennett

I'm the first one here. I know that because all the lights are off inside and the whole building looks as gloomy and ominous as the sky above my head right now.

I swipe my temporary access card on the door panel and enter the office where I spend a nervous few seconds shuffling along in the dark until the automatic lights kick in and the corridor is suddenly so bright that I have to close my eyes for a moment.

As soon as they adjust, I get my bearings and head straight for the lift. Once there, I push the button and hear the clunk of machinery whirring into life above me.

A moment later and the doors slide open, allowing me to step into the small, mirrored space that will take me all the way up to the 14th floor. I press the relevant button on the display panel and the doors seamlessly close again. It's a good job I'm not claustrophobic because there isn't much space in here when I'm alone never mind crammed in with a load of other office workers.

I have been experimenting with taking the stairs lately in some kind of desperate bid to ensure I get my recommended 10,000 steps a day in, but I've quickly got bored of that plan, and the option of taking the lift has started to win again. Plus, I'm in a rush today, so I need to save as much time as I can.

Somebody else on my floor could turn up at any time and then my plan will be ruined.

It isn't long until the lift doors open again, and I step out onto familiar territory. I see the reception desk that I know so well and will spend most of the day sitting at, but for now, I have a bigger purpose, so I walk right past it and through the door that leads into the main office.

As I go, I can't help but shiver. It's absolutely freezing up here. The heating obviously isn't on yet. I'm not sure who is usually the first person here, but I assume whoever it is turns it on when they arrive in preparation for the day. All I know is that by the time I arrive at half past eight each morning, the office is warm and inviting.

But for now, it's even colder than it is outside.

Another swipe of my temporary access card has me inside the next door, and now I'm standing in the expansive open-plan office belonging to Taylor & Wright Lawyers. The only time I ever pass through here is to use the toilet or make myself a cup of tea in the staff kitchen and its usually quite intimidating to walk through when its full of loud, cocksure law professionals all jabbering into their phones and barking orders at their inferiors.

But being here so early means it's a different atmosphere. There's no noise. No movement.

No nothing.

I take a moment to observe the layout of the office. The rows of veneered desks that probably cost more than I make in a year. The high back leather chairs standing like watching sentries at each workstation. The flat black screens of the many computer monitors, currently in a restful state until they are activated and deployed to send emails, letters and reports.

And beyond it all, the floor to ceiling windows offering a truly breath-taking view of the city.

I wonder what it would be like to work beside that view every day. I doubt I'd get anything done for staring so much at the world going by outside. It's definitely a far cry compared to my view on the reception desk which is on the other side of the office and just means that all I get to see is the lift doors opening and closing and a white wall bearing the black lettering of the company name.

But of course, I don't get to enjoy the same view as my colleagues. They're all full-time high earning employees of one of the biggest law firms in London whilst I'm just the low paid temp they have hired to cover their usual receptionist's maternity leave.

There's a clear pecking order here. The more senior and valuable you are to the company the further along the floor you are seated, which is why I'm right by the lift, barely five yards from where everybody gets out. But the opposite end of the floor is where the Partners offices are located because that's where the best views are.

Of course, I've never been that far down before. I know my place, and I always stick to it.

Except today.

I hurry past the rows of empty desks in the direction of the prestigious offices and trigger each set of automatic lights as I go, leaving a trail of pale florescent lighting in my wake. The place is immaculate at this time, as yet undisturbed after the cleaners finished their shift at some ungodly hour in the middle of the night. Soon these surfaces will be a littered mess of coffee cups, sandwich wrappers and legal papers, but for now, they are pristine and clear.

I reach the end of the desks and turn the carpeted corner and the further I go along the natural curve of the building the more I can see of London as it begins to wake from its slumber.

I can see the mighty tower of The Shard, the bottom rising up from the rain-soaked streets and the top disappearing in a shroud of early morning mist. I can see the collection of tall office buildings across the river, seemingly huddling together in the freezing temperatures. The Gherkin is behind them all somewhere, once an iconic part of the skyline but now obscured by newer, bigger competitors. And I can see The Thames, looking as murky and fast flowing as always.

On a summer's day, this would be one of the best views in the world. But it's still impressive in winter, and my heart begins to beat a little faster at the prospect of what I am about to do.

I pass several large wooden doors that all bear the name of some important lawyer who works here until finally, I reach the door at the end. It's closed and, for a second, I worry that it means the occupier is inside and my plan is scuppered. But then I remember how early it is, and the fact that all the lights are off, and the heating is off, and I know that's there's nobody on the other side of that door yet.

But that still doesn't mean I'm not freaking out as I put my hand on the door handle and slowly turn it. I hold my breath as I push it open and pray my boss isn't waiting for me on the other side...

But the office is clear.

Phew.

But even though there's no other soul in here except for me the room is far from empty. Large mahogany bookcases run along the walls, all of them filled with perfectly aligned leather-bound books. There's a side table holding a glass bottle filled with some kind of brown liquid. Whisky perhaps. Two crystal glasses sit on white placemats beside it. Another table is used to display a cricket ball, which on closer inspection seems to contain the autographs of a team, though I'm not sure which one.

Then there is the centrepiece of the room which is undoubtedly the desk. Cut from an Amazonian tree and handcrafted by several highly skilled carpenters, it's sturdy yet sleek, curved, yet rigid, varnished yet natural. It probably sounds more like a car than a piece of furniture.

I only know so much about it because I've overheard the other lawyers talking about it in the kitchen. Someone said they believed it to be worth 50k. Another said it was closer to 80.

One thing's for sure. It's impressive.

And the view...

My god, the view.

I knew it would be good, but this is something else. The way the office is positioned it fits the curve of the building, meaning the more you walk around it, the more you can see. And I feel like I can see the whole of London from here.

There's the Wembley Arch in the North. The Crystal Palace Tower in the south. And everything in between. The tourist sights. The high-rise offices. The apartments by the Thames. The red buses and black cabs queuing on London Bridge. And the tiny, ant-sized pedestrians making their way along the wet pavements far below.

So this is what being the owner of a Law firm gets you.

I'm a million miles away from ever having an office like this myself. But that doesn't mean I can't pretend.

And that's exactly what I'm going to do now.

I get to work, aware that I'm racing against the clock and it's only a matter of time until the owner of this immaculate office enters the room. If I'm still here when they do, then I can kiss goodbye to my crappy receptionist job and my even crappier 20k a year.

If you think that sounds like a measly wage for the cost of living in the south of England, then you'd be right. It's not enough, which is why I'm stuck at my mum's house until I make it as an influencer.

I walk around the desk to the luxurious red leather office chair positioned behind it. This is the seat that you get to sit in when you've made it at the company. But because I'm the only one here, it's now the seat that I'm going to sit in.

I lower myself into the chair, feeling my body sinking into it and realise instantly that it's definitely as comfortable as it looks. I'm surprised the boss can get any work done sitting in this all day. It's so relaxing I could be asleep in minutes.

But there's no time for that. I take my phone out and open the camera. This is what I'm here for. A photo of me, in this chair, at this desk, with this view. My *PhoGlo* account is going to blow up when this hits it.

The way I'd imagined it would be for me to take a selfie of myself in the chair with the backdrop of London behind me but when I try that it doesn't look as good as I imagined. The back of the chair is too high and doesn't show enough of the city behind me.

I need a Plan B.

Think Emily, think.

I look down at the desk in front of me and try to figure out how I can make that the focal point. Then I have it.

I drag the plush chair around to the other side of the desk, so instead of the view being behind it, it's now in front. Then I put my feet up on the desk so that my long legs and black heels are resting on the beautiful mahogany surface with the amazing view of the capital in the background.

This is perfect.

I caption this photo ***Boss Life***.

#SwimmingWithTheFishes

Ivy Lane

The water is the perfect temperature. Just warm enough to swim in but just cool enough to give me some respite from the scorching heat of the midday sun.

It's times like this that my life seems like a dream. Here I am swimming in the ocean in front of my luxurious suite on the beach. It's hard to believe that I'm the same girl that used to sit on the wall overlooking the freezing cold seafront in Grimsby eating a 50p bag of chips and hoping for a miracle in life to take me somewhere better.

Now I've swapped the churning, windswept waves of the North Sea for the calm and tranquil waters of the Indian Ocean and I couldn't be happier about it. But it's not all fun and games. I still have work to do. It's time for another photo.

This one is going to be the trickiest of the day. This one makes me nervous. That's because I'm not the one taking it.

For my next *PhoGlo* post, I've entrusted the camera to one of the employees of the hotel I'm currently a guest of. He's a small and chubby man called Domingo, and he is the one who brought me breakfast this morning. He's a native of the Maldives, but he speaks perfect English, so he was able to understand when I asked him if he would be kind enough to take a photo of me in the sea. And when I say photo, I mean several.

I can only hope his camera skills are as good as his language skills.

I've tried to be as clear with my instructions as possible. He is to take as many photos of me as he can as soon as I give him the signal. That way, I will have plenty of options to choose from when I return to shore and have a look at what he captured.

I've waded out into the sea far enough for the water to be waist height and from my position, I can see Domingo standing on the beach in his crisp white hotel uniform holding my phone and waiting for me to give him a thumbs up.

I'm wearing the bikini that the guys at MyStyle have paid me to promote. It's a dark red strapless number, and I thank god that I doubled up on my Pilates classes before I agreed to model it because it's certainly revealing. I wouldn't have been seen dead in something like this a couple of years ago when I was all flabby and unfit, but now, with my firm abs and my toned bum, I can just about carry it off.

Especially from a distance, which is why Domingo isn't allowed to come any closer than he already is.

The plan is for me to completely submerge myself under the clear turquoise waters before suddenly erupting from the sea and tilting my head back quickly, which should cause my long hair to flail back behind me and create a spectacular arc of water over my head.

It's known as the Mermaid Hair Flick, and it looks as cool as it sounds. But it's not easy to pull off, and I know it's going to take a lot of attempts to get it right.

This idea isn't an original one. There's plenty of girls online that post the exact same photo whenever they are splashing around in the sea. The only reason I'm doing it too is because it looks so damn awesome.

I feel sorry for girls with short hair. They aren't able to get a shot like this.

I take a deep breath. I'm ready for my first attempt, so I look back at Domingo and give him the thumbs up.

It's game time.

I take a deep breath and submerge myself in the ocean. The water is refreshing as it hits my face and I know if I was to open my eyes right now then I'd probably see lots of crazy coloured fish and maybe even a sea turtle, but I keep them closed because me and saltwater don't mix well.

As soon as I know my hair is fully under, I push up off the sandy seabed and burst back above the surface, throwing my head back dramatically and feeling my wet hair flying above my head before slapping against my back.

Then I look over at Domingo and see the camera is obscuring his face. God knows what photos he managed to get. But the more you try, the luckier you get, so I give him another thumbs up and disappear beneath the water again.

I repeat this four times, but it's only when I'm preparing for the fifth and final time that I notice the figure standing at the other end of the beach, just visible amongst the trunks of the dozens of palm trees that line the strikingly white sand.

Unlike Domingo, this man is tall and well-built, and instead of a baggy white uniform, he is wearing a tight black muscle shirt and white chinos. Initially, I think he could be another guest at the hotel, but there's something about the way he is lurking amongst the trees and staring at me that makes me uncomfortable.

As I dip below the water again in preparation for my final attempt at the Mermaid Flick, I hope that the mysterious man will be gone by the time I reappear.

I erupt from the sea one last time and flick my head back hard. This time I actually see the rainbow of water that I've created all above me, and I hope Domingo was quick enough with the camera to get it.

But when I look back to the shore, I can't see any sign of Domingo. In fact, I can't see anybody. Not even the man in the trees.

I'm suddenly all alone.

'Domingo?' I call out.

But there's no response. The only sound is the breeze rustling the palm trees. But whereas before that noise was soothing to me, now it only seems ominous.

I look out to sea, and for the first time during my stay here I see the appearance of clouds on the horizon. But these aren't the wispy white clouds that you sometimes see on a hot summer's day. They are the foreboding, black clouds that tell you a storm is on the way.

I suddenly feel vulnerable standing here in this vast, and otherwise deserted ocean. I need to get back to land. I need to find Domingo.

Most of all I need to find my phone.

I walk back through the waves much quicker than how I had entered them only ten minutes earlier. When I had first stepped into the sea and felt how perfect the temperature was, I had felt like I could have swum in it all day.

But now, I can't wait to get out and the rumble of thunder in the distance only makes me go faster.

'Domingo?' I shout again as I get closer to the beach, but I already seem to know that he isn't going to answer my call.

Where could he have gone? Maybe he went back to the hotel? But surely he would have said something before he left?

I make it back to the beach, and it feels good to swap the sinking wet sand for the firmer, drier version under my feet. But having a stronger footing doesn't help me solve the mystery of where Domingo went.

I'm just about to call out for him a third time when I see it. Sticking out of the sand, the sunlight glinting off the screen, just a small distance away from where the waves are lapping at the shore.

My phone.

I rush towards it and scoop it up as quickly as I can, terrified about the damage the minuscule grains of sand could do to my expensive piece of technology. Shaking the phone hard, I blow on it several times, hoping that none of the beach went up inside the charging port.

But it must have done.

It was in the sand.

After several more frantic puffs of air and a load more shaking, I stop and inspect my phone. At first look, it seems okay. No scratches. Still working. But it's impossible to know what damage might appear in the future as a result of it being left in a hazardous location.

Only time will reveal that.

How dare Domingo do this with my phone. If he didn't want to take any more photos, he should have just said.

Is this the kind of service you should expect from a 5-star resort?

I'm furious. I'm going to speak to the manager. This is an expensive phone. Not only that, but it's my job. Without it, I'm nothing. No more photos. No more posts.

No more money.

I suddenly remember why I was even out here in the first place and go to check the photo album to see what images Domingo captured before he got bored and threw my phone on the floor. I'm expecting there to be nothing of use. His heart clearly wasn't in it.

But to my surprise, I see the photo album is full of photos of me in the sea, and many of them are good. More than good, in fact. Some of them are amazing.

I've smashed the Mermaid Hair Flick.

Go Ivy.

I feel relieved that this whole scenario wasn't a complete waste of time, but I'm still angry at Domingo for leaving my phone like he did and will definitely be speaking to the manager later. I should expect better than this considering how much exposure I'm giving their hotel this weekend.

With the dark clouds moving in quickly and the rumbling growing closer, I realise that an afternoon of sunbathing and swimming isn't going to happen now, so I'm just about to head back to my room and edit my next post when I notice it.

A marking in the sand, right in front of my suite.

It's a symbol. A circle with four dots in the middle.

I recognise it immediately. It's the logo of my employers. The people that got me to where I am today. But what is it doing here, in the middle of nowhere?

And why is it right outside my bedroom door?

I think of the message I received before I left England. The unknown man watching me from the trees. The mystery of Domingo suddenly vanishing. And now this.

I head back to my room as quickly as I can, but I'm not doing it to escape the raindrops that are starting to fall onto the sand all around me.

I'm doing it because I need to escape this island.

I need to get out of here.

And I need to go now.

Before it's too late.

#Screwed

Emily Bennett

God, this day is dragging. Monday mornings are always the slowest, but this must be some kind of record. I feel like I've been here days yet the clock on my computer screen tells me it's only 10:02. Seven hours to go, minus an hour for lunch.

Whoop-dee-do.

It doesn't help that I got into the office so early this morning. Usually, I'd be rushing to my desk with only seconds to spare at this time of the week, but of course, I'd been a lot more punctual today in my bid to get the perfect photo. But while that decision had added an extra hour onto my time in the office today, I have to say it was worth it.

The post has only been on my *PhoGlo* page for just over an hour, but it's already on track to be my most liked one yet.

1387 and counting.

It's a smash hit. A big success.

Maybe this influencing dream isn't quite so far away after all.

It confirms what I've been thinking for some time. I need to take more risks. Photos of me standing in front of famous landmarks aren't going to cut it anymore. I need to be at the top of the damn things, hanging off the edge, making it impossible not to look and like.

Okay so maybe not literally. I'm not planning on scaling The Shard any time soon. But I definitely need to up my game. My post today has proven it. People don't just respond to any old thing that they can see or do themselves.

They respond to things that they *aspire* to see or do themselves.

A photo of me with my feet up on an expensive desk, overlooking one of the best views in London is what they want. Because they can't do that. They can't get a view like that. Because they aren't the boss.

Technically neither am I, but online I can be whatever I want to be. And today I was the boss. And today I am bossing my social platform.

My follower count is growing exponentially, far quicker than it has grown before. Yes, I did well with my hashtag choices, but I know most of it is down to the picture.

It always comes down to the picture.

So now I know what I need to do. I need more posts like this one. Not necessarily me pretending to be a boss but something with that kind of power and prestige.

Something aspirational.

It's time to brainstorm.

I open up a new window on my computer screen and prepare to type. I should really be looking at my email inbox and the calendars of the lawyers that are expecting clients to meet them this morning, but this is more important.

I'm only a temp here after all. I know they'll ditch me as soon as the usual receptionist gets back from her maternity leave, so it doesn't really matter how hard that I work. I'm out of a job in three months whatever I do.

So I might as well do me.

My fingers move across the keyboard as I type out every idea I have for my future posts.

Michelin star restaurants. 5-star hotels. Boats. Private planes.

Okay so that last one might be a bit of a stretch, but I have to think big. That's what I did with my post today. Just because it wasn't my office, it didn't mean I couldn't pose like it was so just because I can't afford to eat at fancy restaurants or stay in swanky hotels it doesn't mean that I can't pretend I can.

I'm well aware that most of the influencers out there use deception and pretence to boost their following. Not everyone starts out with access to the finer things in life. You have to earn it. And in this world of social media, you earn it by posting a photo. It didn't matter whether you actually paid for the things in that photo or not.

You just have to look like you did.

I'm getting into it now, my fingers flying across the keys as more and more ideas come to me, each one crazier than the last. It's all going well until-

'Emily?'

I look up my screen to see Rebecca, a mousy haired girl the same age as me. I met her on the day I signed up to the recruitment agency that got me this job. We were sat next to each other in the waiting area before we were seen by one of the many recruiters and killed time by talking about the kinds of work we were looking for.

She'd told me she'd left university eighteen months earlier but struggled to find employment, even with her degree in business management. I'd felt a little sorry for her, even though that type of degree is about as useful these days as one you could have made up on a piece of paper yourself at home. Of course, I didn't say that at the time.

She had seemed like a nice girl, and I'd wished her well as I'd been called into my pre-assessment interview. But I hadn't seen her since that day. Until now, when she was standing right in front of my desk wearing a smart office dress and looking unsure about her whole reason for being here.

'Hi,' I eventually say. 'Rebecca wasn't it?'

'Yeah.'

She's nervous. Fidgeting. What is she here for? An interview? Perhaps that business management degree wasn't such a waste of time after all, not if it can get her in the door of a big fancy lawyer company like this one.

'Are you here for a job?' I ask her when it becomes clear she isn't going to say anything else.

'Yeah,' she says again but doesn't elaborate further. She's going to have to be more talkative than this in the interview if she wants to impress them.

'Who are you here to see?' I ask, switching from casual acquaintance mode to professional receptionist mode. I might as well do if she isn't going to be chatty.

''Erm...'

I look up from the call list of the company's employees and notice that she is struggling to maintain eye contact with me.

'Rebecca, there you are. Thank you for getting here so quickly.'

It's Margaret, the sixty-one-year-old office manager and the woman that showed me the ropes on my first day here. It makes sense that she would be the one that Rebecca needed to see. But I'm still not sure why she didn't just tell me that.

They shake hands and I smile, playing up to my role as the grinning dumb receptionist that places like this seem to enjoy. At least until Margaret leaves again and I can return to my bored, sleepy face persona instead.

But Margaret doesn't leave.

Instead, she turns to me and asks me to come with her.

'Okay,' I say, unsure why but happy to get away from this desk for a minute.

Maybe she wants me to show Rebecca where the kitchen is. Maybe make her a cup of tea. One of those tedious little jobs that she can't be bothered to do herself, especially when she can get me to do it instead.

But then she tells Rebecca to take the seat that I've just vacated and informs her that someone will be with her in a moment to show her the ropes and suddenly I see what is happening here.

Rebecca isn't just here for another job.

She's here for my job.

No wonder she couldn't look me in the eye properly. She feels sorry for me.

Because I'm being let go.

Margaret confirms as much after she has taken me to one of the empty meeting rooms and given me all the reasons they have come to their decision. Poor timekeeping skills. Too many toilet breaks. Too much internet browsing. Not enough reception work. Yadda yadda.

I stop listening after a couple of minutes and instead start worrying about how I'm going to get another job. This one didn't pay much, but it was something.

Now I've got nothing.

I'm going to have to go home and explain to my mum that I'm unemployed again. That I'm stuck living in my childhood bedroom for the foreseeable future. She'll make me a sandwich and tell me it's okay. But it's not. I have dreams. I don't want to live with my mum forever, no matter how nice she is and how many sandwiches she makes me. I want to be my own woman. I want to be able to afford my own damn sandwiches.

'Do you understand?' Margaret is asking me impatiently.

And so I nod even though I don't and then sign whatever they need me to sign and before I know it I'm shaking Margaret's limp hand and making my way to the lifts that will take me down to the ground floor. A quick ride down and then I'll be back outside into the harsh reality of being unemployed in one of the most expensive cities in the world.

I can't even buy a drink to cheer me up because the pubs around here aren't open yet. I guess I could just buy a can of Gin & Tonic for my train ride home.

Drinking alone on the train at mid-morning. The life of an unemployed bum.

Go me.

As I go, I pass reception and collect my possessions from under the desk where Rebecca sits awkwardly in my old chair beside me, not daring to speak. But I put a brave face on and wish her all the best in her new job. And I mean it. She's a nice girl, and it's a rubbish place to work.

Good luck.

As I walk away, Rebecca calls after me. 'There was something on the screen when I sat down. I'm not sure if you need it?'

She holds up a piece of paper, and I see that it's my wish list of future *PhoGlo* posts. The restaurants. The hotels. The private planes.

Oh god, she must have read it. She even printed it off for me.

How embarrassing.

It's evidence of me dreaming about living a millionaire lifestyle, and yet I can't even hold down a poorly paid receptionist's job.

I think about pretending it isn't mine, but it's too late for that. I thank her and take it, telling her it's something for my younger cousin's school project. It's a pathetic excuse, and she doesn't buy it for a second, but I had to try something. This whole situation is cringeworthy enough.

I press the button for the lift and stare at the closed doors, waiting impatiently for them to open and take me out of this situation.

By the time it arrives, I can hear someone explaining the switchboard system to Rebecca, and I step inside the small space and reach for the button for the lobby when I see Margaret suddenly appear in front of me, putting her hand across the doors so they can't close even if I want them to.

'And one more thing Emily. Putting your feet up on the boss's desk is an extremely disrespectful thing to do. I don't care how many *PhoGlo* followers you have.'

And with that, she takes her arm away, and the automatic lift doors slide shut.

Thanks for the send-off.

As I descend, I wonder how she knew about my post this morning. Did she follow me? Surely not. Then I remember I had logged in to my *PhoGlo* account once on the reception computer, just to see what my profile looked like on a desktop screen rather than on my small phone screen.

Maybe she checked my internet history. Maybe she found my page that way and had a look at my profile.

To the outside world, the office in my photo would have been unrecognisable. But to someone who worked in the company that the office was a part of, it would have been obvious.

Was that the real reason for my firing? Or was it just the final straw?

Whatever the reason, the result is the same.

No matter how many likes that photo gets me today, it isn't going to help me pay any of my bills now.

#TroubleInParadise

Ivy Lane

My bags are packed. I'm ready to leave this island.

Except I can't. The airport is closed. No flights in or out.

The storm outside is bad. "It's a big one," the man on the reception desk told me. Potentially catastrophic. I have to stay in my room until it blows over. Or until the hotel is blown over.

Whichever happens first.

So here I am, hunkered down from Mother Nature's angry behaviour outside. The wind is rattling the doors and windows of my suite, and I can hear the rain hammering against the roof.

The man wasn't kidding. This is a big one. But I don't have time for this.

I need to get out of here.

The message in the sand has spooked me. The fact it was there means they are here. And if I'm stuck in my room, then there's nothing to stop them from getting to me now.

After I'd retrieved my phone from the beach earlier, I'd gone straight to reception to demand to speak to the manager. I wanted to know why Domingo had just left my personal belonging so carelessly as he had. But I didn't get to see the manager.

Instead, I got to see Domingo.

He was walking through the reception area as I waited, wheeling luggage that belonged to a young couple who were smiling so much it looked like they were just beginning their honeymoon. I hadn't wanted to spoil their first day of wedded bliss, but I had needed answers from Domingo, so I had approached him as he stood by the lifts and demanded he explain to me what had happened.

But I almost wish I hadn't now. Because what he told me confirmed my worst fears.

They are here.

And they are coming for me.

Domingo had told me how just after I had gone back under the water for another one of my Mermaid Hair Flick attempts, he had been approached by a man who told him he was required urgently at reception and that he would give the phone back to me himself.

Apparently, he had told Domingo he was a guest at the hotel and knew me from the pool area and would be okay to look after it. Amazingly Domingo had taken his word for it and ran back to the reception area, only to find there was no issue but when he had tried to find the man again, he was nowhere to be seen.

Domingo had apologised and assured me he was going to call by my room later to check I got my phone back okay, but he had been too busy to get around to it yet. So I had asked him to describe the man that had spoken to him.

Black shirt. White chinos. Tall. Well built.

The man in the trees.

I'd mumbled something at Domingo and ran back to my room to start packing. Then I'd hauled my suitcase to reception and asked for a taxi straight to the airport. But the storm had stopped me getting any further and now here I was, taking refuge in my opulent suite that was being bombarded by the elements while that man was out there somewhere, biding his time, waiting to make his move.

I take a bottle of champagne from the mini-bar and pop the corkscrew. It's not a time to celebrate, but I need something to calm my nerves. At these prices, it's an expensive way to do it, but I don't care.

I can settle the bill later.

When I'm safe.

I feel the fizzy bubbles going down my throat and keep drinking until the first glass is gone. As I pour my second, I think about what the man could possibly be planning to do.

If he had wanted to get to me, he could have done it at any time. He could have done it at the beach instead of just leaving my phone lying on the sand. No, he had done that to give me a message. Just like the symbol on the beach that accompanied it. He was giving me another warning, one that went further than the one his employer had sent me just before I left England.

I felt slightly reassured by this as I drank half of my second glass. They're still at the warning stage. Yes, it's escalating slightly by sending someone to the hotel I'm staying at, but it's still just all warnings. I can live with that.

The problem is I don't know when the warnings will stop. Because they have to at some point.

They won't let me keep getting away with this forever.

I look at my phone lying on the bed across the room. Normally it's never far from my right hand but ever since this afternoon's events, I've been finding myself avoiding it.

My next post is overdue. My followers will be waiting. The companies paying me to promote their business will be waiting. But right now, social media is the last thing on my mind, because it's the thing that got me into this mess in the first place.

When we are young, we believe that we can achieve all our dreams with a lot of hard work and a little bit of luck. But when we get older, we realise that it's not as simple as that. Hard work doesn't guarantee anything. And luck is an elusive and terrifying mirage, fleeting in its appearance and just as likely to err on the side of the bad kind.

I learnt that the same way as everybody else. After setting the goal of becoming a famous actress, I was soon worn down by the years of regular rejections and the constant crushing of my dreams. But with the arrival of social media suddenly there was a new way to become a celebrity and become idolised by millions of adoring fans, and it didn't involve auditions or callbacks. It just required a good eye for a photo and the ability to grow your presence online.

I was one of the first people in the UK to set out to become an influencer. Back when I started, the whole concept was still new and apart from a few savvy celebs in America no one had really figured out how to turn posts on your page into money in your bank account.

But the potential was clear for anyone willing to work for it, and I'd done my best to jump on the gravy train before it took off. But there was only so much a girl in Grimsby could do to get some attention online and while my posts of food, fashion and North Sea sunsets were edited and hashtagged to within an inch of their lives, they couldn't compete with my rivals who were posting from more glamourous places like LA, Sydney or London.

There's no filter in the world that can make a beach in Grimsby look like one in the Bahamas.

And so with my follower count respectable but still a million miles away from what I needed it to be I'd resigned myself to the fact that this would be another one of my dreams to fall by the wayside.

Until the private message had arrived in the inbox of my *PhoGlo* account...

Hi! I see you have a strong following and we want to work with you! I represent a global marketing company that works with a number of popular influencers like yourself! If you are keen to grow your social media platform and monetize your brand further, please reply to this message for more details!

The message had been sent from a mysterious person called 'SS', and a quick look at their profile page didn't show a name or photo, though it had confirmed that they worked for some kind of marketing and media company, although it wasn't clear what the name of that company was either.

There was just a lot of generic captioned photos promising great results and higher profits as well as images of influencers that had supposedly used their services before.

While I hadn't recognised any of the influencers in the photos, it had been exciting to be chosen for this opportunity out of the many other wannabe social media stars just like me, and the way the message was worded had made it impossibly alluring.

We want to work with you! Popular Influencer like yourself! Grow your social media platform and monetize your brand!

Back then, I was by no means a popular influencer, but they were already treating me like one. They wanted to work with me. They wanted me to grow.

They wanted to monetize.

And so, of course, I had replied and asked for further details and the next message I received had given me a time and meeting place.

2 o'clock tomorrow afternoon in Leeds.

I guess it had been too much to expect this powerful figure from a global marketing company to come to Grimsby.

I also presumed I hadn't been the only person they had sent the message to and figured the meeting in the city was likely to be an open affair, with several wannabe influencers like me all vying for whatever service they could provide for us.

So the next day, I had made the two and a half-hour train journey from my hometown on the Lincolnshire coast to the Yorkshire city of Leeds. I'd been there once before with friends for a weekend but hadn't seen much of the place that time unless you counted the six pubs, two nightclubs and one kebab shop we visited and I'm not sure you should.

It had been a grey and drizzly day, and by the time I'd got off the train, I had begun to worry that the whole thing was going to be one big hoax. Or even just a mistake. That the message had been meant for somebody else, somebody that actually had a large following on social media and possessed the power they needed to sell their products instead of a girl from Grimsby whose last post had been in her bedroom as she attempted to give makeup tips to her measly amount of followers.

But when I had arrived at the café not only was there somebody waiting for me, but I was the only person they were meeting.

He was a well-groomed man, someone that clearly earned the kind of money that allowed him to wear the type of suit he had on. His blonde hair was slicked back, and he was tanned but not the orange kind of tan so many people in this part of the world get from the inside of a bottle. This was the deep brown tan that only comes after spending several weeks in an exotic location.

He spoke with an American accent as he introduced himself as Sebastian. Then he told me he liked my page. Said he saw the potential in me as an influencer. Wanted to accelerate my growth.

It was all so exciting. Not only what he was telling me but just him in general. His voice. His blue eyes. His passion for what he did. I hadn't met anyone like him before. Someone that had the same ambition as me. Someone that wanted to do more than just live and die in the same town they were born in without making any impact on the wider world.

I said yes before I even knew what I was saying yes to.

And even as things progressed, and the months went by, and I realised Sebastian and his company had darker motives for using people like me, I had still said yes. I had still done everything they had asked of me.

Everything.

Until I'd eventually learnt to say no. My conscience had finally caught up with me.

But only after they had given me everything I had ever wanted.

And after I'd already done some terrible things.

I look up at the roof, convinced that the rain is going to break through at any moment now. The storm is getting stronger. There's no way I'll be able to sleep through it, which might be a blessing.

At least if I stay awake, then I'll know if the man tries to get into my room.

I make my way over to the huge bed and fall onto the soft duvet. My phone lies beside me, but I don't pick it up. I just lie there with my eyes on the door. Waiting for the storm to pass. Waiting for the morning when everything will seem better.

Hoping that I'll still be alive long enough to see it.

#LoverNotAFighter

Emily Bennett

What a rubbish day. I'm glad it's over. Not that tomorrow will be any better. With no job to go to now all I have to look forward to is a slow day phoning recruiters and trying to avoid another argument with my mum.

She's mad at me for losing my job. I told her that they had just wanted a receptionist with more experience working with lawyers, but she didn't buy it. She knows something must have happened for them to let me go. She suspects I wasn't working as hard as I could have. She knows my heart wasn't in it.

And she is right, of course. My heart wasn't in it. Whose would be? Nobody dreams of being a receptionist.

But I can't say that to her. She already thinks I'm silly enough as it is wasting my time on social media, trying to turn it into my job. She doesn't understand that people can make money from posting photos and videos. Her generation never understands that. They still think the only way to make a living is working all day long in an office, shop or warehouse.

But there is another way.

There has to be another way.

I hate arguing with mum. We are usually so close. But neither of us are happy, so arguments are the natural result of two unhappy people sharing the same house together.

I'm unhappy about the fact I have no money, no dream job and no dad. She's unhappy that she has a small amount of money, a crappy job and no husband. As you can tell, it's not exactly laugh-a-minute in the Bennet household right now, which is why I've squirrelled myself away in my bedroom ever since the latest argument ended.

I'm lying on my bed, my mum's downstairs on the sofa, and neither of will say another word to each other until the morning, because both of us are stubborn, and both of us are hurting.

What a mess.

I should be job hunting, but instead, I'm on *PhoGlo* scrolling through the profile of Ivy Lane. I know envy is not an attractive emotion, but that's the one I have right now. I'm envious of her photos. Her follower count. Her life.

I want to be her.

I'd do anything to be her.

While I'm stuck in my childhood bedroom ten minutes from the hospital that I was born in, she's halfway across the world in the Maldives, getting paid to live a life of luxury. Her last photo was several hours ago and was an amazing image of her in the sea, flicking her hair back, and yes, she looks unreal. The post was a paid promotion for retail chain MyStyle, and the bikini she is wearing is a part of their newest range.

I wonder how much she got paid for that one post. Five thousand? Ten? Fifty? More? I don't know because I don't get paid to promote anything. I have a fraction of her followers. And I know I'm supposed to be all positive about it and believe in the law of attraction but the way I'm feeling right now, I just can't.

I'm doing everything she did. I'm posting regularly. I'm using the right hashtags. I'm liking and commenting on other people's posts to get their attention and show that I'm engaging in the online community.

So why aren't I getting the same results she did?

As tempting as it is to just keep throwing hard work at the problem, I'm concerned that hard work has nothing to do it. I'm worried that it's all about luck and nothing else.

Maybe Ivy is just one of the lucky ones. For every Ivy Lane, there must a million Emily Bennetts. Not everybody can make it. I know that. I just really thought I would be one of the fortunate ones.

But my follower count has actually fallen today. It's so disheartening. Especially after what I did this morning to try and increase my audience. The earlier than normal start. The risk I took sneaking into my boss's office. The fact I put my feet up on a desk that costs more than anything I'm ever likely to own myself.

All for nothing.

After an initial flurry of activity this morning, the likes and new followers have stopped coming. It's not uncommon to have people follow you then change their mind. People sometimes do it to get you to follow them, and when they see you haven't done so, they retract their name from your tally. So all the new followers I thought I was getting turned out to be an illusion.

They were probably just people like me. Trying to grow their profile. Vying for attention in an overcrowded market. Giving up when they saw they weren't getting any.

Maybe that's what I should do. Just give up. Delete my profile and uninstall the app. Get a 9-5. Be like everybody else.

Be realistic.

Tears swamp my eyes, and they blur my view of Ivy Lane's profile. Maybe if I could speak to her. Ask her for advice. Find out what she did to get so many followers. There has to be a trick to it. Something I'm missing. There must be a secret.

I could send her a message. It's an option. But what are the chances of her even reading it, let alone replying to it? She must get hundreds of messages a day. Girls like me begging for help in their own influencing careers. Others just saying how much they admire her. Then there's all the men that must contact her, telling her how fit she is and sending her photos of god knows what.

She doesn't need another loser in her inbox. She's too busy for that. I wonder where she will be going after the Maldives.

Miami? Hong Kong? Dubai?

I scroll down through her page and see all the photos she has posted over the past year. The cabana in Cancun. The sunbathing in Santorini. The rooftop restaurant in Rio. She is literally living the dream. Never spends more than a couple of days in one place. Never has to do anything she doesn't want to do.

Never has to sit in her childhood bedroom crying and wishing for someone else's life.

I put my phone down. It's not helping me to see other people's success right now. Either I make my own, or I quit.

It's one or the other.

And right now, I feel like quitting.

I pick up the piece of paper on my bedside table, the one Rebecca embarrassingly printed off for me just after she took my job away. It's the list of ambitious posts I had planned for my *PhoGlo* profile back when I thought I was going to crack the code and post my way to a million followers.

In my current state of mind, I can't even entertain the idea of having the confidence to pull any of them off. So I just throw the paper to the floor and roll over on my pillow.

It's only early evening, but I might as well go to sleep. I won't bother putting a goodnight post or story on my account. There's no point. I'm going to delete it in the morning anyway.

But then I remember that my alarm is still set for the ridiculously early time I got up this morning, and I grab my phone to turn it off.

As I do, I notice I have received a new private message on *PhoGlo* from somebody called 'SS'.

I open the app and take a look at the message, expecting it just to be some guy who's plucked up the courage to contact me after perving at one of my previous lingerie photos. I bet he doesn't realise that I got that lingerie in a half-price sale in Primark and the only reason my stomach looks so good is because I spent forty-two minutes editing the hell out of it.

But when I read the message, I see that this SS character isn't just some guy creeping on my profile. He works for a global marketing company and-

-OHMYGOD, he thinks I'm an influencer and wants to work with me!

I sit up straight on my bed, sleep suddenly the furthest thing from my mind.

I read the message through again to make sure I didn't imagine it.

Hi! I see you have a strong following and we want to work with you! I represent a global marketing company that works with a number of popular influencers like yourself! If you are keen to grow your social media platform and monetize your brand further, please reply to this message for more details!

This is amazing. This person wants me to reply if I am interested in what they have just sent me and of course I am because it sounds like exactly what I have been hoping for all this time.

I type out my response and send it back quickly before they have time to go looking for somebody else, and I miss my opportunity forever.

To my shock and delight, SS messages me straight back and tells me how glad they are that I'm interested and then asks would I be available to meet them in London tomorrow afternoon at a coffee shop on Borough High Street at two o'clock?

Hmmm, let me think about that one. I'm unemployed and have nowhere to go but downstairs to

get another snack from the fridge. I think I'm free to meet you.

I message back to confirm, and then they reply and tell me the appointment is arranged and then I just stare at the message for what must be ten minutes before I finally close it and lie back down on my bed.

I was so close to giving up. I was going to delete my social media platforms and tell my mum that I was going to grow up. But now my dream is still alive. Now I'm closer to being an influencer than I have ever been before. Maybe that vital piece of good luck that is needed in all stories of success has finally come my way.

There's no way I'm getting any sleep tonight.

I'm too excited for tomorrow.

I'm too excited to meet SS.

#TheMorningAfter

Domingo Manik

For someone that has lived in this part of the world their whole life, I never seem to get used to the storms. The ferocity of the wind. The incessant rumbling of the thunder. And the damage they always leave behind.

Last night's storm was a big one, the biggest one in at least two years I'd say. But I'll leave it to the guys at the weather bureau to confirm that. I'm just a modest hotel bellboy after all.

But I can tell from the walk that I've just made around the premises of my employers that it was a big one. Leaves from the many giant palm trees around the grounds lie untidily on the floor. The pool area is littered with debris. There's even a couple of broken windows in the restaurant.

Today is going to be a busy day at the hotel if we are to restore it to the standards expected of its Five Star rating as quickly as possible. Right now, it doesn't look like the kind of place you would want to pay thousands of dollars a night to stay at.

Right now, it looks like a bomb has gone off.

But the storm has cleared, and the blue skies that make this part of the world so popular with tourists have returned, and in a few hours, the guests here won't even be able to tell that a hellish weather system passed through at all. But before the clean-up operation begins, my colleagues and I need to check that those same guests are okay.

I have been assigned to the Palm Suites, the most expensive and decadent suites we have on our site. Rooms in this part of the hotel start from $3000 a night and go all the way up to $15000. Spending that kind of money always seem crazy to me, but I guess people that are willing to do so are the reason I'm in a job, so I can't complain.

I reach the first suite and knock twice on the door. The structure of the building looks intact, and I'm sure the people inside are fine, but it's good customer service to check. The door is answered by a tired-looking man in his fifties with a sunburnt face and a distinct lack of clothing on his lower body, so after quickly confirming he and his wife are fine, I move on to the next suite.

Four more knocks on suite doors are answered, and all occupants are accounted for, so I'm feeling relaxed about my first job of the day.

Until I reach the last suite on the $3000/night block.

I knock three times, but there's no answer. I know a young woman is staying here and so I knock again. But there's still no response.

I doublecheck the guest list that the manager handed to us all ten minutes earlier and see that the woman in this suite is called Ivy Lane. But I already knew that because I've had a couple of conversations with Miss Lane since she checked in to the hotel two nights earlier.

She's a pleasant woman, if a little demanding. I like to help our guests as much as I can during their stays. Carrying their bags. Helping them book excursions. Even applying a little sunscreen on them by the pool if they so wish. But Miss Lane had her own particular set of requests.

She wanted me to take photos of her.

But not just one or two on the beach like most of the other guests ask for. She wanted me to stand there and take multiple pictures while she dipped herself in the sea and jumped out again, flicking her hair back. She said something about Mermaids, but I didn't understand what she meant. As far as I know, Mermaids are the mythical creatures made up of half woman, half fish and from what I could tell about Miss Lane, she didn't have gills or a tail.

But I'm in the business of hospitality, so I had been hospitable to her requests and taken several photos of her pretending to be a Mermaid or whatever it was she was actually doing in the sea.

But I'd also spoken to her a short while after that when she had accosted me in the reception area and demanded to know why I had left her phone lying on the beach unattended. Of course, I would never have done such a thing and had simply explained to her that I had been called away to reception on a hotel matter and left her phone with a fellow guest and supposed friend of hers.

Though it had transpired that the friend was in fact not who he said he was and so I could only apologise profusely for my error of judgement in leaving one of her possessions with him. I'd restrained from going on to stay that while it was my job to ensure the guests had a pleasant stay in the hotel, it wasn't my job to spend half an hour taking photos of them while they splashed around in the sea.

Since that last conversation I hadn't seen Miss Lane but then the storm had moved in shortly after that and I hadn't seen much of anyone as we had all quickly bunkered down in our living quarters and battened down the hatches to wait for the fearsome weather to pass.

But before I had gone back to my room, I had tried to find the man that had pretended to be a friend of hers only to have no luck in locating him again anywhere on the premises. I had described his appearance to the security guards and told them to contact me if they saw him, but I hadn't heard anything since. Apparently, they hadn't seen any man in a black shirt and white chinos. But then again only a madman would have gone outside last night in that storm.

I knock for a fifth time on Miss Lane's door, but there's still no answer, and I wonder if she has gone down to the beach for an early morning swim. It's still a little chilly, but I know from my experience in tourism hospitality that English people will do anything to get a bit of sun and so it's possible that she is already out and about and soaking up the rays as the clouds have cleared overhead.

I put a cross next to her name on the register and plan to circle back here again later this morning, but as I go to walk away, I remember how concerned she was yesterday when I told her about the man at the beach. So instead of leaving, I turn back to her door and try the handle.

It opens easily. Her door was unlocked. Maybe she is in after all. Or perhaps she is on the beach and accidentally left it open. Either way, I've entered her room now, so I might as well find out which one it is. After all, it's one less guest on my list if I find her.

I call out to Miss Lane as I walk into the suite but get no response. From my position by the doorway, I can see half of the expansive room, but there is no sign of the English woman. Just the large wooden wardrobe with both doors closed and the table littered with makeup accessories and stray items of clothing.

I feel bad going any further in case I surprise Miss Lane and catch her in a state of undress, so I remain by the door and call out to her two more times. But there's still no answer, so I'm definitely about to leave this time when I notice the red droplets on the floor.

There's three of them. At first, I think it could be makeup, but then again it could also be blood, so I step further inside to investigate.

As I round the interior wall and catch sight of the rest of the suite, I freeze and cover my mouth in horror.

A young woman lies on the bed, her body still, and her eyes wide open, staring lifelessly at the ceiling. Both her wrists are slashed, and there's blood all over the usually pure white bed linen.

It seems that although the storm has passed, things won't be getting back to normal here any time soon.

This 5-star resort in the middle of paradise has lost one of its guests.

Ivy Lane is dead.

#RIP

Emily Bennett

I slept better than I expected considering today is potentially going to be one of the biggest days of my life.

My phone screen tells me it's 09:07 and I'm surprised my mum didn't want me up before she left for work this morning. I'm grateful she let me sleep in but also worried it means she's still mad at me. I guess I won't know for sure until I see her tonight when she finishes her shift at the supermarket but hopefully by then I'll have some good news to tell her that will kill off any ill feelings she still has towards me.

I'm going to meet SS today, and according to their messages and a quick look at their profile page, they are someone that is going to help me move one step closer to my goal of being a popular influencer. I know mum just wants the best for me and worries that I'll waste my potential chasing a dead-end dream, but once she sees that I'm attracting interest from powerful companies that specialise in social media marketing, then I know she'll support me and stop insisting that I get a 'normal' job.

She might even buy champagne.

I hold my phone in front of my face, and the facial recognition setting allows it to unlock. Some mornings I'm so hungover that it doesn't recognise me, but today I'm well-rested, so it is only too happy to let me in.

Thanks Apple.

I ignore the 31 unread WhatsApp messages from my friends and go as I always do to the *PhoGlo* app, needing my fix of beautifully edited photos by beautifully talented influencers before I can face the more routine aspects of my life.

But instead of colourful sunsets and highly filtered selfies, I see several photos of sad faces, motivational quotes and phone numbers for mental health helplines, all accompanied by respectful captions expressing their shock at the news and offering their condolences to the family and friends of Ivy Lane.

What has happened? Is it Suicide Awareness Day? Why is everybody telling everyone to look out for each other?

And why is everyone praying for Ivy Lane?

I go to her profile to see if I can find out more. But her last post was the mermaid hair flick photo from yesterday.

But then I see it.

The first three comments underneath the amazing photo, all saying variations on the same thing and all written by some of the most popular and famous influencers online

I can't believe this. RIP Ivy!

Oh my god my beautiful girl! Say it isn't so!

RIP you amazing woman! I miss you already!

Wait, what? Ivy Lane is dead? What the hell happened?

Like most things in life, Google will give me the answers, and a quick search throws up multiple news articles containing the grim facts.

Popular Influencer takes her own life in paradise

The body of *PhoGlo* star Ivy Lane, 28, was discovered today in a suite owned by OceanView Resorts, an exclusive 5-star hotel in the Maldives.

Ivy, from Grimsby, England, was staying as a guest of the hotel in exchange for documenting her stay to her vast following on *PhoGlo,* the social media platform particularly popular with young adults.

A professional influencer, Ivy had amassed over a million followers on her account, and her death has sent shockwaves through the online community. It is believed she took her own life.

"I can't believe it, I had no idea she was struggling" said Tiffany Rose, a successful influencer and one-time rival of Ivy, who had since become good friends with the late star. "It just shows that no matter how perfect we can make our lives look online, nobody ever really knows what somebody is going through privately." She finished by urging anybody struggling with mental health issues to seek help and vowed to host a fundraiser to raise money for Suicide Prevention Hotlines.

The manager of OceanView Resorts has declined to comment at this stage, but it is believed several staff at the hotel are being offered counselling to help them cope with the gruesome discovery on their premises this morning.

The concept of an influencer is a relatively new phenomenon and involves somebody with a large following using their platform to 'influence' the spending habits of their audience by promoting particular brands or products. It is believed the industry as a whole is currently worth over $8billion and *PhoGlo* is at the epicentre of its rise.

However, this type of work has had its controversies. In 2018 it was ruled any such posts had to explicitly state they were advertisements and the 'paid partnerships' feature was added to make this clear to users. Amongst the critics of this trend is UK politician David Reynolds who believes the concept of social media figures advertising to audiences, many of whom are of a young age, should be banned.

"It's one thing to let the corporations advertise on these platforms as we all know quite clearly when a brand is pushing a particular product" David said in an interview in 2019. "But putting that advertising in the hands of these 'celebrity influencers' is a much more dangerous game. Young people, like my daughter, for instance, are so impressionable they will often do whatever their favourite celebrity is doing without any concept that they are being sold to. The corporations are well aware of that and are simply exploiting it."

Ivy herself had gone from relative obscurity to social media superstardom in just two years, and it is believed she was one of the highest-paid influencers on *PhoGlo* at the time of her death.

Ivy's mother is currently on route to the Maldives and has asked for privacy at this time.

Ivy Lane 1992 - 2020

This can't be for real.

Ivy Lane is dead.

She killed herself.

That doesn't make any sense. She had everything. She was living her best life. She loved her family and friends too much. There's no way she would have ended it all.

But then I'm aware that everything I know about Ivy Lane has been viewed through the prism of social media and just like the rest of her 1.3M followers I only ever got to see what she wanted me to see.

People don't put their bad experiences online; they put their best ones. You could be having the worst day in the world, but if you upload a photo of a great view then that two-second snapshot of your day represents the entirety of it to a stranger. I know that as well as anyone. There's time I've posted a smiling selfie to my page only to be crying as soon as I've put my phone away.

But still, this is shocking news. A suicide always stuns more than any other form of death because you feel like it was preventable. No one can save somebody from an accident if the injuries are too severe. No number of good wishes in the world can cure an incurable disease. But when someone takes their own life, you always feel like it was avoidable if only the person had opened up to someone about how low they felt.

Maybe Ivy had confessed to dark thoughts. But if so, she would have done so to her closest family and friends, not her followers on a social media website.

I scroll down through her photos as I have done so many times in the past, but none of them offer any clue as to what their owner was apparently thinking about doing. Not even the captions she posted contain anything that could be construed as someone who was battling their inner demons.

Just sunsets and selfies, which when placed alongside this awful news, suddenly feel so pointless.

I'm supposed to be getting ready for my meeting with SS, but right now my single-minded goal of trying to become an influencer seems hollow.

If Ivy had reached the top of the mountain and it still wasn't enough to make her happy, then what hope is there for me?

But she was a hero of mine. Seeing her success was one of my main reasons for wanting to do this myself. Just because she's gone, it doesn't mean that is no longer the case.

She might be dead, but she lives on in the people she inspired while she was alive.

I add my comment beneath her last post, along with the other 117,000 other comments already on there.

This is heart breaking. You inspired me and so many other people to reach for the stars. RIP Ivy xx

Then I put my phone down. It's too upsetting to read any more. I feel so bad for her mum flying out to the Maldives to bring her daughter home. Like me, she had also lost her father a few years ago. Now there's more misery for the family.

Life isn't fair. It's not fair that a young woman in the prime of her life was taken away by mental health problems. It's not fair that a mum has to bury her child. And it's not fair that like me, Ivy had her father taken from her before his time.

But then my mind drifts back to the meeting I'm supposed to attend at two o'clock this afternoon. Just like life can be cruel, it can also be kind. And the message I got last night from the mysterious SS asking to meet me was one of the kinder events in my recent life.

I force myself out of bed and head to the bathroom for a shower. I'm going to the meeting today, and I'm going to give it everything I've got.

It's what I want to do.

And it's what my deceased hero would have wanted too.

#UpInTheAir

Colt Miller

The ice clinks in the glass on my tray table as the cabin shudders slightly. Just mild turbulence. Enough to make some people grip their armrest tightly and say silent prayers. But not me. When you fly as much as I do, it takes a lot more than a bit of turbulence to get your heart rate up.

I pick up the neat whiskey that the redheaded air stewardess served me a moment ago and take a long gulp. It's refreshing, and I've earnt it.

It's a toast to a job well done.

The employees of the hotel where the body was discovered believe it was suicide. The media around the world believe it was suicide. And most importantly, the local police on the island believe it was suicide.

I achieved the task I was given by my employer. Five years after they hired me and I'm yet to let them down.

I return my beverage to the tray table and look out of my window at the startlingly blue sea below. We're currently 36,000ft in the sky yet it looks closer than that. I can even make out a ship forging its way through the Indian Ocean, a flurry of disturbed water trailing in its wake. Sometimes I wish I could stay up here.

Life sure is simpler at this altitude.

There's no Wi-Fi, which means there's no internet, which means it's just the way I like it. No tweeting or hashtagging or liking or commenting or trolling. Just peace and quiet. Or actual conversations done face to face rather than through a phone screen.

For someone who hates the online world so much, it's ironic that I work for an online marketing company. But my job doesn't involve computer screens, keyboards and passwords. My work takes place in the shadows of the real world and uses simpler, more time-tested tools.

Mainly knives.

I leave the networking to the experts in that field. I have my own speciality, and I stick to it. But that doesn't mean my work lacks the glamour of my colleagues. In the past twelve months, I've visited some of the most exotic locations on the planet. Monaco. Acapulco. Bora Bora. Jamaica. Japan. Fiji.

If I had a *PhoGlo* page, I'd never run out of photo opportunities to share with my followers. But I don't. Not many serial killers do. A post of a dead body probably wouldn't get many likes. Or judging by the state of the world these days maybe it would.

But I stay offline in both my personal and professional life. Discretion is the name of my game, and there's nothing at all discreet about social media.

My time in the Maldives went to plan, even with the obstacle of a category four storm threatening to level the island during my stay. After I'd touched down two days ago, I made my way to the room my employer had booked for me in a modest three-star hotel nowhere near the beachfront five-star facilities that so many people who visit that part of the world opt to stay in.

The person picking my accommodation knows that it's best that I don't stay anywhere that could draw unwarranted attention. A single man checking into high-end accommodation might be asked a few questions that a single man checking into mid-range lodgings wouldn't.

Questions like; What brings you to the island? What do you do for work? What's your real name? And the only questions I want to be asked came from my boss or my bartender. Did you complete your task? Did it look like suicide? Would you like another round?

After a day spent mainly sleeping off my jet lag, I received word that the written warning to the subject had been ignored. She was in the Maldives, and she was still ignoring the wishes of my employers, which coincidentally were also her employers. That meant it was time for the next stage.

The physical warning.

After a poor night's sleep which was mainly down to the lack of a quality air conditioning system in my hotel I made my way across the island to the kind of hotel where the air conditioning is so cool and constant that it's almost like a gentle breeze soothing you after a day in the sun.

Almost.

Once there, I obtained a visual on the subject and observed her performing some rather inane activity in the sea while a hapless hotel employee took photos of her on her phone. I watched from the trees, but I made sure to stand just far enough forward for her to notice me in between her dips into the ocean.

As she looked at me, I had remained still and gave nothing away with my expression. I wanted her to know that I wasn't just a passing tourist who was enjoying a sneaky peak at a younger woman while my wife was back at the room. I wanted her to recognise that I was a threat to her.

I was the voice at the back of her mind that told her she really should stop ignoring the warnings.

I hadn't planned on leaving the markings in the sand until later, but I was feeling creative, and so while the subject was under the water, I had relieved the poor bellboy of his camera duties and taken the phone for myself.

Leaving it on the sand served two purposes. One, it would unnerve her and keep the written warning she had received the night before at the forefront of her mind. And two, I knew the sight of her expensive device buried in the destructive grains would piss her off and if there's one thing in life I like to do it's piss off people that are addicted to expensive devices.

By the time she resurfaced from the sea and looked back at where her camera should have been pointing at her, I was gone. But not before leaving my employer's company logo on the sand in front of her suite.

The second warning was in place, and then all I had needed to do was wait.

It can go either way at that point. Either the influencer heeds the physical warning and falls back in line. Or they persist with ignoring what's best for them and make me leave my hotel room once darkness has fallen and pay them a real visit.

This subject had done the latter, which is why she is no longer breathing.

There are a number of ways a person can commit suicide. Hanging. Overdose. Severing an artery or two. And there are a number of ways a person can fake the appearance of a suicide, simply by making it look like one of those aforementioned things took place.

For Ivy Lane, I opted for the artery method. It had been a while since I'd used my knife and there was also the fact that I'd forgotten to pack my rope which ruled out the hanging option. The overdose was the cleanest and easiest way, but that also made it the most boring way, so out came my trusty blade.

Access to her room was easy, considering the suite was made from bamboo wood and straw. It was a miracle no one had ever been burnt alive staying in such a hazardous fire environment, but that was for the hotel manager to avoid, not me. I had found the subject asleep on the bed and while I had delayed my work for a few more minutes just to try and let the buzz build in my brain I eventually mounted her, covered her mouth and held her to the bed as I slashed my weapon across her thin and slightly sunburnt wrists.

The blood poured from her as easily as the likes used to roll in on her *PhoGlo* posts, or so I'm told, and within minutes she was dead.

After ensuring Miss Lane's suicide would look obvious to whoever entered the room after me, I had accessed her phone by holding it in front of her face.

God bless facial recognition technology. Not that cracking her pin code would have taken me much time but still, small victories.

Once in, I had deleted the warning message that my boss had sent to her twenty-four hours earlier and a quick check through her other recent messages confirmed that she hadn't forwarded it on to anyone else. Not that it would be too much of a problem if she had. The account it had been sent from had been deleted well before I had entered her room.

With everything taken care of, I had left the blood-stained suite and gone back to get some shuteye in my humble yet fluid free hotel room. It was a textbook job, and it would have been the perfect night if only I hadn't got so drenched in the storm making my way there and back. But it was just a minor annoyance on what had otherwise been a very pleasurable and productive evening in paradise.

I drain the last of my beverage and raise my empty glass to get the attention of the stewardess. She's surprisingly attentive considering we're in Economy class and she doesn't have to work as hard as her colleagues in First. But I appreciate her speed and my second drink is on my tray table in good time.

Travelling in this manner is just another example of how important it is that I blend in. Nobody cares what a person flying economy does for work. The less people that ask me questions, the less I have to lie to them.

I look around at some of my fellow passengers and see all of them are glued to some kind of electronic device. Playing games. Watching movies. Killing time until they can get a Wi-Fi connection again. But I just look out of my window and think about my next job. The next influencer I have to keep in line. Maybe this one will heed the warnings and fall back in line with what is expected of them.

Or maybe they won't.

It's always more fun for me when it's the latter.

#CaffeineConfidence

Emily Bennett

I'm early. I want to make a good first impression. After all, it's not every day that I get invited to meet with a representative of a global company that has the power to make all my dreams come true.

I'm well dressed for the occasion, wearing a black pencil dress with a high neck and a killer pair of heels. It's professional with a touch of sexiness. I don't know what SS will be like and don't want to risk losing any favour I already have by coming off as too casual, or worse, slutty.

But I also don't want them to think that I'm dour and would be better placed on reception, so I've gone for the type of look that could work in both an office and a high-end bar.

I hope I've got the balance just right.

I'm sitting in the corner by the window of a coffee shop near London Bridge waiting for SS to arrive. It's still ten minutes until our meeting time, but my eyes remain on the door for any sign of them. Not that I know what they look like. I don't even know if it's a man or a woman that I'm meeting today.

If it's a male, then I imagine a balding middle-aged guy in a generic suit who will talk fast and in all sorts of riddles about the power of growth and sales figures. Or if it's a female, I picture a power-dressed, caffeine riddled woman who acts like she's got more balls than any of the males in here. Because that's been my impression of most of the people that work in marketing. But really, I have no idea what they will look like and how many balls they may have.

I need to stop thinking about balls.

Lying in bed last night I had done a full sweep of the mysterious SS profile page on *PhoGlo* but there was no sign of any actual photos of them amongst all the motivational quotes and impressive marketing conversion rate figures.

Finding nothing there I had clicked the link in the bio that took me to a company website although it was just as vague. There was a lot of stylish fonts and clinically coloured pages but not much substance and no tangible information like an address or a contact number and most bizarrely of all, no company name. The only thing I could see was the company logo, which was a circle with four dots in the middle.

Nor was there a list of clients they had worked with in the past anywhere on the site, just like there was no 'Meet Our Team' page that might have showed a photo of SS alongside the other employees of this supposed global corporation.

I had felt the first pangs of doubt about the legitimacy of the message I had received and with no name other than SS to put to this mysterious figure, I couldn't even look for them on other social media channels, in an attempt to put a face to the name that way.

Then I had had the idea of messaging a couple of influencers and seeing if they knew who SS was. After all, their message had claimed that they had worked with a number of them. But in the end, I had resisted the urge, aware that the chances of me messaging the one influencer that had met SS amongst the sea of influencers that hadn't was small.

What's more, the chances of any of them even replying to me, just an obscure wannabe, were even smaller.

The only way I would be able to know what SS looked like and what they were really about was to come to this coffee shop today and meet them, which is what I had done. But it was now two o'clock and there was no sign of SS.

Every man or woman that had entered the shop since I had been here, had either bought their coffee and left or taken it to a table that wasn't mine. If SS had arrived, then they would have seen me and approached me because they knew my face from my *PhoGlo* page.

So the only conclusion was that they weren't here yet.

They were late.

Of course, I would sit here and wait until they arrived. It's not as if I had anything else to do. Well, apart from actual job hunting but screw that. Besides, this is supposedly an interview, so I am technically job hunting now.

They would probably be here at any moment now. They would apologise for being late and explain that they had just come from a meeting across the city and the traffic had been a nightmare.

That's just what busy people did. They rushed from one meeting to the next. This meeting for them is likely to be just one of dozens in their busy calendar today, even if for me it's the one and only thing separating me from lying in bed at home scrolling mindlessly through job seeker websites and watching reruns of some reality show I've already seen.

But I mustn't let them know that. I can't afford to come across as desperate. If SS thinks that I'm already well on my way to becoming a mega successful influencer, then that is the image I have to project when they arrive.

But for now, I can be myself, which means fiddling nervously with the collar on my dress and checking my hair and makeup in the selfie mode on my phone's camera. As soon as they get here, then I'll transform into a confident, powerful goddess.

I'll wow them. I'll dazzle them. I'll-

'Hi Emily.'

I look to my left at the man who has been sitting at the table nearest to mine and working on his laptop ever since I arrived. He's mid-thirties, with slicked back blonde hair and the bluest eyes I've ever seen. So blue, in fact, that I could swim in them for days, but that doesn't matter right now.

Except it does, because I'm just staring at them open-mouthed.

'Sorry if I surprised you. I just had a couple of emails to send, and I really needed to get them off before our meeting.'

I'm still staring. But finally, the part of the brain responsible for speech kicks back into life, and I say;

'Sebastian?'

He smiles and nods before holding out his hand for me to shake, bridging the gap between our two tables.

I shake it quickly and notice how brown the skin on his hand is. And on his face. He's so tanned. I wonder if it's a full-body tan.

But I shouldn't be imaging that.

'Nice to meet you,' he says in his American accent.

I don't know the regional dialects in the United States well enough to figure out which part of the vast country he is from, but wherever it is I want to go there. His voice sounds soothing yet sharp, casual, but clipped. Completely different to my Essex accent, which I find myself trying to dial down as he moves across from his table into the seat opposite me and asks me to tell him about myself.

As I speak, he is still, holding eye contact and absorbing every word I say. It's a sharp contrast to the men I'm used to speaking too. Guys my age are terrible listeners, and no matter what you tell them they just seem to grunt back their responses as they continue to play their video games. My last boyfriend couldn't even take his eyes away from the TV screen as I spoke to him, which is one of the many reasons why he is now my ex.

But Sebastian is listening to me, r*eally listening,* and I find myself telling him much more than I had planned on doing.

About all my hopes and dreams. About losing my last job because I was spending too much time working on my *PhoGlo* profile. And about how I am willing to do anything to make it as an influencer.

I'm talking without a filter right now, and the restrained, powerful image I was originally planning on projecting has made way for a blabbering, mega honest version of myself.

But I can tell by the smile on his face that this is exactly the side of me that he wanted to see.

I can tell by the attention he is giving me this interview is going extremely well indeed.

Most importantly of all, I can tell that he likes me.

#MrChangeYourLife

Sebastian Sawyer

Another fish takes the bait. They always bite. I'm yet to find one that doesn't.

My meeting with the latest in a long line of wannabe influencers has just finished, and like every single one that came before her, she couldn't say yes to my plans quick enough. Nobody ever refuses the opportunity to change their life for the better, which makes this part of my job easy. The other parts of the job are trickier, but so far there hasn't been a single obstacle that my colleagues and I have failed to overcome.

And Emily Bennett is unlikely to fall into the category of unsurmountable obstacles.

She is desperate for fame and glory and is driven by a desire to escape her boring life and break out into the world to be a success in her own right, and holds the belief that if only she could have all those things, then it would make up for any deficiencies or pain in her past.

In other words, she's exactly the type of person we're looking for.

But I knew this before I met her. You can learn everything you want to know about someone by spending a little time browsing their social media profiles. In Emily's case it was on *PhoGlo* that I learnt everything I needed to know about her.

Her first appearance on the platform on December 22, 2018 which was a photo of her chicken salad and a caption 'Carbs are the enemy'.

How enlightening.

The eight posts that followed it, which were a combination of poorly filtered sunsets and plain awful mirror photos that showed her awkwardness both in front of and behind the camera.

The post on March 11, 2018 of her smiling face and the caption saying, 'The hard work starts now', which seemed to be the time she went all-in on her influencing dream and started posting more regularly.

The motivational quote she uploaded a month after that saying, "Don't tell people your dreams, show them."

The June 2018 image of her and two friends staring out across the sea in Greece while on a girl's holiday and reminding her followers to surround themselves with people that lifted them up. This was also the time she started hashtagging all her posts with #FromBillericayToBeyond

The 'Family Is Everything' Quote Image she posted in August 2018 in which the caption revealed how heartbroken she was that her father had been diagnosed with cancer.

The photo in November 2018 of her in a hospital bed beside her gaunt father saying that he was the bravest person she had ever known and that they would beat cancer together as a family.

The photo she uploaded on May 17, 2019 of her father holding her as a baby above the caption that thanked him for being the best dad ever and ended with RIP xxx.

The emotional and drunken video she uploaded on New Year's Eve 2019 when she said that despite everything bad that had happened to her over the last twelve months, she was sure 2020 was going to be her best year yet.

The sad face selfie she posted on January 9, 2020 that said she had never felt so lost.

The makeup tips. The full body mirror photos. The heavily filtered panoramas of London. The famous quotes written across pink backgrounds in heavily stylized fonts. The selfies.

So many selfies.

All her hopes and dreams, darkest fears and happiest memories, splashed all over the internet for anyone to see. The small but slowly growing follower count. The increasing Likes count matching the increasing frequency of her posts. The complete transparency of everything she did.

The sheer desperation of it all.

There were millions of accounts just like hers online, all of them seeking attention and believing that the next post would be the one that got them discovered and changed their life forever.

All of them featuring basic makeup advice in the hopes that an international cosmetic brand would see their latest post and offer them a fortune to promote their newest product.

All of them copying and pasting the same inspirational quotes that they pulled from a quick internet search two minutes before they posted them.

All of them hashtagging in their favourite celebrities on the off chance that one of them might actually notice them and pluck them out of obscurity by featuring them in one of their Stories.

There are a million Emily Bennetts out there, but right now she is feeling unique. Right now, she would do anything I say. Right now, she is putty in my hand.

All of which will make it easier when it comes time to tell her what I want her to do.

But first I have to give her what I promised her. More followers. Once she sees the numbers going up, then she will believe in my magic. She'll think it's a combination of my marketing skills and her 'accessible, girl next door type personality'. Of course, it won't be either of those things, but she can believe what she wants to.

She isn't ready for the truth yet anyway. Very few people are. They think millions of dollars and millions of followers just fall into your lap if you edit your photos a little better and 'network' your way through the online community. That's like believing you can run faster than Usain Bolt if you just train a little longer than him, or you can sing like Beyoncé if you just keep up with the lessons for another year or two.

The truth is the game is rigged. But most people don't know that, so they think their success is down to them. That's okay because it makes what I do much easier.

Right now, Emily Bennett is thinking that all her years of hard work and positive thinking have finally paid off. In reality, I just needed a new influencer to replace the one I just lost.

And by lost, I mean ordered to be killed.

Ivy Lane had gone off course. Sure, she had accepted my offer of help when she was a nobody two years ago, and she had accepted all the riches that came her way when I made her a somebody. But then she stopped listening and wanted to go it alone. That was never the agreement, so now she is dead.

Now it's up to Emily Bennett to ensure she doesn't end up the same way.

#HellYeah

Emily Bennett

Things are looking up. It's been a rubbish couple of years, but I stayed positive and kept at it, and now all my hard work is finally starting to pay off.

The meeting with Sebastian was a success. He seemed to like me, even with all the waffling I did, which meant he hadn't been able to get a word in for the first ten minutes of the meeting. I'll admit I came across as a little over-eager, despite my original plan of playing it cool and letting him do all the selling to me.

But I couldn't help myself. There was something about him that made me open up. He had an easy-going personality and seemed happy to listen to my life story. It made a change from the conversations I have had recently, which have mainly involved taking orders from a team of arrogant lawyers or arguments with my mum.

Then there was the fact that it was great to talk to someone that treated my goal of becoming a successful influencer like an adult instead of instantly dismissing it and telling me to grow up. Family, friends, work colleagues, they all either humoured me or shot me down when I told them my grand plans for a better life.

But Sebastian had listened and nodded and told me there was no reason that I couldn't do any of the things I wanted to do. He had made it sound so easy, which of course I knew it wasn't, but the fact that he was treating my goals like a set of actionable steps instead of the ramblings of a mad person made me feel better than I had in a long time.

As I look out of the train window on my way back to Billericay, I think about the first step he laid out for me in his company's master plan to turn me into one of the biggest influencers on *PhoGlo*. They wanted me to send a post out tonight to my followers. Nothing too flashy or gimmicky. No desperate 'buy this' plea to drum up sales. Just a simple photo which they would provide and a simple caption beneath it.

This, Sebastian explained, would prove to them that I could follow their instructions and would give them the confidence to trust me when it came to uploading the posts that their clients had paid to have displayed to as wide an audience as possible.

I wasn't being paid for this first post, but I would be for the ones that followed, and while I didn't know exactly what kind of things I would be promoting yet, I hadn't really cared when Sebastian had told me what I would be paid in return for my work.

£2,000 per post.

I had almost fallen off my chair and onto the floor of the coffee shop when he had given me the figures.

Two thousand pounds!

It used to take me about five weeks to make that much money working as a receptionist, and now I was being told I could make that same amount just by putting something on my *PhoGlo* page, which was something that I did every day for free anyway.

So I gave Sebastian my bank details before he could change his mind.

It sounded too good to be true, but I knew it wasn't. Not really. This was the job. Payment per posts. Lots of people in the world already had a job like this, and many of them got paid a lot more than £2000 for their work. Those at the top of the influencing ladder could bring in six figures per post. It's estimated that the top social media influencers in the world make half a million dollars with every post they upload to their page, just to promote a product or company to their vast army of followers.

But after I had got my breath back and avoided spilling my coffee all over Sebastian, I had become concerned about how he expected me to give his clients the kind of return on investment that they undoubtedly were looking for.

After all, I only had 4,382 followers.

I imagined the other influencers he employed had followings in the hundreds of thousands, and maybe even millions. My tally looked pathetic in comparison to those kinds of numbers.

Ivy Lane I am most certainly not.

But he had reassured me that my follower count was just right for what they wanted me to promote and he had told me how different clients had different budgets and that at this current time my follower count was perfect for filling a role that had recently opened up for them. Then he had given me the second most exciting piece of information, to go along with the staggering wage he was offering me.

He told me how I could expect to see my follower count climb up all the way to a million over the next year.

One million followers.

I'd spent the last three years doing everything possible to scratch and claw my way to 4k followers and now here was somebody telling me that they were going to grow my following faster and higher than I had ever thought possible.

Doing my best to remain calm in the coffee shop, I had asked him how he planned to do this, and it turned out that the answer was a simple one.

He was going to give me a set of hashtags that I was to use, and they were ones which he said would expose my posts to the widest possible audience. They were hashtags that had been decided on by a team of maths boffins who had devised algorithms to know which ones were the most powerful to use.

It all sounded a little confusing, and even Sebastian admitted to not fully understanding how the team had come up with the equations, but he said that wasn't important. All that mattered was that I used the hashtags in each post, and the algorithms would do the rest.

So that was the job. Post what they told me to post, including the magical hashtags that a team of apparent rocket scientists had come up with then sit back and watch the money roll in.

I'd said yes to all this, of course, and it was only on the seventh yes that Sebastian had stopped laughing and offered me his hand to shake before telling me he had enjoyed the meeting and that he would be in touch.

Then he had stood up, dropped his laptop into a trendy carry case and swaggered out of the coffee shop and left me sitting alone at the table staring open-mouthed at him and everything he had just said to me.

I couldn't wait to get home and tell my mum about the meeting. I wondered how she would take the news. It was obviously positive information that I would be giving her, but I still felt a knot of anxiety in my stomach about her reaction to it all.

Our last interaction had been a screaming match in which she had accused me of being immature, selfish and of throwing my life away on a silly dream. In return, I had told her that she didn't understand me, that she wasn't as supportive as dad had been and finally, that I hated her and couldn't wait to get out of her house.

I'd felt guilty about what I'd said as soon as the words had left my mouth, especially the part about dad being more supportive than her. I shouldn't have said that. Bringing him up in an argument wasn't fair, and besides the fact that it reminded both of us that he was still gone, it wasn't taking into account the different personalities that my parents possessed.

Dad had always been more like me. Creative. Passionate. A daydreamer. Mum was the opposite. Pragmatic. Level-headed. Realistic. I had often wondered what having a brother or sister would have done to the dynamic of the house. Maybe my sibling would have taken more after my mum and made it two v two, balancing out the house. Instead, it had just been me as an only child, which meant I always clashed with my mum and took my dad's side on everything because he was the one that I resembled more.

But he had taken me aside several times as a child and told me that just because I disagreed with mum, it shouldn't mean that we don't love each other. And I knew he was right. Of course, he was. My mum loved me just as much as he did. And I loved her too. Whether or not you are a dreamer or a realist doesn't change the fact that you are parent and child and both of you share what should be an unbreakable bond from the moment you come into the world.

I vow to myself that before I tell my mum about my new job tonight, I will apologise for everything that I said yesterday and then I will give her the biggest hug I can.

Because she's my mum after all and I love her.

Even if she does drive me mad.

#MumKnowsBest

Liz Bennett

I'm dreading going home. It hasn't been the same comforting place that it used to be ever since my husband died. His death has left a massive hole in the family, and it will never be filled. I thought I could do it, but it's clear now that I can't.

It's not supposed to be like this. A family unit should consist of two parents, not one. That way, it allows each one to balance out the strengths and weaknesses of the other. I was good at the cooking. Dave handled the DIY tasks. I would get Emily up and ready for school in the mornings because he couldn't function properly before 8 am. He would tuck her into bed and read her a story at night because I was exhausted in the evenings. He helped with her English homework. I helped with her Maths.

He encouraged her and allowed her imagination to soar to great heights. I encouraged her but ensured she kept her feet on the ground. He played the good cop to my bad one. And that was okay because that is how it works. You can't have two good cops, or your child will have no discipline. You can't have two bad cops, or your child will grow up miserable and hate both their parents. So you split the roles.

A team. Strengths and weaknesses.

Balance.

Now that was gone. There was no balance anymore. Just me trying to do everything at the same time and failing miserably at most of it. Even the things I was good at have suffered because I'm so tired from doing all the other stuff. I barely cook a nutritious meal anymore. Beans on toast is usually as good as it gets these days. Dragging myself out of bed every morning is getting harder and by the time I do get to bed, I'm lying awake for hours, just utterly aware of the gaping space beside me.

And Emily. *Poor Emily*. I know she's hurting just as much as I am about Dave not being here anymore. She's so young. Just starting to make her way in the world. Full of life and ambitions. She needs her father here to bounce ideas off of, another creative mind in the house to dream big with. She needs him here to walk her down the aisle when she gets married one day.

And most of all she needs him here just to give her a hug and tell her everything is going to be alright.

Emily and I used to be as close as a mother and daughter should be, but now I feel the space between us growing. She's twenty-three and still no nearer to picking a career and progressing in it. No boyfriend to settle down with. No place of her own. I don't care about those things if she doesn't, but I know she does and that's what upsets me the most.

She lost her latest temp job yesterday, and we argued. I know she hated it, but I tried to make her see that most people hate their jobs, though it doesn't mean they can just slack off to the point where they get replaced.

That's not how the real world works.

I hate my job. I didn't grow up planning to work as a store assistant in a supermarket. But bills need to be paid, so you take whatever job will help you pay them.

The truth is I gave up on my career in finance to raise Emily while Dave carried on working in his construction career. By the time she was old enough to go to school and I had more time on my hands, I had fallen too far behind in my accounting courses to get a job and even if I had wanted to retrain it was costly and time-consuming. But it wasn't a problem because we had Dave's wage.

I'm not the first parent to give up their career to focus on raising a young child, and I won't be the last. I was happy to do it. Instead of money, I was paid in long days playing with Emily when she was young. That's something money can't buy. But now she's an adult and Dave is gone and all that I'm left with are things that only money can buy and pay for.

Water bills. Heating bills. Food bills. Car payments. Replacing the broken TV in the lounge. Replacing the broken tap in the kitchen. All outgoings and I pay for them all. Me. No one else. And all in the knowledge that I would pay every penny I had just to replace the one thing that I can't.

The presence of my husband and Emily's father back in our home.

Now I've finished work, and I've got to go back to the deteriorating house and make myself another crappy meal and probably have another argument with my daughter before crawling into bed and crying myself to sleep. I don't want to do it anymore. But I don't have a choice. Because Emily still needs me. And I will never let my daughter down, no matter how much we fight.

I just hope she's had some luck on the job front today. A phone call from a recruiter maybe, offering her a new position. Somewhere she can develop. Grow. Build a career. Something stable. Something better than what I do.

Something more realistic than being an influencer on bloody PhoGlo.

It's a silly dream that's she's held on to for too long now. I know she thinks it's a proper job posting photos online all day, but I've told her it's only a proper job if you get paid for it and so far she hasn't made a penny from it.

Social media is just for fun, for keeping in contact with friends, for an escape from the real world. Not something that you hide inside of so that you don't have to go out into the real world and earn a living.

Of course, I've told her this many times before. It's the main reason we argue. She accuses me of not supporting her. I tell her that's not true, but it's impossible to make the transition from bad cop to good cop after playing the first part so well for so many years.

I just want her to be a happy, healthy, normal twenty-three-year-old woman. All her friends are working in steady jobs, moving out to their own places, finding a nice partner to spend their nights with. I don't see why she doesn't want those things too.

Life is short. I know that better than anyone. Dave and I should have grown old together. Enjoyed our hard-earned retirement together. Passed away old and grey in a retirement home somewhere together, surrounded by Emily and her husband and their children.

But Dave had been taken too soon, and none of us left know when it's our time to be taken too. So we have to make the most of the time we do have. That's all I want Emily to do. Make the most of her life. Enjoy it. Live it.

Take regular holidays and see the world. Buy a place and make it her own. Be financially free, so she doesn't have to struggle like I do. But to do all those things you need money, and that's something she doesn't have because she spends all day on her social media apps chasing something that isn't real.

I don't care how often she tells me about other influencers that are earning millions of pounds a year and are getting paid to stay in fancy hotels and wear expensive jewellery, because the fact is that it is other people doing that.

Not her.

Just because some woman in America is getting paid a million pounds to model the latest pair of shoes, it doesn't mean Emily is. I know it's important to have idols, but I try to explain to her that for every one person that makes it, there's a million that don't. That's just the harsh reality of life. There isn't room for everybody to achieve their dreams. We can't all be pop stars, or footballers, or influencers. Only a very select few get to do those things. The rest of us have to stack the shelves in the supermarkets so those lucky people can eat, or fix their cars so they can drive them around, or build the mansions so that they can live in them.

I try to make her see that having a normal job doesn't mean you don't have ambition. It means you are being a responsible adult and paying your way in the world. I just hope that she finally listens to me one day.

For both our sakes.

#HardWorkPays

Emily Bennett

I'm so excited. In two minutes, I will press the share button and upload the newest post to my *PhoGlo* account. But this isn't like all the other posts that I have shared over the last few years. This one won't just be lost amongst all the other posts vying for the attention of the platform's users.

This one isn't a shot in the dark.

This will be my first post for my new boss. My first as a full time fully employed, fully paid influencer. And the first one of many.

And it's a pretty simple one. No advertising. No gimmicks. No begging for likes or comments or anything. Just a selfie of me, no makeup on, wearing one of my favourite baggy red pyjama t-shirts and smiling into the camera. No filter. No editing. Authentic. Raw.

Real.

The caption will be just as honest as the photo. Sebastian has told me what to say, and I've typed it out word for word on my phone:

My name is Emily Bennett. I'm a twenty-three-year-old woman from Billericay in Essex, England. My favourite colour is purple. My favourite film is Legally Blonde. I like Chinese food but have to be careful as I'm allergic to peanuts. I hate pizza. Yeah, weird I know. I

lost my job yesterday. I lost my dad last May. I've spent the last few years trying to project the perfect image of myself to the world. But today I'm being open and honest. No makeup. No filters. No hiding. This is me. And I am enough. Just like you are.

Just reading it over again gives me goosebumps. It's so intimate. I can't actually believe I'm going to post it in a minute's time. I never would have done this myself. The makeup-less selfie. The complete lack of the filter applications. And the admission that I've tried to fake my happiness over the last three years.

But this is what Sebastian wants me to post, and he's the boss, so if I want to keep my job, I have to do what the boss says. As much as this influencing is my dream, I also need to think of it as a normal form of employment, which means there will be good parts and bad parts to it.

The bad part is that sometimes you have to do things that you don't want to. The good part is that you get money deposited into your bank account on a certain time every month. It's called being an adult. It's called the real world, and now I'm fully functioning member of it.

My mum has told me this enough about the real world over the years, and she told me it again tonight when we had a discussion about my job prospects. I listened to her, let her say what she had clearly been waiting all day to tell me then I smiled at her and told her I had some good news.

I told her about my meeting with Sebastian. I told her what he wanted me to do. And I told her what they were paying me to do it.

At first, she had been shocked, which I found funny because that was exactly the same reaction I had when I heard about my new job too. Then she had some words of caution for me, advising me to be careful and protect myself because usually when things sounded too good to be true, it turned out that they were, and I bit my tongue and resisted the urge to argue. But then she smiled, and I saw the tears in her eyes form as she hugged me and told me how proud of me that she was.

And then she had told me how proud dad would be. And then I cried too.

It's almost time to share my first post for Sebastian, so I take one last look back over it for good luck. The honest selfie. The ultra-honest caption. And the new hashtags that they have told me to add at the bottom. The ones that the boffins came up with. The ones that are going to supercharge my platform. The ones that are going to get my post in front of more people than it's ever been in front of before.

I could tell you what they are.

But then I'd have to kill you.

The clock strikes eight and I hold my breath as I hit *Share*. That word has never been more appropriate for what I've just done. I've shared everything about myself in this post, and now it's out there in the world for everybody to see. I breathe out. It's done.

Sebastian told me not to obsess over the post tonight, not to stare at the likes tally or read through every comment or watch my follower count go up all night. But that's easier said than done. There's no way I'm sleeping tonight. I'm too wired. So sorry Sebastian, but I will not be putting my phone down any time soon.

And it's already happening.

In the first two minutes since I posted this is already my most Liked post ever. And the comments. So many comments. All positive. All empowering. All thankful for my honesty.

Then I go to my profile page and dare to take a look at my follower count. I think there's a mistake. It says 4,909. But I only had 4,382 a moment ago. There's no way I could have gained that many new followers within a couple of minutes. These hashtags might be good, but they're not that good.

Or are they?

A minute later and I sail past 5000 followers, and then I start to see what Sebastian was talking about. These hashtags are powerful.

Like, Kardashian powerful.

I throw my phone onto the bed and scream, and within seconds, my mum comes running in with a terrified look on her face. But then she sees how happy I am and when I tell her how many followers that I'm getting from just one post then she starts screaming too.

I know she's happy for me and just relieved that I have a job that I am passionate about. But there's more to it than that; I just haven't told her yet.

I know how little money we have as a family now dad has gone, and I know how much she hates her job. I haven't mentioned it to her tonight, but I have a plan once I've got a few more posts under my belt and the money from Sebastian and his company is starting to land in my account.

I'm going to give her most of it. I'm going to tell her to use it to pay the mortgage, and the bills, and the car payments. Then I'm going to tell her to quit her job at the supermarket and spend her days doing whatever the hell she wants to because she's earnt it.

And there's plenty of money to go around now.

Because I've earnt it too.

My mum leaves to go and text her friends and tell them how proud of her daughter she is, and I collapse onto my bed, my head swimming with so many exciting thoughts. The money I'm going to make. The places I'm going to go. The life I'm going to live.

Goodbye Billericay.

Hello Bahamas.

But amongst all the excitement, there is one thing bugging me at the back of my mind. It's the question that has been there ever since I received the message that they wanted me to type out for my first post.

How did they know everything about me?

My favourite food. My allergies.

My dad.

I rambled on a lot in my interview with Sebastian and can't remember everything I told him, but I'm pretty sure that I didn't mention my favourite types of food and the fact I am allergic to peanuts. And I definitely didn't mention my dad because I find it impossible to talk about him without tearing up and I know I didn't cry in the interview.

Yet he knew it all. I don't know how but he did, and now I want to ask him. It's not necessarily a problem, but it would be nice to understand how and where he got his information on me. But I'm worried that if I do ask, then he might think that I'm ungrateful and might start having second thoughts about employing me.

I don't want that to happen.

Now that I've got my dream job, I will do anything to keep it.

Anything.

#SomebodyIsAlwaysWatching

Sebastian Sawyer

I stare at the bank of plasma screens on the wall in front of me. They all display a variety of numbers, and all of them are going the same way.

Up.

Each screen represents an employee, and there are eight in total. One of the screens was black for a day due to that particular employee's contract being terminated with us. But it is back in action and showing the numbers of her replacement, twenty-three-year-old Emily Bennett from Billericay, Essex.

Her numbers are much smaller than her colleagues on the adjacent screens, but they will get there. The important thing is that they are moving in the same direction as the others, which they are and will continue to do as long as she does what I tell her to do.

Emily believes the rapid rise in her post's engagement figures is down to the powerful use of the hashtags I have given her, the hashtags that I told her had come from the clever minds of a team of mathematicians running impossibly complex algorithms through sophisticated computers.

The reality, in this case, is not as exciting as the fiction.

There is a team of clever minds, although instead of being mathematicians they are computer hackers and the complex algorithms they are tapping into aren't their own but rather belong to the website they are breaking into.

They are hacking PhoGlo's codes.

There are four of them in the team, and they are beavering away behind me, on the other side of the locked door that leads into a windowless room where they can't be disturbed.

Or discovered.

They are the heartbeat of this company. Without them, people like Emily wouldn't get to do all the things she's going to be doing. And I wouldn't possess the vast power at my disposal.

And what do I do?

I am the owner of this small enterprise. But just because I keep the number of my employees limited, that doesn't mean there is any limit on the profits I make each month.

I have two main roles to oversee. One, I recruit the influencers and monitor their progress, mainly ensuring they stick to their tasks, with no margin for error. Two, I am the link between those influencers and my many wealthy clients that dictate the message they are to send.

So you could call me a middleman but if you do then make sure you call me a handsome, fashionable and extremely well-compensated middleman.

Thanks.

I sip my macchiato as my eyes light up from the activity on the plasmas. Each screen contains three numbers. A Likes tally, a Comment's tally and the main one at the top which is of the most interest to me.

The total follower count for that influencer.

Beside each number is a percentage and this shows how much that user's platform has grown since their last post. These figures are, of course, always healthy.

Emily is currently at the bottom of the pile numbers-wise, and as I look across each monitor, I see the pecking order plainly running all the way up to the first screen and the number one influencer on our books.

Mason Manor.

Now she might just sound like a mansion in the English countryside, but she's also one of the most powerful people on social media today. Every time Mason posts is an event in itself, and there's not an update on her account that gets less than a million likes these days.

Mason was the first influencer we hired, and despite all the others that have come and gone over the years she is still the best. But there's no secret to her success. I tell this to all the influencers in the early days of their time with us. All Mason has done is follow the rules that we set out at the start of our agreement, and the rules couldn't be easier to understand.

You do what we tell you to do.

That's it.

No need to overcomplicate it and Mason certainly doesn't. Do what we say, receive your substantial payment and enjoy your life until the next time we ask you to do something. Why anybody would struggle to follow that simple blueprint is beyond me, but there have been a few influencers over the years that have gone against me.

But not before we made a big success of them of course.

It's easy at the start when they're broke and dreaming of reaching the big time. They'll do anything to get it, especially after we have given them a taste of what they can expect, which is what I did with Emily today. Tales of dizzyingly high follower counts and social media stardom are enough to get anyone to follow my commands.

But eventually, after a few years have passed sometimes these influencers start to forget who it was that got them to the top, and they start believing they are so big now that they can go it alone, which breaks our original agreement, and so that's when I have to step in and gently remind them.

I'm a professional, so the first reminder is always a written warning. If that is ignored, then there is a gentleman in my company who I like to send on a little road trip to give them a physical warning.

That's two strikes and just like good old baseball, that beautiful game that they play in my home country which I don't get to see enough of these days, three strikes and you're out.

Ivy Lane had three strikes.

And now Ivy Lane is no longer on any of these screens.

I have a lot of work to do, but I find myself unable to look away from Mason's screen. The numbers are mesmerizing. I feel like a proud father. Not literally.

I'm just the boss, and her real father is no longer around. That goes for all the other influencers on the screens.

Not only do they share the same job, but they share the same background and life experiences. They all come from the same kind of places, and they've all suffered their fair share of emotional heartache in the past. It's the reason I pick them in the first place, and it's the reason they are so compliant once they get here.

Studies have shown that those without a father figure in their lives are more easily persuadable. They have also shown that when many people experience a tragic loss, then they have the urge to get away from where it happened and put as much distance between themselves and the painful memories. And there are even studies showing how many people that live in small towns want to escape them and make a name for themselves in the big cities of the world.

You can do a lot with studies. You can read them in your morning newspaper then go about your day and forget about it. You can listen to them on the evening news then go to bed and lose the knowledge in a haze of dreamy fog.

Or you can take the information and use it to build a company so big and so powerful that you couldn't even comprehend it if you tried.

I chose to do the latter. Each one of the influencers on these eight screens has been chosen carefully after their personality traits, behavioural patterns and life history have been analysed and dissected. I know more about these people than they know about themselves.

Yet none of them ask me how that is when I first approach them. None of them want to know why it is that I can tell them their favourite movie or what type of food they should avoid if they don't want to end up in the hospital. None of them even want to know how it is that I know their darkest secrets and fears.

The date they suffered a tragedy.

The precise time their world was falling apart.

People in my generation and older would want to know these things. But the youngsters of the world these days are the opposite. They don't want to keep facts about themselves hidden away. They don't care for secrets and anonymity. They want to share things with the world. They want total strangers to know everything about them. They want to be read like an open book.

Just as long as you follow them and like their latest post.

And so that is how I assembled this merry band of influencers on the screens before me. They all put themselves out there to be found, and I found them.

Now they are mine.

And there's not a damn thing they can do about it.

#FollowMe

Emily Bennett

Last night was pretty special. I've had some epic nights over the years, but most of them involved alcohol and bad decisions. But there's no hangover here today. Nor is there any shame or regret or frantically texting all my friends to ask them what the hell happened.

My mind is clear. My conscience is too. And I know every single thing that happened because I was wide awake and mentally present for all of it.

At 9 pm, one hour after I pressed Share on my first post for Sebastian's company, I surpassed 7000 followers. At 10 pm that same post had 300 comments, all positive. At midnight it had 5400 Likes. By half one in the morning, I was closing in on 9000 followers.

Then I fell asleep.

I hadn't thought it would be possible to drift off amongst all the excitement, but I guess my adrenaline levels dipped slightly and I crashed. Even with all the notifications on my phone and the messages from my friends who were just as stunned by the developments as I was, I had somehow managed to sleep.

By the time I woke up, it was 08:15, and when I picked up my phone and went to *PhoGlo,* I saw something truly amazing and something that I had been a long term goal of mine ever since I installed the app a few years ago.

I had passed the magical 10,000 follower barrier.

That figure is always one of the most exciting ones to hit for anybody that uses social media apps because once you reach it the way your follower count is displayed changes. Whereas before you had 9,999 followers now you have...

10k.

In the online world where social proof matters more than anywhere else, the 'k' is sexier than a pound symbol. Because it means your account has graduated from being a humble, modest page, to being one that garners respect and attention from others.

And particularly people that run businesses.

With 10 k followers, you become attractive in the eyes of companies looking to promote their products to a wider audience. Now you have that all-important social proof telling them that you are popular on this platform and that's when messages will start to land in your inbox. They are messages asking if you would be interested in promoting something to your followers. Nothing too big at this stage and certainly not anything too lucrative.

Yet.

It could be basic eyeliner for a cheap high street accessory store. Or even a new dog food that's about to hit the market, though it helps if you actually have a dog to promote it alongside. But the messages will start to come in and the more followers you get, the bigger the companies will be that contact you.

And the bigger the payments are that go with them.

I see that there are already three messages in my inbox from business owners enquiring about my availability and interest in promoting something for them. One retail store asks me to wear a new summer dress they are launching. An evening college wants me to say how cool their online courses are that they are offering to new students. And a chocolate bar company want me to film myself taking a bite out of one of their products and share it with my followers.

I want to say yes to them all, especially the chocolate bar one. But I'm not sure what the terms of my agreement with Sebastian's company are exactly. I haven't actually signed anything yet. Not a contract. Not anything.

Am I allowed to promote these things? Or am I exclusive to him? I hope it's the former, but it could be the latter.

I better check.

But I'm still nervous about asking too many questions at this stage. Everything is going so well that maybe I should just be grateful instead of bothering him with my silly queries. He's obviously far too busy for that, and he must have hundreds of other influencers to deal with every day and most of them with much larger followings than me.

I'm glad I didn't message him last night to ask him how he knew so much about me, mostly because I figured it out for myself a short time later. The reason he knows so many personal and private things about me is because I'm not exactly a personal and private person. One look on my *PhoGlo* page will tell you that.

It's all on there, the answer to almost anything you could want to know about me. My favourite food? Chinese of course, which my post from October 2018 will tell you when you see that I captioned it #FavFood.

My favourite colour? Purple, of course, when you see the regular use of it in the clothes that I wear in many of my selfies as well as the multiple hashtags #PurpleIsMyColour.

My peanut allergy? There's even a post for that too, from January 2019 when I was taken to hospital and shared a photo of my arm with the admission bracelet around my wrist.

#PeanutsPutMeHere.

Everything Sebastian asked me to put in my first post was already on my profile page somewhere already. My age, hometown, likes, dislikes, *painful experiences*. All there.

All he had to do was look for it, and that is obviously what he had done. He would have seen the posts about my dad's cancer and the photo when I sat with him in hospital and the picture that I posted of him holding me as a baby the night he passed away in 2019.

It's funny how sharing those things with the world didn't seem such a big deal at the time because they were broken down into manageable, bite size chunks. I think the reason last night's post felt so much more expressive was because it was sharing several personal things all at once.

But now I understand why Sebastian made me do that, because bite-size chunks don't have any impact.

Sledgehammers do.

That's what my post last night was. It was a sledgehammer of truth and because it was so strong and hard-hitting it had a much bigger impact than any of my previous posts combined. People want honesty. Why give it to them in dribs and drabs when you can give it to them all at once?

Sebastian had clearly known this, which is why he had made me do it. And between that and his super hashtags, it had worked. My profile was blowing up, and it was all because of him.

I felt so relieved that I hadn't messaged him last night to ask why he knew things about me. So I will hold off on messaging him now to ask him if I can make deals with these companies that are offering me work.

I'll find out soon enough if I'm able to accept paid promotions and it would be great if I can, but even if I can't it's not as if I need the money. Sebastian is paying me a small fortune every time I post. Although I didn't get paid for the first post last night, he has promised me I will make at least £2000 each for future ones. As long as he asks me to do plenty more then I won't have to worry about money for a very long time.

And by then, based on the way it's already progressing so quickly, my follower count will be so high that if I do eventually decide to part ways with Sebastian's company in the future, then I will be my own boss and able to control who I do business with going forward. The world is my oyster. I'm in a great position right now. So there's no need to rock the boat.

I just wish I knew which other influencers out there were working for Sebastian. I did ask him in our meeting, but he was vague and didn't give me any names. He told me to just focus on my own brand for now and not waste time comparing myself to others. He said that was a rookie mistake that many wannabe influencers made, and I had agreed with him because it was the mistake I had made ever since I had decided to become an influencer.

I would spend days and nights stalking the profiles of the biggest influencers in the world, studying their posts and looking for tips on how to improve my own. Sometimes I would even blatantly steal their ideas and copy them onto my own page just changing their photo for one of me in the same pose. It was taking their creativity and passing it off as my own. And it was the reason I hadn't got anywhere with it.

Because it was amateurish.

Now I am a pro, so I can't afford to make rookie mistakes.

But still, it would be nice to know one or two names of my fellow colleagues on *PhoGlo*. Just to say hi at least. Get to know them a little better. See if they have any advice for me on how to thrive in this crazy online business.

But I have no way of knowing who works with me and who doesn't. Not yet anyway. So for now, all I can do is scroll through my news feed and look at the various posts and wonder if they are working for the same boss as me. People like Stella Robinson. Danny Lopez. Mason Manor. All rich, powerful, mega-successful influencers.

Did they make it on their own or did it all start for them the same way that it started for me?

Are they really successful independent entrepreneurs or did they just get a message in their account one evening like I did?

What I really want to know is, are they also working for Sebastian?

#LadyOfTheManor

Mason Manor

Another day, another front-row seat to a fashion show.

This one is in Venice, but honestly, I can barely tell the difference anymore. Paris. Milan. Madrid. They all look the same to me nowadays. Skinny models tottering down a long catwalk wearing the latest creations of some world-renowned designer.

Lightbulbs flash.

The audience applauds.

Bring out the next one.

I never thought I'd get bored of being in places like this, but I guess everything gets boring when you've done it enough times. And there isn't much I haven't done over the last five years.

I've walked the red carpet at hundreds of exclusive events. I've flown first class multiple times. I've got a phonebook full of A-list celebs who text me on a regular basis to ask for wardrobe advice. I've been around the world and back again at least two dozen times, and I spend more time in an airport than I do at my Manor in the Kent countryside that cost me £3.4 million to buy and is obviously named after me.

I've quad biked through the Saharan desert with sports stars. I've swum with sharks and jet skied with chart-topping singers. I've dined with Presidents and

Prime Ministers. And I've raised over £20million for charity.

And through it all, I've kept my *PhoGlo* account updated with three posts and ten stories a day.

I have over 150 Million followers on the platform. I'm in the top 10 influencers in the world. And I did it all without being related to somebody that was already famous.

I'm just a normal girl from England.

I'm just a normal person like you.

At least that's what I try to make you believe. That's all influencing is about in a way. I make myself relatable. I make you think you can be just like me if you dress like me and exercise like me and basically aspire to be like me. Of course, you never will be like me, but that's not the point.

The point is you spend a lot of money trying.

But that's not your fault. And don't get me wrong, I'm not a massive bitch. I really am just a normal girl from England. A town called Sevenoaks in fact. You'd like it there; it's quaint. Not that I ever get to go home much anymore.

But strip away all the A-list pals and the travel videos and the red-carpet selfies, and you will find that I am almost exactly like you.

Because just like you, I am trapped.

How can I be trapped? I'm never in the same place for more than 24 hours. I always have a plane ticket in my hand. I have more money than I could ever hope to spend in my lifetime.

Yet trapped is the best word to describe my life. Because just like you can't afford to quit your crappy job because you need the money, I can't afford to quit this influencing life because I need to stay alive. If you quit, you might lose your ability to afford decent food and shelter. If I quit, I will definitely lose my ability to breathe.

For all my riches, fame and apparent freedom, I am just someone who works for a company managed by a boss that keeps a tight leash on their employees.

See, just like you.

If this sounds like I'm complaining though then please know that I am not. I love this life. It's the one I dreamed about before I had it and it's the one that I still enjoy to this day. Just because I get bored at a fashion show every now and then doesn't mean I'd rather be an admin assistant or shelf stacker back in England.

The fact I have no escape from it doesn't bear too heavily on me either. It's a small price to pay for having such a life. I know not all influencers live under the constant threat of death but all the influencers that work for the same boss as me do.

There's always eight of us at any one time. It occasionally dips to seven, but they always find a new replacement quickly. We all know why it sometimes drops to seven, but we don't talk about that.

We don't need to.

But I'm number one, the first influencer that was hired by Sebastian and the one that has always had the biggest following. I've worked hard to get to where I am today, and I've done so many things just to stay here. And I'm not just talking about filters and hashtags.

I've influenced political campaigns. I've helped dangerous prisoners get released back into society. And I've killed a man.

But please don't tell anyone.

You don't think Sebastian's company plucks people like me out of obscurity and pays them a fortune just to advertise some makeup product or 5-star hotel in the Caribbean, do you? That would be silly, not to mention a massive waste of money and potential.

No, Sebastian hires people like me to indirectly do their dirty work for them. If there's a politician they want in power, they get me to declare my support of them, take a selfie with them and influence the votes of millions of voters in that campaigner's country.

If there's somebody in prison who one of Sebastian's customer's needs on the outside then he gets me to raise awareness about their plight in jail, the travesty of justice they suffered and how you can help by signing the petition that I've linked to in my bio.

And if there's somebody whom Sebastian wants killed because they don't suit their agenda, then there's no better way of buying my loyalty to him than getting me to do it for them.

Okay, so maybe I'm not just like you, but it doesn't matter because nobody outside of the company ever knows any of this. They just see the photos I put up on *PhoGlo* and aspire to be just like me.

I will be an influencer until the day I die, regardless of whether I try to leave the company or not. But I won't leave because I've got used to the finer things in life now and also, I don't particularly want to end up dead either, so there's that.

Poor Ivy. She thought she could get out. She believed she could just say thanks for all the help and the money and the fame, but I'll take it from here. But it doesn't work that way, and now she is being buried on Friday.

I'm going to be attending her funeral. But not as a colleague of course. Nobody knows that we all work for the same company. No, I will be there just as a friend, mourning the loss of a fellow influencer and British girl done good.

Keep this between you and I, but Ivy phoned me in tears two nights before she died. She said she wanted to get away from Sebastian and asked for my help.

Of course, I told her the only thing I could.

There is no way out. Stick to his rules. That is all we can do.

But she didn't listen, so now I need to find a pretty black dress to wear on Friday. Maybe one of these models at the fashion show that I'm currently attending will give me an idea of what to wear. But it's not likely.

The last model that came out had a pineapple on her head.

As soon as this show is over, and I've uploaded the photo of my view from the front row I will board a private plane back to London where I will meet Sebastian and his newest apprentice. I believe she is called Emily Bennett.

I've already followed her, as per Sebastian's request. I'm sure that was a thrill for her to see. She'll be even more thrilled when I walk into the same restaurant as her and sit down at her table tonight.

After an evening of giving Emily a taste of the life she can expect to lead now she too is a paid influencer just like me, the pair of us will head north to the town of Grimsby where we will pay our respects to the deceased *PhoGlo* star Ivy Lane. The photos that I will share from the day will be poured over by millions of rabid fans online, and the fact that I will tag Emily's profile in some of them will mean she will get tens of thousands of followers almost instantly.

Once the funeral is over and done with, I will hightail it back to the nearest airport and depart the gloomy shores of the UK to spend some time sunning myself on the golden sands of a five-star resort in Mexico while I wait for my next instruction for Sebastian to come through.

It's a crazy life, and it's not for the fainthearted. Fashion shows. First-class flights. Funerals.

So many funerals.

But as long as I keep doing what I'm told to do, then it won't be my funeral, and that's all the motivation I need.

Forcing myself to concentrate on the moment at hand, I take a photo of the model standing high up on the catwalk above me. She's wearing a lilac tutu and has the legs of a goddess.

I caption the photo 'Visions in Venice'.

#FrontRow #TuTu #LegsForDays.

I could do better with my hashtags, but it doesn't really matter. With 150 million followers I could hashtag the most insane nonsense, and I'd still get flooded with likes.

I'm lucky in that I've progressed to the stage where Sebastian trusts me to post my own content in between the messages he tells me to share. Back when I started, I had no control over what I sent to my follower's feeds.

Poor Emily will be in that boat now.

I'm losing concentration again and so I re-focus and press Share on my post, instantly sending it to the pockets and handbags of my millions of followers.

It'll give them something to smile about when they're on their break from work, I suppose.

I can't remember the last time I smiled and actually meant it.

Probably just after I met Sebastian.

Nothing kills smiles quicker than that man.

#MeetYourHeroes

Emily Bennett

I'm so excited I can't sit still. There's just too much going on.

The view in front of me. The £50 cocktail that's gone straight to my head.

And the fact that Sebastian has just told me that Mason Manor is on her way to meet us.

We're on the top floor of The Shard, and I feel like I can see the whole city from here. If I thought the view from my old boss's office was good, then this is something else entirely. I feel like I'm as high as the clouds. Not that there are any today. It's an unusually clear and sunny January day in London and even though it's freezing cold outside the temperature in this restaurant is perfect.

When Sebastian told me to meet him here, I thought it might finally be my opportunity to meet the rest of the company. A team-building gathering perhaps. But when I arrived, I saw that it was just him, sitting alone at the only occupied table in the restaurant and sipping a tall, tropical coloured drink.

He looked as splendid as always, in a royal blue suit that fit him perfectly and his slick blonde hair looking perfect in the rays of sunlight that shone through the floor to ceiling windows all around him.

I, on the other hand, was wearing a simple black dress that cost £15 and wasn't as figure-hugging as his outfit. I knew I would have to dramatically overhaul my wardrobe now that I had the money to do, but I hadn't had the chance to go shopping yet. It hadn't even been twenty-four hours yet since my first post for Sebastian's company, and already my life was becoming a bit of a blur.

My follower count now stood at 14,657. My DM's and WhatsApp's chats were blowing up. And then Sebastian had called and told me to meet him here at three o'clock to discuss our business strategy, so I'd been forced to finally stop looking at my phone, cobble together an outfit and jump on a train into London just to get here on time.

Now the meeting was almost an hour old, and Sebastian and I still hadn't talked business. Instead, we had been working our way through the eye-wateringly expensive cocktail list, and I was struggling to stop giggling as the alcohol content in my bloodstream continued to rise.

Sebastian wasn't just a charming, suave businessman. He was funny and had kept me entertained with some hilarious stories about his many adventures all over the world ever since he had started his company.

There was the story about a private jet owned by a famous hip hop artist having to turn back to the airport after the cabin became so engulfed in the smoke from all their joints.

There was the hotel party in Vegas with the YouTube star who leapt from his balcony into the pool below because somebody had brought a tiger into his room.

There was the post Oscars party in LA when Sebastian had woken up with his head resting on the chest of the Best Actress winner and her angry husband screaming at him from the other side of the locked door.

He was full of stories, each one more crazy than the last but then, after three cocktails and just when I had thought I was going to laugh so much that I would need oxygen support, he had leaned forward at the table and told me the best thing.

'You're going to have your own stories just like these.'

Me. Little Emily Bennett from Billericay. I was going to party on private planes with musicians and trash hotel rooms in Vegas and maybe even wake up with my own Oscar winner one day.

Please let it be Leo.

It all sounded too good to be true and amongst the haze of alcohol and laughing fits, I was reminded of my mums use of the famous saying.

"If something sounds too good to be true, it usually is."

But so far there had been no indication that any of this was anything but true. The followers Sebastian had promised me were already pouring into my *PhoGlo* account, and there was more and more of them by the second.

The chance of a better lifestyle was already becoming evident, what with me sitting at the top of the tallest building in the UK and drinking drinks that I would never have been able to afford before.

And even the money he had talked about was real too. I knew that because even though he had told me I wasn't being paid for the first post I did for him, I had actually received a notification on my train ride in today that a payment had just been made to my bank account.

£2000.

Just like that. No long painful wait for payday to come around each month. And what's more, during our little alcohol-fuelled meeting today Sebastian had told me that the money from each post would be paid in daily.

Daily!

That meant that with one post a day I was suddenly making £14,000 a week and I didn't have to wait to see any of it. I could see it sitting in my account right now, and it was going to keep coming.

So sorry mum, but it seems that sometimes things that sound too good to be true actually can turn out to be as true as can be. And she would see this for herself soon enough when she was able to quit her job at the supermarket and had her feet up on the sofa while I was paying off her mortgage.

I can't wait to make her happy.

And soon enough things would get even better.

Because Mason Manor would be joining us.

I get goosebumps just at the thought of her name. She's a big deal on *PhoGlo*. She has over a hundred and fifty million followers, and I am one of them, of course. I have spent years tracking her remarkable rise from a small town in the south of England to become one of the richest and most influential people on the planet.

From a small town in the south of England.

Just like me.

But there was no way I could expect to ever get to her level of fame and fortune. Now that would be too good to be true. I would settle for less because it still would be a hell of a lot more than what I had yesterday.

Maybe Ivy Lane's level. That would be a good place to get to. She had an amazing life. If I could be like her and have all the things that she did, then I would be happy. Happier than she apparently was anyway.

It's so sad what happened.

May she rest in peace.

Sebastian picks up the cocktail menu, and I can't believe he's thinking about ordering another one. If I drink anymore, I don't know if I'll be able to stand up.

But I don't want to seem ungrateful. I'll have to keep drinking. I'll just have to pace myself a little better. But I must keep drinking. I need to get used to this.

Cocktails in the afternoon. *It's a hell of a lot better than passing calls through a reception desk.*

Then I see Sebastian put the menu back on the table and stand up from his seat and I realise he is looking at the entrance to the restaurant behind me. He is straightening his tie and clearing his throat. Someone important must be here.

OHMYGOD SHE IS HERE.

I try not to vomit. I'm definitely drunk.

But I need to man up and stand up.

I rise to my feet and quickly brush out the creases on my dress. Take a deep breath. Pretend to be sober. You only get one chance to make a first impression, and I need to nail this one.

I turn around.

And then I see her.

She glides through the empty restaurant, her long dark hair flowing behind her and her smooth tanned limbs moving gracefully as she makes her way towards us.

She is wearing a bright red strapless dress and clutching a Chanel handbag. The heels are high. The makeup is immaculate. And the hair.

Jesus, the hair.

The waiters in the restaurant stop and stare. I bet everyone she passed on the way here did the same thing.

She looks a million dollars. She's worth several.

And now she is looking right at me.

'Hi Emily,' she says, holding out a perfectly manicured hand towards me. 'I'm Mason.'

#BossOfTheYear

Sebastian Sawyer

I call the waiter over again and tell him to bring us three espresso martinis before he serves us dessert. He smiles and hurries away to give the bartender my order, and I can tell he's just desperate to get to the part where I give him his tip. But we're not quite there yet. I've got a lot more money to spend before I cover his rent for the next three months.

I sit back in my chair and rest my hands on the full stomach that's currently still trying to digest all the lobster and caviar I put into it over the last half an hour. As I recline, I listen to Mason finish the story she has been delivering so expressively to a rapt Emily.

Miss Manor can talk for England. She will probably run England one day too. That's my plan, anyway. But let's not get ahead of ourselves.

Right now, she is doing exactly what I asked her to do.

She is *selling the dream to Emily.*

She has told her about the fashion show she just got back from in Venice. She has told her about how she sat on the front row and that her post from the side of the runway got over 10 million likes.

She has told her where she is going next, which is a 5-star resort in Mexico that has seventeen pools and a suite that leads straight out onto the sun-drenched shores of the Caribbean Sea.

She has told her all about her celebrity pals, and her first-class travel, and her never-ending lifestyle of cocktails, clear blue skies and crazy parties.

And while she hasn't expressly told her how much she makes per post, she has hinted at her enormous wealth enough times during the conversation to let the new girl know that she's in a very lucrative business and she would be stupid not to keep it that way.

Of course, it's probably nothing that Emily didn't already know about her. You can find most things online these days, particularly if the name in your search bar is Mason Manor.

Net worth? £120 million.

Properties? Penthouse in Miami, yacht in Monaco and of course her manor in Kent.

Cars? Yellow Lamborghini. Pink Porsche. Black SUV.

Preferred charities? Parkinson's, Cancer Research and Support for Abused Woman.

Reasons for wanting to be an influencer? Ambition, a desire to see more of the world than her small town and a passion for sharing positivity with her followers.

Ultimate goals? Number 1 influencer on the planet.

Biggest fear? That it was all a dream and to have to go back home with nothing.

The life and times of Mason Manor, out there for all to see. And see they do. She was the most searched for person in 2019. The official studies might not have said it, but my hackers told me it was so, and I believe them because there's not much they don't know.

But she didn't lay it on too thick. She played it just perfect. So perfect in fact that as the waiter brings us the three martinis, I interrupt her to raise a toast which is the signal for her to press pause on the storytelling and let me take it from here.

'Wow, and I thought my life was crazy,' I say laughing at Mason's last story as I hold my cocktail in the air and wait for my two employees to do the same.

When they do I carry on:

'I'd like to raise a toast. To social media and everything that it has given us. To you, Mason, for interrupting your busy schedule to come and welcome our newest joiner into the company. To health, because without it, none of this would matter. And finally, to you, Emily...'

I see her hanging on my next word as she waits for me to finish my sentence.

'Welcome to the company.'

She breaks out into a silly, drunken grin, and I wink at her as I take a long sip from my cocktail. She does the same, as does Mason until we all return our glasses to the white linen tablecloth and recline in our seats.

'So Emily, what would you usually be doing right now at half-past four on a Wednesday afternoon?' I ask, well aware that such a question will only cement further in her mind just how much I have changed her life in such a short space of time.

'Oh god,' she says in between a mouthful of caviar that's dribbling down her chin. 'Well, if I wasn't working in some shitty job, I guess I'd just be at home at my mum's house.'

'Wow, so this is slightly better then?' I cheekily ask, and she nods her head in agreement and tries to stop any more caviar escaping her mouth.

'What's your mum's name?' Mason asks, after she has finished eating her bit of caviar in a much more lady like manner than her colleague.

'Liz,' Emily answers, taking another large gulp of her cocktail. She is going to be incredibly hungover tomorrow, but she is the happiest girl in London right now.

'Awww no way, my mum's called Liz too!' Mason tells her excitedly, like they're already well on the way to being best friends, which of course in Emily's world would be the best thing to ever happen.

'I know,' Emily replies, before looking mortified that she said that out loud. 'Sorry, I mean, I've just seen on your page, you know, when you've wished her a happy birthday message.'

Mason smiles. 'Of course. Yeah, I tend to get a bit gushy when it comes to family.'

'Me too,' Emily, replies, and I know that's certainly true because I've seen every single post that she has put online over the years.

'And what's your dad's name?' Mason asks her, finishing her cocktail and picking up the menu to make her next selection.

I keep my eyes firmly fixed on Emily because I know the question will affect her, and I would like to know just how much.

Mason looks up from her menu and notices Emily's perma-grin has suddenly disappeared. Then she reaches out and gently rests her hand on Emily's shoulder and asks if she has said something she shouldn't have. It's exactly how I told her to do it over the phone just before she boarded her plane from Venice.

Emily looks at Mason, and for a second it looks like she has completely sobered up and is remembering where she is, which is a world-class restaurant at the top of one of London's most famous landmarks sitting beside one of the most famous *PhoGlo* stars in the world.

And so she pulls herself together.

'No, it's fine. Sorry, it's just, well, my dad died two years ago,' she finally says to Mason but not without shooting me an awkward glance too. She knows that I am aware this is difficult for her to talk about because she knows that I have read every single thing she has posted to her profile over the years.

It's why I made sure to tell Mason to bring it up today.

'Oh, I'm so sorry,' Mason quickly replies, playing the mortified best friend part as well as I'd anticipated. 'Me and my big mouth just blurting things out without thinking that other people might be just like me.'

Emily tries to understand the last part of Mason's sentence.

'Just like you?' she asks, wondering how in a million years she could ever be just like the incredible Mason Manor.

'My father passed away a few years ago too,' Masons tell her, but only by keeping her eyes on the plate in front of her. She's showing another side to her uber confidence. A vulnerability.

A side of her that Emily can really relate too.

'Of course, I'm sorry,' Emily said, taking her turn to apologise. 'I should have remembered.' Again, she has let slip just how much she has stalked Mason's profile over the years. She is forgetting that you should learn about a person piece by piece, only by the snippets of information they offer to you themselves in their company as they get to know you. But she's part of the generation that forget this because they already know everything about somebody just by looking at their *PhoGlo* page.

Not that Mason cares. She depends on people like that. She makes her incredible living from people wanting to know everything about her.

But now Emily feels like she is *really getting to know* this impossibly successful influencer and she is learning that she shares many things in common with her. The same background. The same fear about being liked on social media. The stress over what to wear in each post.

And of course, the fact that they have both lost both their fathers.

I beckon the waiter over again because it's time for another round. This 'meeting' is going perfectly, and

Mason is proving once again that she is my number one employee.

And Emily? Well, she is still trying to eat the caviar without getting it all down her dress and slowly realising that if she stays on this track, the one I have now placed her firmly on, then she can be just as successful as Mason Manor in the coming years.

It can be as easy as that.

#SleepOver

Emily Bennett

I'm so drunk the room is spinning. And this is one big room.

Scratch that. You can't call this a room.

It's more like a house within a house.

I guess it's technically the kitchen, but this isn't like any kitchen I've ever been in before. All the surfaces are gleaming. Tiles upon tiles. The floor. The walls. The ceiling isn't tiled, but that's only because there's a huge skylight cut into the centre of it.

There's a fridge the size of my bed, at both ends of the room.

A glass cabinet housing the fanciest glassware I've ever seen.

A set of knives so sharp I feel like they could cut me from across the room.

It's modern. Pristine. *Perfect.*

And the centrepiece is the marble breakfast bar that runs across the middle of the room and could easily seat a family of thirty. But right now, it's just seating me.

Me and my lifesaving bottle of water.

I take another swig of the ice-cold liquid, and it's a relief to be drinking something other than alcohol. I don't know how many cocktails I had. Eight? Nine?

And I don't know how I made it back from London all the way to the Kent countryside without throwing up.

I'd done my best not to. There was no way I wanted to have to pay the soiling charge in the transport me and Mason had taken back from The Shard.

It was a goddamn Limousine.

She had called for it after our boozy afternoon meal when it was home time, and we had said our goodbyes to Sebastian in the city. I found it crazy that she had the number for a Limo company saved in her mobile, but of course it wasn't. This is Mason Manor we're talking about here.

She was hardly going to call for Mick's Taxi's now was she.

So somehow, I had managed to get through the half an hour ride in the back of the Limo without throwing up, and now I was sitting in this palatial palace in the middle of nowhere. I could hardly believe it. I was in Mason Manor's home.

Mason Manor. Literally.

It's the mansion that has featured on MTV Cribs and a hundred celebrity entertainment websites. It's the one that has two swimming pools (indoor and outdoor), two Jacuzzis (same) and twelve bedrooms, (yes, twelve).

The property is named after its millionaire owner. The same owner that was now my colleague, cocktail companion and most amazingly of all, *my friend*.

But she wasn't with me right now. She had disappeared somewhere into this enormous place she called a home, and left me sitting alone at her kitchen table, nursing a bottle of water and a spinning head. This was after she had invited me to stay the night with her and I had jumped at the offer.

It's not every day one of your heroes asks you to sleepover. It's never really. *It's happened to me precisely zero times before today.* But now it has happened, and here I am, sitting in the home of a *PhoGlo* superstar and having the pick of twelve bedrooms to sleep in.

Even better, she has promised me that we can spend tomorrow enjoying the many amenities of the manor because her and Sebastian don't want me to go home just yet. In fact, by the sounds of it, I won't be going home for quite a while.

Tomorrow evening I will join Mason in the First-Class carriage of a train that will take us up to Grimsby, where after spending a night in the best hotel the town has to offer, we will be attending the funeral of Ivy Lane.

I was surprised when she and Sebastian asked me if I would like to go to the event, mainly because I'd never known Ivy and occasions like that should only be for family and friends.

But they had told me that I wasn't just some stranger off the street poking her nose around at the funeral of a deceased celebrity. I was one of them now. I was what Ivy had been.

An influencer.

And it wasn't as if I didn't know her. Not really. I'd spent hours looking at her photos and reading her posts over the years just like the rest of her million followers had. I did know her. Not directly. Not personally.

But I did know her.

Besides, Sebastian said, it would be great exposure for me to be seen there because I would be standing side by side with Mason Manor, one of the most recognisable people on the planet. Once the photos from the funeral leaked out, which of course they would because there were bound to be a zillion camera phones there, then the world would want to know who the mysterious blonde girl in the black dress standing beside Mason was.

And just like that, Sebastian had said as he clicked his fingers, I would be well on my way to my first million followers.

A million followers.

It sounded exhilarating. It sounded amazing. And if I'm honest, it sounded a little cheap too.

Using someone's funeral as a way to increase my exposure wasn't really what I had in mind when I wanted to grow my following, but in the end, it only took me five seconds to say yes to it because it meant that I got to spend another couple of days with Mason.

I was never going to say no to that.

Plus, it will be nice to pay my respects to Ivy and her grieving family. She was a hero of mine, and I'm sure they will be pleased to hear just how much she inspired me and so many other young women around the world.

But before all the pools, and the five-star hotel tomorrow and the paying of respects the day after that, I needed to get some sleep and give myself the best chance possible of not starting tomorrow with the worst headache known to humanity.

With that in mind, I push myself up from my breakfast bar stool and stagger out of the kitchen, into what I think is the hallway, but it could just as easily be an aircraft hangar such is the size and length of it.

'Mason?' I slur, calling out into the humongous home for any sign of its owner. But there is no reply.

I hadn't expected one. I didn't have the loudest voice in the world and a loud voice was the minimum requirement you would need if you wanted to get someone's attention in a building this size.

I decid not to call out again in case it came off as a little needy and figure I'd just make my way up the stairs and find a bed to crash on. She had told me to take my pick of the bedrooms when we arrived here, so I guess that's what I will do. I'm also guessing that I'll just pick the first one that I come across because I feel like I could fall over at any moment and the sooner I'm horizontal on a mattress, the better.

But then I see the staircase, and I realise it's not just as simple as going upstairs to bed. Most people's staircases only consist of around ten steps and are narrow enough for you to hold on to both the handrail and the wall as you move up them if you so wish. But this staircase?

Not so much.

It must have consisted of at least thirty steps, but that's just my drunken estimate. It was probably more. It was also by far the widest staircase I had ever seen, so the option of holding on to both sides of it on the way up was out of the question. I would have to pick a side and hope that was the right one to get me up to the bed I so desperately craved.

I opted for the side with the handrail and put both my hands on to its sturdy metal frame and began to climb up. I must have looked pretty awful with my makeup-stained face, caviar-stained dress and dirty bare feet trying to coordinate my intoxicated body up a basic human construction.

This was one event in my life that definitely would not be going on *PhoGlo*.

Somehow, I was managing to stay mobile, and before I knew it, I was halfway up the monstrous staircase. In any other house, I would be at the top by now, but here I still had some way to go and so I forced myself on, all the while taking deep breaths and praying that I didn't throw up all over her marble steps.

Then finally I made it. I was at the top. I felt like Rocky when he reaches the top of that staircase in that film. I don't know what it's called. I'm not a boxing movie fan. I just had to sit through it once with an ex.

But anyway, I feel like Rocky.

Seconds later, I have stumbled into one of the many bedrooms up here and fallen face first onto a king-size bed, and that's how I will remain until the morning when I will be woken up by the owner of the house with my black eyeliner and slobbery saliva all over her pristine white linen duvet.

Lols.

#HangoverFromHell

Mason Manor

Poor Emily. She overdid it last night, and she has been a wreck all day. I hoped a swim in my indoor pool might have helped her, but it actually seemed to make her worse. Then the Jacuzzi was too hot and, in the end, she had just returned to the spare bedroom upstairs to try and sleep it off.

But I had been forced to wake her up around 4 pm because we needed to get going if we were to catch our train up north to Grimsby. When I had awoken her, she had seemed to be in an even worse state than before her nap, but there was no time for sympathy.

I bundled her and my travel bag into the back of the Limo and headed into the city.

I could have paid the Limo driver to take us all the way to Grimsby and cut out the train journey altogether, but I had wisely decided it wouldn't look good to roll into town for a funeral in a vehicle as flashy as this one. The train was more respectable, and more in keeping with the working-class ideals of the people that would be attending Ivy's funeral. But we would be travelling first class on the train.

They didn't need to know that bit.

Now we were speeding through the English countryside on the 17:20 service, and I was rather enjoying the more down to earth travel I was participating in, which was more than could be said for Emily who was hiding behind a pair of my Gucci sunglasses and looking like she wanted to be sick again.

She'd already visited the toilets once since we had left the station and, in her words, it had been "horrific" in there. Just to be safe for the rest of the trip I had asked one of the train employees to give her a sick bag, and she was now clinging on to it for dear life. I, on the other hand, was sipping my glass of red wine and staring out the window at the lush greenery whizzing by.

It felt good to spend some time in the UK. It was a shame about the circumstances of my visit, what with Ivy's death and all, but still it was good to be back on home soil. I lose track of how many countries I visit in a year, and even a look through my *PhoGlo* posts doesn't easily give me the answer. There's too many of them to go through, and sometimes I post them out of order so it's hard to retrace my steps as easily as it could be.

All I know is I've visited every continent except Antarctica over the last twelve months and multiple times. Asia is my favourite, but I have a soft spot for North America. Everything's just bigger and better in the good old US of A.

Canada not so much.

But now I'm headed to Grimsby. It's different to what I'm used to, but it will be nice to see where Ivy grew up. I knew her well, and so it won't seem weird that I show my face at her funeral. She was an employee in Sebastian's company, just like Emily. She stayed over at my house after our first meeting with

Sebastian just like Emily. And she was absolutely terrible at handling her alcohol, just like Emily.

I can only hope that's where the similarities between them will end.

But that isn't my concern. It's up to her to make the most of this opportunity, just like I have. I don't always agree with the things Sebastian wants me to do, but the positives easily outweigh the negatives. I would have thought Ivy would have understood that too, but then if she had, I wouldn't be on my way to her funeral right now.

I liked Ivy, but she knew the rules. You post what Sebastian tells you to post. Most of the requests are fun and the sort of thing you would be posting anyway. Selfies, full mirror shots, sunsets, poolside views. But occasionally he will ask you to post something with a darker motive than the usual one of growing your following.

He might want you to criticise a policy being debated in a certain government because he knows your legions of followers will then criticise it too and the volume of numbers can sway the politicians into rejecting it when it comes time to vote. If you actually read up on what the policy was about you will find it would have negatively impacted part of Sebastian's substantial investment portfolio, but of course, we're just dumb influencers, we shouldn't be reading about stuff like that.

He might want you to be seen exclusively flying on a new airline that has opened up, and again, it's probably because he has invested in it and wants to make quick profits when all your followers start trying to book their holiday flights with the same company.

He might even want you to give a bad review of a restaurant somewhere just because the waiter was rude to him when he visited and so he knows a bad review seen by millions of people will mean that restaurants profits will take a massive dip into the red.

They might even end up closing altogether.

Vindictive? Yes. Cruel on the owner? Most definitely. But I'd rather be posting bad restaurant reviews than some of the other stuff he could be asking me to do for him. And make no mistake, once Sebastian has you under his spell, he will ask you to do a lot of things. And if you value your life and the lives of your loved ones, then you better make sure you do them.

Because it's not just your life that is at stake when you enter into employment with Sebastian. It's the lives of everyone you care about too. There's a reason why he always picks people that have lost their father, and it's not just because he wants a strong parental influence out of the way when you are deciding whether to accept his offer of employment.

It's because then you only have one parent left and so you will do anything not to lose that one too.

But I know he prefers not to punish the mothers of his influencers by ending their life. He just uses that as a threat. He much prefers to punish the mothers by ending the life of their influencer child. That's what he did with Ivy. Now her poor mother will be putting on a black dress and a brave face tomorrow and burying her daughter, and it's all because Sebastian gave the order for her to be killed.

She had gone rogue. Refused to post any more of Sebastian's requests. She had told him she was out. Done. *Thanks for all the help Mr Sawyer, but I'll take it from here.*

But of course, that's not how it works. You can't just use Sebastian and his team of hashtag crazy hackers to build yourself a massive following before saying thank you and riding off into the sunset to live a life on your own terms.

Ivy obviously thought she could. She believed that she was her own boss now. That she could pick and choose which companies she promoted. That she could negotiate her own earnings. That she could travel on her own timetable and live life as a free, independent spirit.

Now she is lying in a morgue somewhere in Grimsby after her body was flown back from the Maldives.

It was so avoidable. So unnecessary. All she had to do was follow the rules. Listen to Sebastian. Please Sebastian.

Obey Sebastian.

I look at Emily dry heaving into the paper bag across the table from me and wonder how compliant this new girl will be. She doesn't fully understand the scope of what she has signed up for yet. But she will do soon. They all do. Then it's up to them to either end up like me or end up like Ivy.

I know which one I would prefer.

#SorryForYourLoss

Emily Bennett

I'm dressed in black, and so is everybody else. A sombre mood hangs over the church. People greet each other with handshakes and hugs, but there's no smiling. Maybe in a few hours, when the body is in the ground, and the mourners are in the pub raising a toast to the deceased. Maybe then there will be a few smiles, once the alcohol relaxes the mood and the fun memories start to be discussed.

But for now, there is no smiling because there is no place for smiling at funerals like this.

Not when the person being remembered was so young when they passed.

I'm sitting on the sixth row of pews, in the middle of the large gathering. It's a big turnout. Ivy Lane was popular. Not just online but in real life, where it actually counts.

The first few rows are made up of who I presume are her family. There are elderly relatives, maybe her Grandma and Grandad. There are middle-aged relatives, aunties and uncles perhaps. And there are youngsters too, possible her nephews, nieces and cousins.

And sitting closest to where the vicar will stand is Mrs Lane, Ivy's mother and someone who is clearly struggling as much as any mother would do in the circumstances.

She hasn't stopped weeping since the moment she came into the church, and if I was to guess, then I'd say she hasn't stopped weeping since she received the phone call from the authorities in the Maldives a few days ago.

It's struck me that Ivy's body has been repatriated relatively quickly from halfway across the world back to her hometown of Grimsby, but then again, she was extremely wealthy, and so perhaps any issues over cost were dealt with quicker than usual.

However it was done, her body is now inside the wooden coffin lying in front of the pews, just a few feet away from the sobbing Mrs Lane.

I notice there is no husband or partner sitting beside the grieving mother, to hold her hand or offer a shoulder for her to cry into, and I wonder if Ivy's dad is even in the church at all today. Perhaps he is separated from her mother. Or maybe he is no longer with us either.

I hope that's not the case. The thought of Ivy's poor mum being a widow as well as losing a daughter is too much to bear. But I'm also aware that if I scrolled far enough through Ivy's Lane's still active *PhoGlo* page, I could probably find the answer as to the mystery of her seemingly non-existent father.

But I might give that particular online search a miss.

Behind the family members come Ivy's closest friends, and I guess their relationships were formed in many different places. From school, from sixth form, from the university she graduated from. All the normal places a normal girl goes too.

Before she went into the world of influencing and nothing was ever normal for her again.

All the people here are the same age as Ivy was when she died, late-twenties, looking youthful yet weary, creeping towards the age when the first wrinkles begin to appear, and the fast metabolism of youth starts to betray you.

But they are still so young, and it's another reminder of how much life Ivy Lane had left to live before she tragically decided she could no longer go on.

Behind the friends come the rest of the mourners. The friends of friends, neighbours, acquaintances, work colleagues. The latter is the category Mason Manor falls into and apparently that is the category I fall into too.

I look at Mason sitting beside me, her tanned, picture face obscured by a black veil and her beautiful dark locks flowing out from under her black hat.

I asked Mason how close she was to Ivy last night as we were lying in our beds at the hotel that she had arranged for us. She told me that she had met her several times over the years, in various places around the world. While they were far from best friends, they had a close bond, formed from the fact that the both of them came from similar backgrounds to make it big in the crazy world of social media stardom.

I could tell by her voice when she spoke about Ivy that she felt upset about the whole thing and so I hadn't probed her any more for information about the deceased. She had been invited to the funeral, so I took that as a sign of how close she had been to the tragic woman.

The fact that I had no invitation had been a concern to me however, and I had mentioned this to Mason as soon as she had told me that I could attend the ceremony with her. But she had told me not to worry about it and that there would be so many people there that I would blend in with the crowd and be able to get inside.

Quite how I was supposed to blend in beside one of the most famous figures in the world wasn't clear, but Mason had certainly been right about the number of people here.

The church was full, both in terms of seating and standing space. But that was only the half of it. Outside, all around the grounds of the church and lining the streets on the way to the service, were thousands of people, all coming out to pay their respects to one of Grimsby's most famous daughters.

Ivy had over a million followers on *PhoGlo* at the time of her death, and unsurprisingly, many of those people came from the same town as her. They had followed her progress online, through their mobile screens, as she had transformed herself from local girl to international influencer in the space of a few years.

Most of the people that had come out from their homes to show their support to Ivy's loved ones are female and mostly in the age ranges of early teens to early thirties. That makes sense, as that was the target audience for someone like Ivy, a young woman herself who lived the kind of dream life that would appeal to so many other young women, particularly those who lived in a nice but fairly dreary northern town like this.

As the driver of the car Mason had hired for us had taken us through the streets of the town and all the way up to the church on the top of the hill, I had looked out of the window at all these women outside and wondered how many of them wished they too could have a life like Ivy's. I had been just like them of course, only a few days earlier, until Sebastian had picked me out of the online crowd and now here I was sitting beside the all-powerful Mason Manor.

The service eventually got under way, and it was clear just how large the crowd inside the church was by the fact that the vicar seemed to be a little nervous while giving his sermons. After a couple of hymns, and the playing of Beyoncé's *Halo*, which was Ivy's favourite song, we had all risen to our feet and watched solemnly as the coffin was carried down the aisle to the waiting grave outside.

The burial itself was to be witnessed by only the closest family members, so me and Mason had stood with the rest of the mourners on the path that wound through the graveyard, making small talk as we waited to move on to the wake.

It was a grey, freezing cold day, but there was no rain, and that seemed to be a source of comfort to some of the people that stood around me and talked in gruff regional accents about winter in this part of the world.

Mason was on her phone for most of the time that we waited, and I wasn't sure if she was replying to messages or preparing another post for her page. I hope it was the former but also remembered that she never went more than a couple of hours without adding something to her account and I had been aware of her taking selfies in the church just before the service had begun.

Part of me thought it was a little rude that she was spending so much time on her phone while we waited, instead of making conversation with the family and friends all around us. But I was also aware that several of the mourners were looking at her and whispering amongst themselves, and it was clear that they recognised her.

Perhaps Mason being glued to her phone was her way of avoiding unwarranted attention or at least a distraction from all the gawping.

After about twenty minutes we saw Ivy's family members making their way back across the frosty cemetery, and that was our cue to head to our waiting transport and make our way to the pub that was holding the wake.

I hoped that Mason would be more talkative when we got there, otherwise I would probably be left alone to converse with the rest of the mourners and that wasn't something I felt confident doing considering the fact that I had never met Ivy before.

I was worried that they would accuse me of being a hangar on, or just another influencer there to take some photos and garner some sympathy with my series of hashtags like #TooYoungToDie or #FuneralsAreTheWorst.

But I wasn't there to do any of that. I was merely here because Mason had told me to be here.

But then I got the message from Sebastian telling me it was time for my next post and when I saw what he wanted me to upload to my *PhoGlo* account, I felt almost as sick as Mrs Lane must have felt when she got the phone call about her daughter in the Maldives.

#Its12oClockSomewhere

Sebastian Sawyer

It's a typically busy day in my world. I've got an 11 am conference call with my fellow board members at *GloryGen*, the fitness retail company that we hope will one day rival *Adidas* and *Nike* for the market share of the global fitness industry. Then I've got a lunch reservation at 1 pm with Michael Spratini, the politician I am throwing my support behind in the race to be the next Governor of New York City. And on top of all that I've got the accounts of eight *PhoGlo* influencers to run.

But before all that I have my regular 10 am meeting with Ivan Ilghiz, a middle-aged Russian investment banker and the man in charge of my substantial portfolio. He flies in from Moscow to visit my Los Angeles office on the first Friday of every month to go through my positions and discuss our investment strategy going forward.

We could hold this meeting over the phone, via a video call or even by email but then all those things can be hacked, traced or recorded and so I ensure we hold the talks in person, face to face, alone in my office, where this is no chance of anything we discuss ending up in a courtroom.

Even then, I still take my precautions.

Every morning when I enter my office and before I begin my day's work I perform a methodical sweep of the room with an Anti-Bug detector, the instrument that tells me if there any recording devices anywhere that I need to be wary about.

So far there haven't been any, but I'm never going to stop checking. When you travel as much as I do it leaves plenty of opportunity for ambitious detectives or nefarious business rivals to sneak in and bug my place of work, and as much as I trust my security staff I know that there are always ways of getting into a room that you just have to get inside.

With the rate at which my operations are growing it's only a matter of time before I start getting heat from the authorities or blowback from my competitors and so it's imperative that I stay one step ahead of them at every turn. It's one thing trying to run a multi-million dollar empire from behind my desk here in my native California, but it's another thing altogether to have to try and run it from the jail cell of a maximum-security prison.

Life inside could be relatively comfortable for someone as rich and powerful as me, but still, it's nowhere near as comfortable as it is on the outside. I sure didn't fork out $20million for my new private jet only to see it seized by the LAPD when they pull a recording from my office detailing all the ins and outs of my astute but criminal business activities.

The clock hits 10:55, and the call from my receptionist tells me that Ivan is here for our appointment. I thank her and tell her to send him in, before rising up out of my comfortable leather desk chair and making my way over to the glass table that holds two crystal whisky glasses and a bottle of eighty-year-old malt that was a gift from a well-known politician in South America.

I pour two measures and hold one of them out for the severely balding man in the grey suit who has entered my office, looking sweaty and harassed after a no doubt torturous taxi ride through the traffic-clogged streets of LA.

I notice his drab attire and the ever-increasing hairless patch on the crown of his head and wonder as I always do why he doesn't invest some of his sizeable personal wealth in himself. Give him money to put into a start-up business, tech company or political campaign, and he's happy to do so but give him money to buy himself a decent suit and a hair transplant, and he's suddenly useless.

But that's not my problem. I have a full head of hair and a wardrobe full of expensive suits, and it always makes me look even more impressive when I'm sitting in the same room as someone like Ivan.

What the man lacks in fashion and personal pride he more than makes up for in knowledge and business sense. After a lifetime of making Russian oligarchs even richer than they already were, he decided it was time to go out on his own and be his own boss and so he started his own investment fund.

But swapping high-pressure trading and underhanded business tips for stuffy boardrooms and low-risk ventures didn't give Ivan the pleasure he initially thought it would, so he had discreetly re-entered the illegal world of insider trading and market influencing, and after several recommendations and clandestine meet-ups in freezing cold eastern European venues, I had picked Ivan as the man to help me run my growing empire.

And run it he had. The start-up money I had initially trusted him with had soon been turned into a much vaster sum, and once I had started to capitalise on the opportunities it was giving me, I had made sure he kept the gravy train rolling. With his network of in-the-know informants, he always got the latest investment opportunities first, before the market heard of them, and so he could easily double and triple the returns on my money on a weekly basis.

With his help and my influence, my company was turning over vast sums of money. Of course, most of it was undisclosed and off the books, but it still existed and was able to be spent on the continued growth of my business.

I shake the sweaty Russians hand and offer him a glass of whisky, which he drinks with all the gusto of a man that has just got off a thirteen-hour flight before he sinks back into my leather sofa and pulls a small USB stick from his suit pocket.

He plugs it into my laptop and enters the encrypted password before turning the screen around to show me what is on it.

Numbers. Lots of them.

All the money our latest ventures had made for us. All in the black. *All positive.*

I study them as sharply as I always did before walking back over to the glass table in the corner and pouring another two glasses of malt. We are celebrating, after all.

47 million dollars' worth of profits since our last meeting. Over eight hundred million in total revenue since we had begun this five years ago. And by the way it was trending, we had a chance at reaching a billion dollars total worth by the time we met again.

We clinked glasses and drank to our success, and enjoyed the refreshing liquor just as two wealthy, privileged men should do. We had all the money in the world. We could buy anything we wanted. Life was sweet.

But neither of us were in this for the money. Not me, who while enjoying the finer things in life had much grander ambitions than just being another rich businessman. And certainly not Ivan, who I would guess barely even touched any of his vast wealth if his haircut and suits were anything to go by. I mean, would it kill the guy to visit a tailor and a decent barber?

No, we were doing what we were doing for much bigger reasons.

We were in it to change the world.

I know that sounds pretentious and what every villain in a James Bond movie says right before 007 blows up their island hideaway and disappears off into the sunset with their estranged wife on his arm.

But we weren't villains. We had estranged wives for sure, but we didn't have island hideaways. And there was no superhero spy out there trying to put an end to our cruel and evil ways. Not that I knew of anyway.

We were just two men who saw an opportunity to not only take from the world, but to give back to it. We wanted to create change. Real change. The kind that impacts on multiple generations and alters the destiny of everyone on the planet.

My business investments weren't just there to make a profit; they were there to make a mark on the world. It's complicated. It's confusing. So I'll let Ivan try to explain it a little better.

Just as soon as he's finished his second glass of whisky.

#LetsTalkBusiness

Ivan Ilghiz

Let's say you want to change the world. Where do you start?

First, you'll need money, and a lot of it. A million is a good place to jump in. That's how much Sebastian had when he first made contact with me. So now you're going to need to double that first mill. Then double it again. And so on and so forth until now you're starting to get the kind of money that can make a difference.

But how do you get there?

I'm an investment banker and have spent over thirty years investing my client's money and turning their underperforming portfolios into high-value assets that will keep their children's children living like kings long after the owner has passed on.

How do I make such great returns? I could talk about diversification and equity investments and the importance of calibrating and so on, but we want to get great returns, not just good returns. And there's only one sure-fire way to guarantee those.

Insider trading.

Yes, it's been around forever, and yes, it's still just as illegal as ever, but it still works just as well as ever, and if you want to see your profits skyrocket quickly then there's no better way of doing things.

I'm not going to tell you who my contacts are, but I'm sure you can figure out that after three decades spent working in the business, my network of informants that are ready and willing to give me juicy nuggets of priceless intel is expansive.

And I'm from one of the dodgiest countries on the planet too, so that helps.

Once your pot of money has grown to a more respectable size, then you can start to implement your strategies on how you are going to change the world. Sebastian's strategy was simple. He was going to capitalize on the growing rise of the 'influencer' in modern society.

Here's an example. Say you want to get someone into power because you know their political party's manifesto will mean great things for the investments you already have. Yes, you could just donate to their campaign, but that's no different to what every rich businessman does and even then, there no guarantee that will have any sway on the public's voting come election day.

So, what can you do instead?

You can use your hugely influential team of social media influencers to tell their millions of followers who to vote for when the polls open.

Because social media is predominantly used by the youngsters of the world, *PhoGlo* in particular, it means you can have an impact on a vast demographic of the voting population. Older generations usually have their lifetime affinity to a particular party, so there's not much anyone can do to sway their votes, but the younger generation are as ever-changing as the wind and will often just jump on whatever it is that their favourite celebrity tells them to do.

So when they open up *PhoGlo* and see someone they admire talking about who they are voting for and why it matters so much to them, studies have shown that it has an enormous impact on the results come voting day.

What studies? The studies that tell us that every candidate our influencers have backed so far has won, by a huge majority, and all of them claimed victory due to their overwhelming votes tallied by the population members aged between 18-30.

Another example: Say you want to grow a brand into one of the largest in the world, but the field is already dominated by one or two major competitors that got in before you. You could just accept your place in the food chain and grow your business where you can, accepting that you will forever be in the shadows of the global giants. Or you could use your merry band of influencers to turn down all offers from the competitors in favour of promoting your brand and reaching an audience that is equivalent to your rivals and for a fraction of the cost that they are paying.

While the famous corporations are spending hundreds of millions a year in advertising costs just to hold their position at the top of the tree, Sebastian's new companies are closing on them all fast because he has something they don't. People that will advertise anything he wants them to and for a lot less than the going rate.

How much do drinks companies pay a movie star to film an advert sipping from one of their cans?

How much do sports giants have to pay the latest basketball star to wear their shoes? How much do electronics manufacturers have to throw at the world's biggest DJ just so he will wear their headphones on stage?

Millions.

How much does Sebastian pay his influencers, many of whom have the same or even bigger following on *PhoGlo*, to advertise his new companies?

Mere thousands.

He's saving a fortune even though he's already in possession of a bottomless pit of cash.

And so within five years, that's why every area of business Sebastian has gone into he has closed rapidly on the market leader. It's why many kids these days are wearing the shoes he wants them to wear. It's why they're buying the phones he wants them to have. And it's why they're voting for that politician and not the other one.

Because the biggest influencers on the planet are telling them all to.

And Sebastian controls the influencers.

The best thing about all this is that no one even knows who Sebastian is. He isn't the face of any of these companies he promotes. He doesn't get filmed shaking hands with the newly elected Prime Ministers he gets into power, and he doesn't feature on any Top 100 Rich Lists alongside all the other successful businessmen of his generation.

But he's coming for them all, and he's already passed many of them already. They just can't see it yet.

And they probably never will because Sebastian keeps his identity a closely guarded secret.

He lives in the shadows.

He's probably not even called Sebastian.

I think the man's a genius but then again anyone that pays me 30million Russian Rubles a year is a genius in my eyes. But he's also dangerous, more dangerous than some of the men I've come across in my time back home and trust me; I've been around some animals.

The power he holds over these influencers is scary. The fear he instils in them to get them to do his dirty work is frightening. The things he has made them do just to keep them and their families alive?

Terrifying.

But it works. His eight influencers barely even know the full scope of what they are involved in. They know it's not legal and they know Sebastian is bad news, but the trick is they don't know any of this until it's too late. Once Sebastian has them where he wants them, then he starts to manipulate them. Any failure to comply with his orders means they are erased, and a new influencer takes their place. And there's another influencer desperate to take their place and be skyrocketed to fame and riches beyond their wildest dreams.

He picks them carefully. He chooses wisely.

All potential influencers come from small towns and are desperate to escape. All potential influencers have been trying to grow their brand for years with little to no success. And all potential influencers will do anything to protect themselves and their loved ones.

It's ruthless. It's brutal.

It's brilliant.

So far, I haven't tried to sway Sebastian to further any of my own interests outside of financial ones. I just receive the illegal trading information from my shady contacts, invest his money for him then show up at his office once a month to reveal exactly how much I have made.

But I too have ambitions of my own. I want to change the world, just like Sebastian.

Ivan Ilghiz, President of Russia.

That has a nice ring to it. Just like Sebastian Sawyer, President of The United States has a nice ring to it too. I have no doubt that is where he is headed if he stays on this path.

Of course, he won't be quite as secretive then. Eventually, he'll have to step into the limelight and reveal all his many talents. But by then, he will be so rich and so powerful that he will get the respect of anybody he meets.

As for his influencers?

They'll just be lucky to stay alive long enough to see it.

#WakeUp

Emily Bennett

I'm mad at Sebastian. I'm mad at the rude and shallow message he wants me to post at Ivy's funeral. And I'm mad at the fact that he isn't returning any of my texts or calls to discuss it.

I'm also irritated with Mason. She has barely spoken to me since we left the church and arrived at the pub that is hosting Ivy's wake. If she hasn't been glued to her phone, updating her *PhoGlo* account with images from the day, she has been posing for photos with some of her admirers outside and even signing a few autographs.

The whole way she has been today seems disrespectful. Not just to me, I mean we're not exactly best friends although it would have been nice for her to keep me company seeing as I don't actually know anybody here.

But mainly disrespectful to the person we are supposed to be remembering.

Funerals are about paying your respects, offering kind words to fellow grievers and swapping memories to lighten the mood. In other words, they're all about the dead. But Mason has made today all about herself.

So far, she has added ten photo videos to her *PhoGlo* page, starting from the hotel this morning where she put a full-body image of herself in the mirror online, wearing a black dress and a sad face emoji.

She documented the journey from the hotel to the church, filming Grimsby as it passed by outside her window and asking her followers to guess where she was.

Then upon arrival at the church, she posted a photo of the service booklet, with a crying face emoji but also a congratulations to her followers who guessed where it was that she had been going.

Like it was some kind of exciting competition to be won.

She even tagged one of her posts with the location, St Johns Methodist Church, as if she was just tagging herself at a hotel or beach bar. The whole thing seems to be more about growing her following online rather than engaging with the family of Ivy Lane in the real world.

For somebody that was supposedly a friend of Ivy, she hasn't once spoken to or offered kind words to the family of the tragic woman.

She had also been tagging me in some of the photos, and of course, there had been a selfie of the two of us in the church, both in black and both looking glum. Okay so I'll admit I played up to the camera for that one, but we all do silly things when someone's recording us.

Of course, the fact I was photographed and tagged alongside one of the biggest stars of *PhoGlo* meant that my following had skyrocketed today, just as Mason had predicted it would when she told me why I had to attend the funeral. I'm already closing in on 40k followers, and I've only been working for Sebastian for a few days.

I'll admit it was a little exciting to see my account blowing up every time I took my phone out, but I was trying not to look at it too much. There would be plenty of time for that after the wake. Right now, I would rather be smiling at the kind people around me and striking up a few conversations wherever I could.

I wasn't here to sell myself or grow my brand. I didn't even know what my brand was yet. That was one of the many things that I wanted to discuss with Sebastian except I couldn't get through to him. The only messages he sent me were the daily ones telling me what I was to post on my account that day along with the hashtags that would propel it and make it more visible to potential new followers.

I had been doing this for the first few days without any problem, but then all he had been asking me to do was post fairly plan stuff. Day one was the makeup-free selfie with the caption detailing some honest facts about myself. Day two had been an old photo of me and my parents, along with the simple message 'Family' (love heart emoji), which had obviously made me reminisce about my dad. Then yesterday I had been instructed to post a video of myself trying to jog down my street, which I thought made me look like a sweaty mess, but Sebastian had obviously seen that my lack of fitness would make me look like I was into self-improvement while still appearing to be just as unfit as most of my followers.

He was obviously trying to make me relatable to my growing audience, and I'd posted them all without argument. Until I had received his message today, telling me what he wanted me to post while I was Ivy's funeral.

He wanted me to post a photo of myself smiling into the camera, with my black dress visible as well as a few mourners in the background, with the caption:

Sad day but we have to keep smiling. If you were a fan of @IvyLane_UK I give you my condolences. All you need to give me in return is a follow xx

The post felt wrong on a number of levels. I didn't want to upload a photo of my smiling face at a funeral. I also didn't want to use the whole day as a chance to gain more followers, even though I knew that's what Sebastian and Mason wanted. And I certainly didn't want to put the kisses at the end of the caption and show complete disregard to the seriousness of the occasion I was attending.

Even the hashtags caused me concern. Alongside the ones that his team of computer geeks had come up with were a few that seemed downright insensitive.

Like #LifeGoesOn.

Or #FollowsNotFunerals.

And worst of all #TheNextIvyLane.

The whole thing just didn't feel right. Not only was this type of post not me and didn't fit with my personality, it shouldn't really fit with anyone else's either. It was insensitive and definitely fell into the category of if you can't say something nice then don't say anything at all. The throwaway line about me sending my condolences didn't disguise the fact that it was a blatant grab for new followers.

I said as much to Sebastian in my reply, telling him I didn't feel comfortable with his request and that if I had to post anything at all from the funeral, then I would have preferred it to be an uplifting quote or maybe even one of my favourite photos from Ivy's account that had cheered me up in the past.

But there had been no reply. So I had waited an hour and messaged again. I wanted to know if I was okay to go ahead and post my own thing instead of his.

No answer.

Now two hours had passed, and I still hadn't posted anything. But he had seen the messages. What was his problem? Just let me know what I need to do Sebastian.

But with each passing minute, I was realising what the lack of response meant.

He had given me my instruction for the day. There was nothing more to be said.

I either had to post it, or I was out.

I took a sip from my glass of Diet Coke and looked around the room. It was busy but not as much as the church had been. Some of the mourners had drifted away, either shortly after the buffet had opened or just after the first round of drinks had been paid for by the family.

But there would have been more people in here if it wasn't for the security guard standing on the front entrance, keeping out all the local fans of Ivy Lane, and all those who wanted to get inside and tag themselves at such a potential *PhoGlo* event, never mind catch sight of anybody famous inside.

But of course, Mason had forgone being in here with a load of old relatives of the deceased to instead be outside, standing amongst the crowds of young and impressionable fans, posing for photos and happily being tagged in a zillion videos and pictures.

I was just about to head back to the buffet for a second time when I saw Mason re-enter the room and make her way over to my table. She looked great, although she was shivering, which of course is what happens when you spend half an hour stood outside in January wearing nothing more than a slinky dress and heels.

She sat down beside me and didn't look up until she had finished typing the message on her phone. Then finally, after what had felt like forever, I was finally worthy enough to get some of her much-sought-after attention.

'What's up?' she asks as she notices the glum expression on my face.

'It's a funeral,' I snap back, slightly irritated that she expected me to be all smiles at such a sad occasion.

'Doesn't mean you can't smile,' she replies, shrugging her bare shoulders which were visible in her dress, the one that had seemed entirely inappropriate for a funeral when I saw her putting it on this morning.

I barely had any skin on show, out of respect, but also because mine was ghostly white in comparison to my tanned companion today.

'Life goes on,' she adds, and I'm instantly reminded of the caption that Sebastian had told me to write a couple of hours ago but was still currently unsent.

'Mason, can I ask you something? I say tentatively, before she has a chance to go back to her phone.

'I got the dress from Mrs Maguires and the shoes from Zyo,' she tells me, smiling.

I raise a smile of my own, even though I don't feel much like it, before I continue.

' 'These messages that Sebastian wants us to put on. Do we have to go along with every one of them or can we say no occasionally?'

I've only just finished asking the question, but I already have my answer by the look on Mason's face.

'You do what he tells you to do at all times,' she finally tells me, after giving me a long, hard stare.

"Or what?' I ask. 'I'm fired?'

Mason laughs and then picks up my glass of Diet Coke and finishes it herself.

'No, you don't get fired,' she says as she stands to go to the bar. 'You just end up like Ivy.'

And then she saunters away to the bar, leaving me sitting alone again in the corner of the musty function room, wondering what the hell she meant by that.

#TruthBomb

Mason Manor

Strictly speaking, Sebastian should have been the one to tell Emily what the consequences are if she fails to comply with his requests. But it doesn't really matter who lets her know. The important thing is that she does know, and now she definitely does.

We had to leave the funeral pretty quickly after I'd made my remark to her about ending up like Ivy if she didn't listen. I'd been hoping to stay for a little longer and had been on my way to get a drink from the bar, but Emily had become agitated, and it was best that we continued the conversation somewhere more private than a pub full of people.

We'd gotten a cab back to our hotel, and I'd managed to get her to stop asking me questions in front of the driver, but once we were back in our room, then I was able to speak more freely.

'What happened to Ivy?' she had demanded to know as soon as the door to our hotel room was closed.

'She went rogue,' I told her as I'd changed out of my dress into something more comfortable.

I had a flight to America tonight, and there was no way I was going to travel looking like I'd just come from a funeral. Life goes on, just as easily as a more colourful dress goes on.

'She stopped listening to Sebastian. Stopped posting what he wanted her to post. That's against the rules, of course. That's not what we all agreed when we signed up for this,' I had continued as I kicked my heels off and felt the soothing softness of the carpet beneath my aching feet.

'So Sebastian made Ivy kill herself?' Emily had asked, and I had shaken my head that the poor girl still couldn't see that it hadn't been suicide that had taken Ivy Lane out of this world.

'Ivy didn't kill herself,' I had told Emily, finally looking her dead in the eye, so she actually started to understand what I was trying to tell her. 'Sebastian has someone that takes care of it. He sends them to find you if you ignore the warnings. And that person is really good at making murder look like suicide.'

It was at that point that Emily had finally grasped the seriousness of the situation, and her silence had allowed me to go into the bathroom to gather up my makeup accessories that were strewn all around the sink. When I had returned to the bedroom, she was sitting on her bed and had tears in her eyes. I'd tried to continue packing as much as possible, but eventually, her sobbing had become too loud, and I'd been forced to stop and take a seat beside her.

Then I'd told her everything. How Sebastian had picked me and taken me from a life of obscurity to the life I had now, and how he had done the same with Ivy, and Emily, and dozens of other people like us over the years. I had told her what he was getting out of it, which was a team of powerful influencers that would do and say anything he wanted them to. And I told her how he kept them all in line; with threats to them and their one remaining parent.

I had explained how I had once tried to do things my own way, after I had built up a large enough following, only to receive two warnings from Sebastian.

A written message on my phone and a physical one written on a notepad which I found in the room I had been staying in at the time.

I had immediately fallen back into line and returned to posting what he wanted me to, and that meant that I was still here, instead of it seeming like I was just another one in the long line of fallen stars that cracked under the pressure of fame and chose to end it all alone in a hotel room miles from home.

That had been two years ago, and since then I had gone on to be Sebastian's number one influencer, a position I planned on keeping, for mine and my mother's sake.

Emily had wiped away some of her tears and asked me why I didn't just go to the police to tell them what was happening. Maybe they could stop Sebastian, she said, and maybe they could uncover the truth about what he had been doing all these years.

But it wasn't that simple. Not only would Sebastian get to you and your family in the end, regardless of whether or not he was in prison, but speaking to the police would only serve to implicate the influencers in his crimes too.

The next thing I had told Emily had been difficult because I hadn't spoken about it with anyone but Sebastian ever since it had happened years earlier. I swore Emily to secrecy before I told her, and she had nodded, looking at me with tear-stained eyes with fear about what I was about to tell her.

I had taken a deep breath and then told her that Sebastian's mysterious henchman isn't the only one in the company that is required to kill and make it look like something else.

The influencers are too.

After I had calmed Emily down again, I had explained to her that about six months after working for Sebastian, he will visit you in person and give you a task. The methods he wants you to use may vary, but the end result will always be the same.

He wants you to kill someone for him.

As Emily had remained silent and scared, I had gone on to tell her about the time he had visited me in Barcelona and given me my task. He knew I was scheduled to visit a party in the Middle East a week later. It was one of those events where a rich Sheikh pays to have a load of celebrities come and party with him and his friends at their mansion and I was on the guest list. I liked to think I had been chosen due to my increasing influence on social media, but in reality, it was probably because I was just another good-looking woman to get into his home.

In Barcelona, Sebastian had told me who the Sheikh really was. He was responsible for several human rights scandals in his home country, and while he remained free from any form of prosecution, his crimes had directly caused the pain, suffering and deaths of a great number of people in the nation.

Sebastian told me he had to be stopped, and then he had told me I was going to be the one to do it.

He wanted me to put something in his drink during the party. Something that he wouldn't know was in there and wouldn't be able to taste when he drank it but something that would kill him within 48 hours of consuming it.

Something extremely hazardous. Something untraceable.

Something I would get away with because I would already be out of the country by the time he died.

Ethylene glycol. A colourless, odourless liquid most commonly used as an ingredient in antifreeze. Extremely poisonous to humans and capable of killing one in 24 hours if medical assistance isn't sought immediately after it is consumed.

Then he had given me a small capsule containing the poison and told me that while he would only ever ask me to do something like this once, failure to comply would result in the deaths of both me and my mum back at home.

'Did you do it?' Emily had asked me, almost shaking beside me on the bed as I had told her the story.

When I nodded at her, she had raised her hands to her mouth in shock. But I had continued because she needed to know the full story.

I told her how I had done research into the Sheikh after Sebastian had left and read online about all the terrible things that he had done to the people in his home country. Women had been persecuted for the simplest of things. Not covering their faces in public. Not walking behind their man on the street. Not bowing to him and showing respect in his presence.

And many men had suffered just as much. All the buildings that the Sheikh had demanded be built had resulted in the deaths of many workers due to the inhumane and unsafe working environments he made them work in. He treated many people like slaves. There was no doubt he was a bad man.

And there was no doubt he deserved to die.

So I told her how I had attended the party and had seen many famous faces there. A superstar DJ was providing the music, and I saw multiple movie stars swimming in his pool. We were all being paid to party with him. Then several of the most attractive women were called to sit with him in his cabana. I had been chosen. That was where I had been able to slip the poison into one of the many drinks on the large table in front of us. There were already so many drugs at the party that even if anyone had seen me, they wouldn't have thought it was strange to see me pouring something into a glass of champagne. Everyone was high. Everyone was relaxed.

I had handed the Sheikh his drink, given him a kiss on the cheek and thanked him for my invitation. Then I had sat back down in between a French supermodel and a Spanish pop star and watched him drink it all.

Two days later, when I was sitting at an airport halfway across the world from where I had done it, I read the news that he had died. No one had looked for antifreeze as a cause of death because no one knew they had to.

That was the same day I received $1 million in my bank account.

It was also the day that Sebastian allowed me to reach 1 million followers on PhoGlo.

It was a few months later before I learnt the real reason that Sebastian had wanted the man dead. It had nothing to do with the Sheikh's human rights abuses. It was because he was the favourite to win the contract for a new oil pipeline that would run between his country and the next. With him out of the way, the pipeline was awarded to another company.

Of course, the winning company was the one Sebastian had all his shares in.

I knew this because I saw the company' brochure in his briefcase the next time I saw him. When I had asked him about it, he had just smiled and said that there were many reasons to want a man dead and I shouldn't dwell on any of them.

I'd told Emily how what I had done meant that I was forever in Sebastian's control. If I was to speak to anyone about what he was doing to me and the other influencers, then the evidence of what I had done would be leaked, and my mother would die knowing her daughter had murdered a man. Then I would die, or perhaps worse, end up in a prison in the same country where the Sheikh was from.

Then I explained to her how Sebastian was just getting started with her. That if she thought the message that he wanted her to post at the funeral was bad, then there was a lot worse coming.

I told her to do as she was told and that everything would be okay if she did. She would get to live the life of her dreams. She would be able to support her mum and pay her back for everything she had ever done for her.

Most of all, *she would get to live.*

As we checked out of the hotel and I said goodbye to Emily, I hoped that I would see her again. Somewhere far away from this chilly, emotion-filled day in Grimsby. Maybe in a beach bar in Miami or in a sushi restaurant in Tokyo.

But as we departed and I saw how shaken up she was about what I had told her, I also knew that the next time I might see Emily Bennett could be at her funeral, with her lifeless eyes looking up at me from the inside of a wooden box.

#WhatWouldYouDo?

Emily Bennett

After speaking with Mason, I uploaded the post that Sebastian wanted me to do.

Shortly after it, I had begun to receive several nasty comments about how it was rude and disrespectful to Ivy and her family and that I was a bitch for using her death to try and improve my popularity.

But I also received over fifty thousand followers in the first 24 hours after it went online, many of whom commented and told me how awesome I was.

That's the internet for you, I suppose.

The train journey back down south from Grimsby had been a long one, and by the time I had walked through the front door of my mum's house in Billericay, I had been exhausted. But of course, my mum had wanted to know about everything I'd done in the time since she had seen me last and so I'd done my best to fill her in, keeping back only the part of the story about hers and her daughter's life now being at risk.

Obviously.

It had been three days since I had seen her last and a lot had happened in that time. I'd had my second meeting with Sebastian, the one where Mason swept in and put me under her spell. I'd stayed at the real Mason Manor for one night and swam in her indoor pool before we took the train up north together. And I'd attended a funeral, one that was as bleak and sombre as any other, and it had brought back memories of attending my father's funeral last year.

I'd also posted another three times to my account since I'd last seen mum and as a result had earned another six grand in my bank account, not to mention a ridiculous number of followers. Then I'd made my way back home, leaving Mason to head to the airport to fly to America, and me to pack my bags before Sebastian told me where I was to go next.

Mum listened to it all with her mouth wide open and a look of disbelief on her face. While she'd been slaving away in a supermarket and coming back to an empty house, I'd been mingling with rich celebrities and travelling up and down the country. Of course, I'd texted her about all this as most of it had been happening, but she still seemed as surprised as if she was hearing about it all for the first time.

By the time I'd got her back up to speed on the events in my life it was approaching midnight, and all I wanted to do was curl up into my bed. Not that I expected to get much sleep. The things Mason had told me were still bouncing around in my exhausted brain.

Threats. Fear.

Murder.

But just before I headed upstairs to my room where I could close the door and try to make sense of it all, my mum stood up from the sofa, crossed the living room towards me and opened up her arms to give me a hug.

As we embraced, she told me again how proud she was of me and that she had been wrong not to support my dream of being an influencer.

It made me want to cry, and I felt like confessing everything to her right there and then. Tell her she had actually been right. How I wished I had listened. How we were both in danger now, and there was no way out of it. How I was trapped working for a man with frightening power and, at some point in the next year, he would meet with me and tell me that I was going to have to kill somebody for him.

How I had no choice but to obey him now.

But instead, I just hugged her back and told her to wake me up in the morning because I wanted to see her before she went to work.

I knew that tomorrow I would get my next instruction from Sebastian and head back out into the world on the next part of his plan for me. But unlike what I had done this week, this next part was likely to involve me visiting more glamourous places than Grimsby and also require me to be away from home for more than just three days.

Therefore, I wanted to see mum before she left in the morning, because who knew when I would be able to see her again.

She promised me she would wake me before she went to work and we said goodnight before I closed the door in my bedroom and then finally, I was on my own. I put my phone on my windowsill, as far away from my bed that I could get it, then climbed under my duvet.

Somehow putting a little distance between me and Sebastian's messages, however small, felt like a minor victory in the moment.

I turned off the light but kept my eyes wide open in the darkness. I needed to think. I needed to make a plan. It was clear I had two options. Either I go along with what Sebastian wants me to do and throw myself fully into my new life as a social media influencer just like Mason has done. Or I rebel and try to get away from him now before he has further opportunities to get me to do the kind of things that will leave me in his debt forever.

But according to Mason, getting away isn't really an option.

Not if I want to keep myself and my mum safe.

So what choice do I have? I have to carry on working for Sebastian.

I try to remain open-minded and think about how bad that would really be. *You know, if I take all the killing and constant fear of retaliation out of the equation.*

I've always wanted to be popular on social media. Now I am. I've always wanted to see more of the world and not be chained to the small section of the planet I was born in to. Now I can. And I've always wanted to be rich and to help make life easier for myself and others, and I'm on my way to that now.

From what I know just by looking at Mason, the money I'm getting now is just the tip of the iceberg compared to what I'll be making in the future.

Even if I did find some way out of this mess, and even if I did it without bringing any harm to me or my family, then what? I'd be back to where I was before all this. No job, no money, no future. Stuck in my childhood bedroom scrolling through *PhoGlo* wishing my life was as fun as the people I saw online.

But if I choose to go with it and obey Sebastian's every command, then what? I know now that he wants a lot more from me than just uploading a specific post to my page every day. Being used as a pawn to further whatever business interests he has is one thing. But killing somebody? That's another thing entirely. That is something that will stay with me forever.

No amount of editing, filtering and hashtagging can remove that memory from my brain.

But the way Mason had described it had made it sound like it wasn't even that difficult. You just put a bit of poison into a drink. You aren't even there when they die.

If I kill a stranger who probably deserves to die anyway, is it really that bad?

I think back to something Mason told me, when we were sitting on my bed in the hotel room in Grimsby this morning. She told me how she had grappled with her decision as well. How it had kept her awake at night and caused her to debate the rights and wrongs of everything she had done and was going to do in future. But ultimately, she had decided to go along with it.

The reason was that once she had experienced a taste of the life that she had always dreamt of, then she had found it impossible to give it up.

The exotic holidays. The private planes.

The money. The fame.

The respect.

Even if there was some possible way to get out of Sebastian's grip, she didn't want to give it all up. And that was the only thing you could do if you somehow managed to escape him.

You would have to hide. Go off the grid. Remain elusive. Forever. Because Sebastian and his men would be looking for you and as soon as you popped up in public or on a *PhoGlo* page then they would find you, and they would kill you.

I didn't want to go back to a life of obscurity. I didn't want to hide away somewhere forever and give up on all the goals and ambitions I had.

I wanted to pay off my mum's mortgage. I wanted to start a cancer charity in memory of my dad.

And I wanted to be the first person in the Bennett family to become a millionaire.

I roll over onto the other side of my pillow and close my eyes. I will try and sleep on it. By the time mum wakes me up in the morning, I will have made my mind up.

By the time Sebastian sends me his next message, I will know what I am going to do with the rest of my life.

#OutOfHere

Liz Bennett

It's not often I go to work in a good mood, but I did today. I couldn't stop smiling as I drove the four miles to the supermarket where I work and, by the time I was unloading the fresh produce onto the grocery aisles, I was positively grinning like a Cheshire Cat.

The reason for my happiness was all down to my wonderful daughter Emily. She has endured a dreadful time since her father died, but she has never stopped aiming for a better life, and now she has it. She is a full-time, fully-paid influencer, and as I left the house this morning and headed to my dreary job, she was packing her bags before taking a taxi to the airport and boarding a flight to Amsterdam.

My little girl has finally grown up. She finally has a career. And she is finally leaving home, although I am a little upset about that part.

But it's time. She's in her twenties, and I know she couldn't go on living in the bedroom she had grown up in forever. Of course, I'll miss seeing her every day, but I know she is happier now and therefore, so am I.

I'll admit I had given up a little on life since I lost my husband. I'd stopped caring about things that I used to enjoy so much. I'd lost connection with all my passions and the things that made me who I am. My love of cooking. Playing netball with the girls down at the local club. And having wine and cheese nights with our friends and getting so tipsy I often forgot how I got home.

Most of all, I'd been letting Emily down. I hadn't been a good mother to her since becoming a widow, and there had been far too many arguments between us, most of which were as a result of my grief and my fear at growing old alone with no money and nobody to share my later years with.

But that had all changed now. It should have been me to make that change and turn around the fortunes of my family, but it wasn't. It was Emily. She has done it all herself. She deserves all the success that is coming her way, and I wouldn't blame her if she just wanted to disappear off into the world and get as far away from me and Billericay as she could.

But bless her, she is a kind soul, and she is a great daughter, and she has told me that no matter how much she is away from home now, and how little she gets to see me in the coming months, she isn't going to forget about everything I have done for her since I brought her into the world twenty-three years ago.

She told me what she wanted to do for me as we said our goodbyes this morning. She told me how she wanted to use some of the money she was making now to go into paying off my mortgage. And she told me to hand in my notice at the supermarket because she was going to take care of me now, just like I had taken care of her for so many years.

I had cried as she told me all of this and I had even tried to refuse the offer, telling her that the money she was making now is hers to spend on herself and not for me. But she hadn't taken no for an answer and made me promise her that I would quit my job today and stop working so hard because I didn't need to anymore.

She hadn't let me leave until I had promised her that and, now here I was, at work, and plucking up the courage to walk into my manager's office and tell him that I'm leaving.

He'll be shocked. He'll be confused. And most of all he'll want to know how I expect to support myself without the measly wage that I make every month.

I will smile. I will relax my weary shoulders and put a hand on my aching back. And I will tell him.

My daughter is a social media star now. My daughter wants to pay me back for everything I have done for her in my life.

My daughter loves me.

Then I will walk out of that office with my head held high and send a text message to Emily, telling her I have done it. Then I will shed a little tear because the only thing that could make this day any more perfect than it is going to be would be if my husband was waiting for me at home.

But life isn't perfect. It has its ups and its downs. Emily and I have been on a massive down for the last two years. But now it's turning around. Now we are headed in the right direction.

Finally, after all this time and all that sorrow, finally, things are looking up.

#LifestylesOfTheRich&Famous

Emily Bennett

I count forty yachts before I give up and decide to just enjoy the view. From my balcony in Monte Carlo, I can see the whole of the harbour area and the calm blue waters of the Mediterranean are littered with the pristine white bodies of million-pound vessels occupied by millionaire owners.

I was on one of those yachts yesterday. It was called *The DreamCatcher,* and it was owned by one of the richest men in Britain. He was throwing a party for his 60th birthday, and I was one of the lucky 300 souls that were invited aboard to celebrate the occasion out on the sun-soaked ocean.

But unlike the birthday parties that I'd been invited to as a child, this one was different. Instead of the guests being given a piece of cake folded up in a napkin or maybe a goodie bag full of sweets to say thank you for coming, each person on the yacht had been gifted with a small memento to remember the party by.

Every man on the boat had received a watch estimated to be worth around 20,000, and all the ladies on board were given a bracelet worth roughly the same amount.

It seems that people who have everything choose to celebrate their birthdays by giving out gifts, and not just receiving them. But when you have a net worth of over three billion pounds, then I guess handing everybody a piece of dry sponge cake in a napkin just doesn't cut it anymore.

I look at the diamond-encrusted bracelet on my tanned left wrist and chalk it up to being just one of the many insane things that have happened to me over the past six months. Ever since I made the decision to go all-in with Sebastian and his vision for my future, I've been living the kind of lifestyle that I used to read about in the 'Showbiz & Gossip' articles on the online newspaper sites.

Been on a private plane? Yes, three times.

Been paid to stay at a luxury resort and document my stay? Every week.

Caused several large companies to get into a bidding war over my advertising services? Guilty as charged.

Pool parties in Vegas? Check.

Swimming with dolphins in the Dominican? Check.

Courtside seats to a Lakers game sitting close to Justin Bieber and some old movie star called Jack Nicholson?

Check. Check. Check.

I've visited five of the seven continents with only South America and Antarctica to tick off the list, although while I have plans to attend the Rio Carnival at some point, I'm not sure I will be making any to visit the South Pole anytime soon. But I never know what Sebastian will have in store for me, so I can't rule it out.

I'm a full time, fully paid influencer now and I have almost just as much money in my bank account as followers on my *PhoGlo* account (just over half a million if you really want to know).

Life has been good to me ever since I teamed up with Sebastian. And the best thing is that even though I'm half a year into my new career now, I know that really, I'm just getting started.

But don't get me wrong, I've still got my feet on the ground. I'm still the same old girl from a small town in Essex who loves her mum and misses her dad. The facial recognition system on my phone still sometimes fails to recognise me after a particularly heavy night. And I'm still living in fear for my life every day from Sebastian and his mysterious henchman that closely monitor my every move.

But I'd be lying if I said the events of the last few months haven't changed me a little. I have more confidence now. I expect better for myself. I demand better. But most of all, I just feel like I belong in the world now. I've found my place, and for the first time ever people look at me with respect instead of disdain, or worse, ignoring me completely.

No longer am I the timid little girl who got fired from her crappy temp job and replaced by someone they thought had a better work ethic than me. Now I am the confident, proud woman that others aspire to be. I'm using my platform to motivate and inspire all the other people in the world that lie in their beds every night and dream of a better life, just as I did for so many years.

And I'm using my profile to make real changes in the world. Not just the changes that Sebastian wants me to make but actual ones that matter to me. I have started a charity in memory of my father and help to raise funds and awareness of the cancer that took his life. I have set up a scheme to help disadvantaged women in Britain have a chance at a better life. And then there's mum, who has quit her job and now gets to spend more time doing the things she wants to do.

She's currently writing a book about the struggles of being a widow. And she's even started dating again. I couldn't be happier for her.

I close my eyes as the one small cloud covering the sun drifts on, and the warm rays of light hit my face again. I'm supposed to check out of my room now but five more minutes on this balcony won't hurt. I would sit here all day and watch the yachts in the harbour coming and going in the middle of this millionaire's playground if I could.

But there's another reason why I am putting off grabbing my bag and leaving this hotel. Another thing preventing me from rushing to catch my flight back to the UK. And no, it isn't just because I'm avoiding the cloudy, drizzly weather in my home country. It's because I have a meeting to attend when I get there, and I already know what the agenda of discussion will be.

I received a message from Sebastian last night telling me he wanted to meet me in Manchester this afternoon. He didn't say why, but he didn't have to. I already know because Mason told me this day would come.

It's time for him to tell me I have to kill someone.

I'm six months into my employment with him, and just like Mason warned, that is usually the time he requests a face to face meeting to discuss a private matter.

He is right on schedule.

I haven't seen Sebastian since we met for cocktails and lobster at the top of The Shard back in January, the same day I also met Mason and back when I was still just plain old Emily Bennett with a few thousand followers and no discernible income to speak of.

Since then, there have been daily messages from my boss but no physical contact. No meetings. No lunches. No parties. I haven't even seen Mason since Ivy's funeral, but at least I can follow her adventures online. But Sebastian has no social media account. The only way I know he is still alive is because he texts me every morning with the post that he wants me to upload to my page.

The man operates in the shadows. But now he is coming out into the light.

Now he wants to see me again.

I've been counting down to this day ever since I made my decision to allow Sebastian to be my puppet master and pull my strings in exchange for a life of glamour and profit. I knew I wouldn't see him before this meeting, and I know it could be a long time until I see him again after it.

We have much to talk about. Goals that have already been accomplished. And goals yet to be ticked off. But I have done everything he has asked of me so far, and so I'm not worried about the meeting with him later today. I've been a model employee and have even sent him a few messages back telling him how grateful I am again for the opportunity he has given me. He never replies. He just lets another day roll by then sends me my next job.

He's all business. I respect that about him. It's a good way to live your life.

It's just like the famous expression. The one I'm sure he'll appreciate just as much as I do. The one where they say; *"it's not personal, it's just business."*

That's my motto now, and it's the one I'll keep in mind as I leave Monaco and board my flight to Manchester.

#GrimUpNorth

Sebastian Sawyer

You wouldn't think that it was the middle of summer in England based on how stormy the weather was as my flight came into land. I'd left twenty-eight degrees, blue skies and sunshine in LA for 14 degrees, charcoal skies and a drizzly rain in Manchester.

If there had been any other way of handling this upcoming meeting that would have seen me avoid having to be here, then trust me, I would have taken it. But I'm cautious, and sticking to the rules that have served me well so far, so here I am, ready to hold the meeting face to face, instead of any other way that could cause the contents of what I am about to discuss to be leaked out into the public domain.

I'm checked into my room at one of the finer hotels in the city and am fresh out of the hot, soothing water of the shower that was of much more comfort to me than the cold, irritating rain outside. Now I'm standing by my bed with just a white towel wrapped around my waist trying to get the hotel employee on the other end of the phone to fetch me a good quality bottle of bourbon.

From the way he's stuttering and stammering back his replies I'm guessing that either the hotel has run out of their supplies of good alcohol or he's new in the job, and he doesn't realise that I'm paying almost

£1000 a night to have a much better service than the one he is currently providing me.

In the end, he gets the assistance of one of his colleagues who apologises for the delay and assures me a fresh bottle will be sent up to me immediately. I put the phone down while they're still apologising and go back to the bathroom to finish drying off.

Standing in front of the mirror, and under the full beam of the enthusiastic lighting in here, I notice what appears to be a grey hair on the top of my head, lying amongst the rest of my thick, freshly washed follicles. I use a pair of tweezers to remove it and am more than a little relieved to see that it appears to be a lone wolf, nothing more than a solitary rogue hair amongst thousands of well-behaving ones.

But I know that eventually the rest of them will turn against me too.

It's just a matter of time.

But just like everything else in life that has turned against me, I will find a solution to it and eliminate the problem. That's what I do. I'm a problem solver, amongst many, many other things and so as I shave my beard, my mind moves on to the problem that has brought me here, to this god-forsaken part of the world that summertime seems to have forgotten.

Her name is Florence Lee, and she is currently one of the biggest obstacles in my company's next action plan for world domination. As the host of the UK's most popular podcast, *The Florence Lee Show*, she has access to the ears and minds of her twelve million listeners per episode.

Her rise to the top of the podcast charts is remarkable but perhaps understandable, as before her journey in broadcasting, she was a popstar and appeared on reality TV shows in Britain. After gracing the gossip pages of numerous magazines and newspapers, she decided to mature a little and start her own podcast in which she would invite various people on to discuss topics relevant to the country at the time.

Using the connections she had made from a brief career in music, she was able to get C-List celebrities onto her early shows, but they were nothing more than tame, click-bait type podcasts where the conversations never got more in-depth than who was wearing which brand of dress on the red carpet that week.

But as the years went by, Florence Lee started to branch out and invite more credible guests on her show.

Nurses to discuss the problems with the National Health System.

Scientists to chat about diet, sleep and exercise.

And even politicians, taking advantage of the huge audience Florence has, to talk about their political party's plans should they ever get into power.

She came to my attention when I was doing my research into strategies to get my preferred candidate for the upcoming general election in the UK into 10 Downing Street. With the polls opening in three months' time and my preferred candidate, Simon Forster, currently trailing in the polls I needed a way of turning the tide.

In short, I needed a way of stopping Florence telling her listeners to vote for Simon's opponent.

One of the things about independent podcasting is that the speakers on the show aren't restricted by any TV network or media giant's agenda. If you host your own podcast, and you own all the rights to it, then you can basically say whatever the hell you like. You can talk about who you love, who you hate, what products you recommended, which ones you avoid, and you can even try and brainwash your listeners into voting for the man you want to be the next Prime Minister of the United Kingdom.

It's the same all over the world and even in my own country. Long gone are the days when presidents were chosen based on how much money they had to run their campaign or which media sources they managed to pay to report favourably on them. This is the age of free speech, and not just the kind that campaigners fought so hard for decades ago, but it barely made any difference if they got it. This isn't the free speech where someone stands on a street corner and shouts at passers-by. This is the free speech where if you have a microphone and the ability to transmit your messages, then you can get them into the podcast app on millions of people's phones instantly.

Florence Lee was a problem for me because she was telling her 12 million listeners to vote for David Stopp, the candidate she believed was the best person to lead Britain for the next four years while I wanted current PM Simon Forster to be re-elected and remain in power for the foreseeable future.

That was 12 million people every week who were listening to someone telling them to vote for my opposition.

And the prediction polls showed that it was having an impact. Simon's lead was being consistently whittled down over the weeks and it was reaching the point that many experts now believed the final result of the election was too close to call.

It was 50/50. It could go either way. I needed those 12 million followers to stop listening to Florence and start making their own minds up.

I needed to shut her up and fast.

Some people might wonder why an American businessman such as myself would be so interested in who became the next Prime Minister of the United Kingdom. But those people don't know that I have a large amount of money invested in industries that are thriving under Simon's leadership right now. If Florence's candidate got voted in instead of mine, then his party would put an end to most of that money because they wanted their policies to go in a different direction, which meant budgets would be cut and my profits would take a huge hit.

There's a reason I've spent so many years painstakingly putting together a team of powerful social media influencers who will obey my every command. It's for situations just like this one. It's to help my candidate win elections just like this one.

And it's to eliminate problems, just like Florence Lee.

I've managed to get one of my influencers on Florence's podcast tomorrow morning. They have been invited on to discuss the world of influencing, talk about the pros and cons of social media, and also tell some of the crazy celebrity stories they have accrued during their time travelling the world.

What Florence doesn't know yet is I will have instructed my influencer to bring up the rumours that she is being paid to promote one political party over the other and that she possibly even had an affair with her candidate of choice several months earlier.

Of course, it's all complete rubbish. I know it, and Florence knows it. But the listeners won't know it and often, planting just one seed of doubt in somebody's mind is enough to see it grow into a whole forest of controversy.

But the guest will have another duty to perform during their time on the show, and it's one that requires a little more skill than simply gossiping into a microphone.

My influencer is going to poison Florence while she is live on her show.

With her gone, and the rumours that my influencer brought up spreading like wildfire through the public, my candidate will start to regain control in the election race and my many investments will continue to pay off as profitably as before.

Several of my influencers have already killed for me before. Now it's the turn of my newest one.

It's time for Emily Bennett to demonstrate her true worth to me. She will be the one that ends Florence Lee's life, and I will tell her this as soon as she arrives at my hotel today.

Yes, it's murder, and I'm sure Emily will have her doubts. But I will tell her what I told all the others.

It's not personal.

It's just business.

#HotelRendouzvous

Emily Bennett

Some women would love to be secretly meeting up with a handsome man in a plush city centre hotel in the middle of the afternoon.

But I'm not one of them.

While I like handsome men and I definitely like plush hotels, I'm not a fan of secrets, and I'm certainly not a fan of anything illicit. So being in this room in Manchester with Sebastian isn't as exciting as another woman might find it to be.

Especially when I know that as soon as the pleasantries are over, he is going to tell me that he wants me to kill somebody.

But for now, I'll force a smile on my face and accept his offer of a drink as I take off my wet coat and hang it on the back of his hotel room door.

'How was Monte Carlo?' he asks me as he pours two measures of bourbon from the bottle that I can tell he already started drinking from before I arrived.

'Stunning. I can see why they call it the playground of the rich and famous,' I reply as I make my way over to the chair in the corner of the room.

'Please, take a seat on the bed, it's more comfortable,' he tells me, and so I do, but only on the edge of it, on top of the duvet, beside the towel that I can tell he used for his shower before I got here.

He turns and hands me my drink.

'Do you have any mixers?' I ask, knowing there's no way I can drink neat whiskey without throwing up all over his bed immediately afterwards.

'Of course,' he replies and opens the door to the mini bar, where he finds a small can of cola and opens it for me.

'Thanks,' I say as I pour the fizzy liquid into my drink, no doubt nullifying whatever expensive taste the whiskey held and making me seem stupid in the eyes of my boss.

But I don't care. I'm more of a white wine kind of girl. If I have to drink spirits, then I will do it on my own terms.

Sebastian lowers himself into the chair that I had been planning on sitting in and takes a long sip from his glass as he keeps his eyes on me from across the room.

'So you're probably wondering why I asked to see you,' he finally says, after draining half of his drink and placing the glass on the table beside him.

'Yeah, a little. I mean, it's been so long since we last met,' I tell him, playing the role of the dumb employee even though I know exactly why I'm here. I just hope Mason was telling the truth when she told me she hadn't mentioned our early conversation with him.

The one in which she told me he asks his employees to kill for him six months into their contract.

'Too long,' he says, maintaining perfect eye contact with me and I take long sip from my glass just to break the intensity of the moment.

I screw up my face a little at the taste but if Sebastian notices he doesn't let on. Instead, he just continues. 'But I've been extremely busy this year, and I know for a fact that you have too.'

I smile. 'Busy is an understatement. But I'm having fun.'

'Good,' he says, nodding his head before picking up his glass again and taking another hearty gulp. Unlike me, he doesn't screw his face up at the strength of the alcohol. He's a big drinker. Mason told me that about him too.

As he polishes off the contents of his glass, I think about how weird it is to see him dressed in something other than the expensive suits he normally wears. Today he's just in a white t-shirt and dark jeans, which although are probably almost as expensive as the suits, give him a more approachable demeanour.

The businessman look can be a little intimidating. But today he just looks like an average guy. An average, good looking guy, with a great tan. I force myself to remember who it is I'm dealing with here.

He stands to pour himself another glass. 'Someone's thirsty,' I say, before instantly regretting it. But he doesn't acknowledge my comment, which is probably his way of telling me that his drinking habits are none of my business.

When he sits back down in his chair, he takes a deep breath before finally getting to what he really wants to talk about.

'Tomorrow you will be a guest on the Florence Lee show,' he tells me. 'Do you know who she is?'

'Of course,' I reply, surprised at the news he has just given me.

Florence Lee is one of the biggest celebrities in the UK. I love her podcast. Getting to go on her show would be a dream come true. But I'm confused. I thought he was calling me here because he wanted me to kill someone. Some rich Sheikh like Mason had, perhaps. Or some dodgy businessman getting in the way of whatever deal he is trying to do. I'm not sure what going on Florence's podcast has to do with any of that.

'Good, then you will know she is a fan of health products,' he says, and I nod the affirmative.

Then he opens the draw on the table beside him and takes out a small bottle of Turbo X Juice, a new Energy drink popular with gym bunnies and paid social media influencers.

He hands it to me, and I study the bottle. I see the recognisable branding. The red and black colours. The large X that features in all the 'X-Rate Your Life' adverts that have been running on international television channels.

I've drunk a few bottles of it myself in the past, mainly after a heavy night of partying. It's great if you need something to get you through an intense gym session or even just a tough morning, which is normally what I use it for. But I'm not sure why Sebastian has just handed me a bottle of it right now.

'Tomorrow morning you will give that bottle to Florence, and you will make sure she drinks from it,' he tells me.

'Why?' I ask, even though it's obvious that he wants me to advertise it for him. Florence's podcasts are streamed live on her website as they are recorded, so I'm guessing he has a sizeable investment in this new product and wants to me showcase it to the millions of viewers watching online.

'The liquid in that bottle you are holding contains a small amount of Ethylene glycol,' he says. 'It is otherwise known as antifreeze. You are going to make sure she drinks it, and in about forty-eight hours she is going to be dead.'

I stare at him open-mouthed from my position on the bed. He wants me to kill Florence Lee. Not some nameless Sheikh with a sordid history of human rights crimes. Not some despicable businessman with a dodgy past.

Florence Lee.

One of the most famous figures in Britain.

On her show.

Live.

'What?' I blurt out, putting the bottle down on the bed as if just holding it is enough to contaminate me with its contents too.

'How does a million followers sound?' he asks me, and despite the look of horror on my face right now, I notice that he is actually smiling.

'I can't do this,' I tell him, but his smile is unshakable.

'That's how many followers you will have after you have been on her show,' he says, like that makes up for the fact that I'm also going to kill the woman who actually owns the show.

I don't know what to say,' I tell him, putting my drink down on the floor and trying to stop the panic attack I feel is only seconds away. 'I need some water.'

'Sure,' he says and stands up to open the mini bar fridge again.

'No, tap water, I hate bottled,' I say in between my deep breaths, and he shrugs and heads into the bathroom with one of the empty glasses from the side table.

As I hear him running the tap in the other room, I pull myself together. I knew he wanted me to kill somebody.

Nothing has changed.

I can do this.

By the time he walks back into the room and hands me my glass of water, I am more relaxed, and eventually, I am calm enough to tell him that I will do what he has just told me to do.

I will kill Florence Lee for him.

#PrincessOfPodcasting

Florence Lee

Summer has finally returned to Manchester. Yesterday was a horrible, rainy day but now the blue skies are back, and instead of coats and jeans I can actually go to work today wearing a flowing dress and with the wind from my open car window blowing through my red hair.

I love my home city, but even I have to admit that it's a struggle to live here when the weather is bleak, which it usually is for a good proportion of the year. But on days like today, when the sun is glinting off the side of the Beetham Tower, and the drivers of the cars around me are in such a good mood that they are happy to let me pass, then it's the best city in the world.

I'm on the way into my studio to record another episode of my podcast *The Florence Lee Show,* and I'm excited about today's guest. Her name is Emily Bennett, and she is a social media influencer. With just over half a million followers on her *PhoGlo* account, she is fast becoming one of the highest earners on the platform, thanks to all the paid advertising she gets off the back of her fame.

But just like me, Emily is a young woman from England, and despite all the success she has experienced this year in rising from obscurity to being one of the most recognisable faces amongst the country's population, she still seems down to earth and as relatable as she was before.

I haven't met her previously, but as I do with each of my guests before they come on my show, I like to complete an exhaustive amount of research on them before we go live. If they have given up time in their busy schedule to come and talk to me and my 12 million listeners, then it's only fair that I take some time to learn as much as I can about them in return.

From what I have found online so far, I know quite a lot about Emily. She is 23, four years younger than me. She has been trying to grow her platform for over a few years on *PhoGlo* though it seems it was only around six months ago that she started to see some tangible results from all her hard work. She doesn't promote as many products or businesses as a lot of other influencers online, but apparently, she is well paid for the ones she does.

She has an estimated net worth of somewhere between £250,000-£500,000, which is a little less than me, but I'd say that if she carries on the way she is going, she will be a millionaire within a year.

She spends most of her time abroad, as most influencers do, but originates from Billericay in Essex and likes to go back and visit her mum whenever she has time. I also saw some posts about her father who passed away a few years ago but I won't be discussing that with her unless she brings it up herself.

I'm excited to get her in the studio and really get her to open up about what it is like to be a social media star. After all, the whole concept of being paid to live your life online is a relatively new one and a completely different type of career to the people I'm used to interviewing.

I've had everyone from movie stars, musicians and comedians on my show, to dieticians, sleep experts and conspiracy theorists but I've never had an influencer on before. I'm fascinated to learn about the daily realities of such a job and whether her life really is as picture-perfect as her profile page would lead you to believe it is.

I know many people in my audience will be keen to hear all about it too. While the demographic of my show's listeners covers all ages and genders, it is predominantly made up of females aged 15-30. I know the majority of Emily's followers fall into the same age range and the main reason for that is that many young women these days want to become social media celebrities just like Miss Bennett.

They will all be eager to learn how Emily was able to take her profile and break through into the mainstream amidst an overcrowded sea of other young women trying to do the same thing. I would be doing my listeners a disservice if I didn't get her to open up and give her honest breakdown of how she became one of the biggest influencers in Britain.

Some people are coy when it comes to sharing the secrets of their success, and while I don't expect Emily to be elusive and hold much back, I am prepared to press her if she is too vague with any of her answers. My shows aren't conducted like an interview and are more of an informal chat between two friends, but I always have avenues of conversation in mind and will lead my guest down them at some point in the show.

But first of all, I will make Emily feel comfortable with opening up to me, so it's important that me and my team of assistants make her feel welcome the moment she arrives at the studio.

I check the clock on my dashboard and see it is 9:15. We aren't due to start recording until ten so as long as the dregs of the rush hour traffic aren't too obstructing, I should be arriving at my studio with almost half an hour to spare.

Just how I like it.

As I drive through a green light and onward into the city that seems to be growing taller by the day based on all the high rise buildings that are springing up everywhere, I'm struck again by the thought of how lucky I am to be doing something I love for a living.

I never grew up dreaming of having the number one podcast in the UK. I don't even think podcasts were a thing when I was a child. My original dream had been to be a pop star. I know, it's cliché. Every little girl dreams of being a pop star. Except I went a little further than most other people and actually found myself in a proper girl band with a proper recording contract.

The group was formed of me and four other girls after we had all entered a reality TV show set up to find Britain's next great pop band. There was even a Spice Girl on the judging panel. Unfortunately, my group didn't win and bowed out in 7th place but not before we had made it to the live studio stage and got to perform our songs in front of millions of viewers on national television.

After we were eventually voted off the show, a recording studio signed us up to the rights for our first album, and when it was released, it made it as high as number two in the UK album charts. I thought all my dreams had come true and I was destined to tour the world with the girls and release several more albums before branching off on my own and having a crack at the obligatory solo career.

But our second album flopped, and suddenly the group was no more. In a desperate bid to keep myself in the public eye, I made a few regrettable appearances on other reality TV shows, but by the age of twenty-five, I was branded a "has been" and left facing an uncertain future.

That was until my best friend had the idea that changed my life forever and put me in the position that I find myself in today, which is that of a highly paid, highly respected podcast host. Even though the group had ultimately failed, I still got together with the rest of my bandmates from time to time to drink wine and catch up on events in our lives, and my friend said I should record these conversations for the few fans that we had originally had.

So that's what I did and so what started two years ago with a dodgy microphone in my front room eventually grew into me having my own studio in the centre of Manchester talking to famous and significant people and being paid thousands of pounds in advertising revenue for every show I put out.

Some people call me the "Princess of Podcasting" because I'm dominating the charts at such a young age, but I don't know about that. I'm just a down to earth Northern girl living a dream. And now I can't wait to meet and chat to a down to earth Southern girl that is also living hers.

#KillerMood

Emily Bennett

I slept surprisingly well last night considering I am going to be the person responsible for the death of another human being today. I hadn't expected to get much shut-eye with all the adrenaline flooding my body after my meeting with Sebastian in his hotel room, but somehow I had drifted off, and now it was almost 9:30. I'd overslept, even with my alarm.

Damn the snooze button.

I throw back the duvet on my king size bed and rush over to the curtains, praying that when I open them, I won't see any of the rain that tormented me so much yesterday. Amazingly, the weather is great, and suddenly the five-minute walk from my hotel to Florence's studio doesn't seem as grim as I thought it might be.

I could always get a taxi to take me the short distance from here to there, but the podcast host knows where I am staying, and I'm worried she might think I'm just another rich, overindulged celebrity if I'm too lazy to walk the 0.2 mile gap between my place and hers.

I'm always eager to show people that I'm still a normal, regular girl and so a normal, regular girl would just walk it, so that is what I shall do. But unless I get a move on and get dressed, then not even a taxi won't be enough to get me there on time.

I need to be there for ten, so I better hurry. I take a four-minute shower, being extra careful not to get my hair wet because that would be a disaster considering how little time I have to play with. Then I put on the green dress that I have chosen especially for today and manage to get the zipper at the back all the way up myself.

Green might seem a strange choice of colour, but I've seen a previous podcast by Florence before, and in it, her guest was wearing a green dress, and the colour looked great under the studio lights. I've been sure to get the same shade as the guest wore, which is called Parakeet, and once it's on it has me looking as bold and confident as the actual bird it is named after.

I comb my hair and give it a revitalizing lift with some hairspray, but I'm purposefully keeping it simple today. Florence used to be a pop star, but now she likes to go for a more natural look, and I want to do the same. I add a touch of bronzer to my face just to cover any minor blemishes, and then I'm almost good to go.

It's 9:48. I don't think I've ever got ready that quickly before. And I doubt I'll ever get ready that quickly again. I suddenly pause in the bathroom door and wonder if the reason for my speed and productivity so far today isn't just because I overslept. Maybe it's because I'm trying to distract myself from what I am about to do.

Perhaps, but I can't afford the luxury of dwelling on it now. I have a job to do. Sebastian was clear with his instructions, and if I want to keep myself and my mum safe, then I need to do what he says. I need to give Florence the can of energy drink, and I need to get her to drink it live on the show.

I'm sure Sebastian will be sitting in his hotel room watching the stream on his laptop. He will probably get a strange thrill from seeing me hand over the can that contains the poison, and I'm sure he'll enjoy watching Florence take a long, thirsty sip from it too.

I'm not exactly sure why he has picked her as the next person to fall victim to his company's seemingly unstoppable desire to achieve world domination. But I know she has millions of listeners, so I can only assume he wants to stop her talking about something that goes against one of his business interests. Because that's the normal way of dealing with obstacles in the business world apparently. You just kill them.

Yeah right.

But I'm not here to judge. I'm here to do a job. I knew what I was getting myself into when Mason opened my eyes to Sebastian and his influencers. For six months, everything has been great. All I need to do is get over this little hurdle today and then the rest of it will be great too.

I know that because Mason told me so. She has done this. She has killed someone for Sebastian before. If she can do then so can I.

But Ivy did this too, and look what happened to her. Eventually, she had enough and tried to get away from Sebastian, but it was too late. She had already sold her soul to the devil, and in the end, the devil had come calling for her.

I've heard the tales of the mystery man that Sebastian sends to give the warnings when one of his influencers starts to disobey him. I know that is the same man that ended Ivy Lane's life, even if the rest of the world believe it was suicide. And I know that is the man that will come after me and my family if I don't go through with this and so I have no choice.

I pick up the tainted can of energy drink and squeeze it into my handbag. Then I take one last look at myself in the mirror before turning and heading for the door.

As I open it, I gasp at the sight of the person standing on the other side of it.

#Surprise

Sebastian Sawyer

I walk through the open doorway, forcing Emily back into her hotel room. Just before the door closes completely, I make sure to put the 'Do Not Disturb' sign on the handle. The last thing I need right now is a cleaner walking in and overhearing what I'm about to say.

Emily looks up at me, and I can see the fear in her eyes. I savour the silence for a moment, enjoying the power that I hold over her.

What's better, influencing the behaviour of millions of people from behind a phone screen, or influencing the behaviour of one person stood right in front of you?

'Good morning,' I say as I stroll past her, going further into the room.

'I need to go,' she tells me as if I wasn't aware that she has somewhere important to be in ten minutes time.

'This won't take long,' I assure her as I sit down on the edge of the bed and tap the duvet beside me.

She stares at my hand on the bed but doesn't move closer.

'This means sit,' I tell her, and reluctantly she walks over and takes her seat beside me.

'Do you have the can?' I ask her, and she nods. 'Where?' I demand to know until I see her tap the side of her handbag.

'Good,' I say. 'Here, take one for yourself.'

I reach into the inside of my suit jacket and take out another can of TurboX.

She stares at it as suspiciously as she stared at me when I walked into the room a minute ago. Then I laugh to break the ice between us.

'Don't worry, I wouldn't poison you' I reassure her, and she slowly reaches out to take the can from my hand.

'I figured it would be easier to get her to drink it if you had one yourself,' I tell her, and she nods.

'Good idea,' she says as she tries to fit the extra can into her handbag. But it's too full. It won't go.

'It's better if you keep that one separate,' I say to her. 'You don't want to mix them up now, do you? Or your mum will have another funeral to arrange.'

She looks sick at my comment, but I don't care. There's no time for pleasantries. Not today.

'One more thing,' I say, checking my Rolex and making her hold her breath as she waits for what I'm going to tell her next.

'I told you yesterday that being on Florence's show would get you to surpass one million followers, didn't I?'

She nods. I've never seen her this quiet before. I quite like it.

'One million followers is cool. But you know what's cooler?'

She shakes her head. She really is quiet now, so I just get to it.

'One hundred and fifty million followers.'

#NumberOneShot

Emily Bennett

My head is spinning. Thank god it isn't raining today because my body is feeling so weak right now that I could be swept away by the water. Down into a sewer. Down into the abyss....

I'm on my way to the studio, and I'm only just going to make it on time. I wasn't expecting Sebastian to visit me this morning. I thought he'd told me everything that I needed to know in his hotel room yesterday. But when I opened my door to leave, there he was, and it seems his plan for me to murder one person for him just wasn't enough.

Now he has suggested a second victim. But unlike the first one, this is somebody that I actually know.

Mason Manor.

It seems that Mason has started to walk down the path that Ivy Lane perilously chose to go down. She has stopped complying with Sebastian's orders. She has been given a written warning today after failing to post what he has asked her to. Shortly she will be given a physical one.

But if that doesn't work, then she will have to be eliminated.

As if all that hadn't been surprising enough to learn then Sebastian had hit me with the kicker. He was giving me the opportunity to be the one to eliminate her from the equation and in doing so put myself on the fast track to her throne.

He wanted me to be his number 1 influencer.

Of course, I'd refused the offer. Told him that I couldn't kill Mason. That she was a friend. A colleague. Not just some stranger he picked out from the crowd. She was a real person that I knew and had spent time with.

I told him to give Mason another chance. She was his oldest employee and his best. Surely, she had earnt an extra chance after her years of loyal service.

But Sebastian had shaken his head and refused my pleas for her reprieve. He told me that she had gotten too big for her boots and needed to be dealt with. If I wouldn't do it then somebody else would.

'Who?' I had asked him as he had stood up and brushed out the creases in his suit trousers legs.

'I have many employees,' he had told me. 'I was just offering you the chance of a lifetime. Maybe I'll ask one of the other influencers instead.'

Then he had headed for the door and perhaps I should have just let him leave. But I hadn't. I told him to wait. Then I told him I'd do it, right after I was done with Florence.

Sebastian had smiled and nodded his head. Then he had wished me luck for what I was about to do, told me he would be watching and that he would be in touch after the show, then walked out of my room.

I'd followed quickly behind, taking the elevator all the way down from the eleventh floor of my hotel before running through the reception area and out of the revolving glass doors into the bright morning sunshine.

I had the can of energy drink in my hand, the one I was supposed to drink in a few moments time. And I had the other can in my handbag, the one Florence was due to drink right alongside me. I had everything that I needed to complete my mission.

I was about to go live on the biggest podcast in the UK. The exposure it was going to give me would mean my follower count was easily fly past the one million mark at some point later today.

In two hours' time, when the show was over, I would leave the studio and head back to the hotel where I would call at Sebastian's room again on the sixteenth floor and listen to the next part of his plan. The plan that involves how I'm going to kill Mason.

But first things first.

I press the buzzer on the entrance to Florence's studio and smile at the assistant that is there to open the door for me. She looks to be around the same age as me, and I wonder what she did to get such a cool job as being Florence Lee's assistant on her mega-successful podcast. Maybe she contacted her online. Maybe she turned up outside and begged. Maybe she just submitted her CV like everyone else does when they want to get a job.

Whatever she did to get this gig I doubt she had to kill for it. Not all bosses are as crazy as mine. And not employees are willing to the things that I am.

The pleasant assistant leads me through another set of doors, past the Green Room where guests that are early can sit on the sofa and enjoy a drink from the vending machine while music videos play on the flatscreen on the wall.

But there is no time for me to take a seat and watch the pop stars on screen. I'm barely on time as it is. I'm heading straight into the recording studio.

And now I'm shaking hands with Florence Lee. She's just as pretty as I knew she would be. She isn't wearing nearly half as much makeup as she had been made to wear during her brief music career and she looked a lot better for it. More natural. *More real.*

She points out a couple of cools photos that are hanging on the wall and have been gifted to her from previous guests, and I show my interest even though I've seen them before from watching her show online.

Then she asks me to take a seat at the impressive glass table in the centre of the room and tells me how everything is going to work. We will just start chatting on her cue, and while she has a couple of topics she wants to get on to at some point in the two-hour show, generally we should just talk about anything that happens to be on our minds today.

I smile and say that sounds nice, well aware that there is no way I can talk about any of the things that are on my mind on this particular day.

Then her assistant shows me how close to keep my head to the microphone so that the sound quality comes out just right, which I practice until she nods her head to tell me that it is perfect.

Then finally everyone is in their seats, and I clear my throat one last time just before we go on air until Florence tells her assistants to pause for a second before turning back to me with a sheepish look on her face.

'I'm so sorry,' she says, with her head to the left of the large microphone in front of her so that I can see her face properly. 'We haven't offered you a drink.'

I smile and tell her not to be silly. In fact, I've brought my own. Then I put my can of TurboX on to the table before taking the second can out of my handbag and passing it across the table towards her.

She thanks me and says she loves this drink.

I say I love it too.

Then she gives us all the thumbs up, and we are live.

#Showtime

Florence Lee

We're twenty minutes into the show, and things are going well. I always worry about keeping the conversation flowing with first-time guests, but Emily is a friendly, chatty girl, and so far, so good. There's nothing worse than awkward pauses when you've got millions of people tuning in, but I don't think I'll have to worry about that today.

'Wow that sounds incredible,' I say to Emily after she has just finished telling me about the yacht party she has been to in Monte Carlo.

'It was,' Emily replies, fiddling a little nervously with her headphones. Most guests find they take some getting used to. I barely even notice them now, but then this is my 234th show.

'So I have to ask right here because I know many of my listeners will be desperate to know. How did you get so many followers on *PhoGlo*?'

I figure I might as well put the question out there early. And I know the comments under our live stream are full of people asking the same thing because my assistant plays the video on a screen which is visible to both me and my guest.

'I get asked that a lot,' Emily says laughing while glancing at the screen to her right.

'I'm sure you do. There are so many women out there that want to be able to do the kinds of things you're doing. Get paid to travel the world. Go to fashion shows in Paris. Yacht parties in Monte Carlo,' I say, almost wondering myself how I would get to do things like that too. 'So, what's the secret?'

Emily stops smiling, and for a second I worry that I've somehow offended her by implying that there is some secret method to success that she has employed and now she is on the spot having to talk about it. But then she lights up again, and I see she is okay with this line of questioning.

'I wouldn't say there is a secret. It's just a lot of hard work, practice, dedication to getting better. You know, all that boring stuff.'

I laugh. But I'm not going to let her off so lightly. I've spoken to enough guests in my time to detect when one of them is holding something back from me.

'Sure, of course. But there must be something else. Because there's thousands of young women out there that are on social media every day, posting photos, trying to get attention for modelling agencies or advertising companies. How did you make yourself stand out from the crowd?'

I smile at Emily to keep things light as I wait for her response. I see her glance at the TV screen again, and it surprises me that someone with over half a million followers seems so self-conscious.

'Well, I'm not sure how to answer that,' she begins, finally looking away from the screen and back towards me again. 'I sometimes ask myself that same thing you know? Like why did I get picked to be an influencer when I was just doing the same thing as everybody else?'

I nod but keep quiet, letting her know that she should continue.

'I guess the one thing I would say is that it's important to be authentic. You have to be yourself. You can't hide behind filters and editing skills because that isn't real life. If you can show a different side to yourself, a more vulnerable side, then I think that really helps to make you stand out, you know?'

I smile. 'I like that,' I say. 'It's easy these days to fake everything online, but being real is still the best thing you can do to get people's attention.'

'Of course,' Emily agrees, and I notice her relaxing again now that the question is dealt with. But I have one more thing I really want to know about as to how she got to where she is today.

'You said a moment ago that you sometimes you asked yourself why you got picked to be an influencer. Who exactly was it that picked you?'

I see Emily's shoulders instantly stiffen again, and it tells me there is a good answer there if I can just find a way of getting it out of her.

'Well it wasn't exactly just one person,' Emily says, 'It usually starts with a few messages. People saying that they are interested in working with me. Want me to advertise something for them. That kind of thing.'

'Okay cool. How many followers did you have when you started to get messages?'

'Almost five thousand.'

'Right. But what if someone has more followers than that and they haven't been sent any messages yet?'

'Erm, I'm not sure,' Emily replies, and I can tell we are getting into it a bit too quickly. There's plenty of time left in the show. I can bring it up again later. It's time to settle her down again. And I see the perfect opportunity to do that.

I pick up the can of TurboX that Emily handed me when she arrived and hold it up so the camera can see it clearly.

'Before we go on, I just want to say thank you for bringing me this today.' I say to her. 'I love this drink.'

'Me too,' Emily replies, smiling and picking up her own can from the table as well.

'I have to ask, where did you get this from? Isn't this still banned in the UK?'

'Yeah, it is. A friend gave it to me in Monte Carlo, so I brought them back. They're allowed to drink it over there.'

'So jealous,' I say, and I mean it. TurboX is a really tasty energy drink, but due to the sugar content, the UK government have prohibited it from being sold in this country. The only times I've tasted it before was when I was on holiday in Italy. I posted a video to my website at the time telling my fans how great it was and urging the politicians to let us buy it in our own country. But no luck so far.

'Shall we have a little drink?' I ask Emily, and she says she would love that.

'We won't get in trouble for this will we?' I ask my assistant who has far more of an understanding of legal issues than me.

'No, we'll be fine,' she tells me. 'It wasn't bought in this country. And anyway, it's only illegal to sell it, not to drink it.'

'Great,' I say and open my can, hearing the loud popping sign of the cap in my headphones. Then I hear Emily do the same with hers.

'Cheers,' I say as I hold up my can towards her.

'Cheers,' she says and bumps her can against mine.

Then I take a long, thirsty swig of the fizzy, refreshing liquid. God it tastes just as good as I remember it. I see Emily drinking hers too and pause a second before continuing our conversation.

When I'm sure that I'm not going to burp as soon as I open my mouth again, I put my face back in front of the microphone.

'It's so good isn't it?' I ask her as we both put our cans back down on the table in front of us.

'It's the best,' Emily replies, before looking back at the TV screen on the wall for what must be the fiftieth time since she came in here.

'Is there somebody watching that you want to say hi to?' I ask her.

'Yeah there is actually,' she replies. 'I'd like to say hi to my mum, Liz. I know she's at home now watching in Billericay. If she's figured out how to find the video. Love you mum.'

'Aww that's great,' I say. 'Anybody else watching? You must have loads of family and friends tuning in too. I can see that we have over seven million people watching live right now. Is there anybody else you'd like to say hi to? Maybe a boyfriend perhaps?'

I know it's a little cheesy of me but forgive me. I like to try and get any juicy gossip from my guests if I can, and Emily Bennett is no different. From my research online I haven't seen anything about her being in a relationship, and so it's worth a shot to find out if there's potentially something new that I can get her to talk about that not even her half a million followers know exists.

'A boyfriend?' Emily repeats, looking away from the screen and back at her can on the table.

'Or just somebody special?' I add, trying to make her more at ease. I can tell by the way that her posture has stiffened up again that there is somebody she has in mind.

'Well there is one guy,' she finally confesses. 'But he's very shy. Doesn't really like the attention.'

'Interesting,' I say, knowing that all of her fans will be desperate to know more about this mystery man. 'Could you give us a name?' I ask, trying my luck and knowing that if she does give me one, then this clip will probably go viral in the crazy world of my listeners.

'Yes I can,' Emily says, suddenly sitting up straight and looking me right in the eye for the first time in a minute. 'His name is Sebastian Sawyer, and he is staying in Room 1507 at the HillBridge Hotel just around the corner from here. In fact, he's in his room right now watching the show.'

Then she turns to the camera that is responsible for the live stream going out over the internet right now and waves at it. 'Hi, Sebastian. I hope you're not mad at me for telling everybody about you. I'm just grateful for you giving me the chance to be an influencer. And I know you are willing to help so many other young women just like me if only they ask you nicely. Maybe they can come and ask you right now?'

Then she blows a kiss right down the camera before sitting back in her chair and laughing.

#Raging

Sebastian Sawyer

What a stupid girl. Saying my name on a podcast with millions of listeners. It's insane. It's reckless. And giving away my address like that. There must be a hundred women on the way to my hotel right now, desperate for me to make them the next big star.

At least she has done what I asked her to do. I saw her give the can to Florence and so at least that's one problem taken care of. But she has just created a thousand more. I will have to deal with her shortly. She won't get away with this. I warned her about what would happen if she went off-script. Now she will see that I meant everything I said.

Now her dear old mother will suffer the consequences of her actions.

But first I need to get out of this hotel before a hoard of screaming girls turn up and try to get to my room. I've got enough on my plate today already without any extra hassle like that.

Emily picked a bad day to go rogue. Mason Manor is causing me problems, and even though I floated the idea with Emily about getting here to do it, I already have my man on the way to her right now to take her out of the equation. I just wanted to see if Emily had that desire in her to become my number one influencer. And it had seemed like she had.

Right up until the moment she had given my location out to millions of listeners in the UK.

But that's not all. Three of my other influencers have also stopped posting what I've told them to and have started promoting things that they don't have permission to promote.

You'd think that the warnings I gave them were enough. Threats to them. Threats to their family. I've made them rich. Successful. *Somebody*. But still, there are some that disobey me. No matter. I'll take care of them like I took care of the rest. It's not as if there aren't enough people out there who don't want their jobs.

Like it or not there's probably a whole crowd of them heading my way right now.

I throw my laptop, clothes and toiletries into my suitcase in a disorganized fashion. There isn't time to pack properly. Emily has seen to that. As soon as I get out of this hotel, I can get myself more organised. But I'm running out of time.

I take a quick look around the room and figure I've got all of my belongings. Then I head for the door, but just before I can open it, I hear the telephone in my room start ringing.

I think about leaving it but then realise it might be Colt calling to give me an update. The mobile signal in here is terrible so he might be trying to reach me that way. I drop my suitcase on the floor and rush over to the bedside table before picking up the phone.

'Yes?'

'Mr Sawyer. It's Sally on reception. I'm sorry to bother you, but it seems there are a number of people down here in reception who are asking for you.'

My hand grips the phone tightly.

Damn Emily. How dare she do this to me.

I can hear the noise of chattering female voices in the background of the call and wonder how so many people were able to get here so fast. But a big proportion of Florence's listeners are in Manchester, so they wouldn't have had far to come to find me once Emily had told them where I was.

'How many are down there?' I ask the receptionist, wondering if it's still possible for me to somehow sneak through reception and get outside before the situation gets any worse. They don't know what I look like after all. But I'm sure they all have camera phones and are filming every man that walks in that might be me.

'There's eleven people here in reception,' Sally tells me. 'They'll all asking me to let them come up to your room.'

'Well tell them no!' I bark down the phone at the increasingly frazzled hotel employee on the other end.

'Yes, of course, sir, but there's more of them arriving by the minute.'

I feel like throwing the phone against the wall but know that isn't going to help me get out of this situation.

'Is there a back entrance I can use? I really need to get out of this hotel, and I'd prefer to do it without having my photo taken by anybody.'

'Of course, sir. I will arrange for one of our employees to come to your room and show you out.'

'Great,' I say sarcastically then slam the phone down back on the receiver.

I look at my watch and see that it is 10:45. I had planned to leave her about midday, after making sure Emily had given the can to Florence, before heading to the airport for my flight back to LA. I've still got time, but things have been made trickier now.

Getting out of here without having my photo taken is one thing. But handling the issues with Emily, Mason, and the three other influencers that have let me down today is another.

Perhaps it's better if I skip my flight and stay in the country. I've got a lot to take care of suddenly and being on a plane for eleven hours won't help me handle all these problems that have suddenly cropped up. I've got a new plan. I'll get out of here and go to the airport. But instead of boarding my flight, I'll stay in the Business Class Lounge until I know that Colt has taken care of Mason down in London. Then I'll give him the instruction to head to Billericay and pay Emily's mum a little visit.

Once she is taken care of, I'll tell him to get out of the UK and head in the direction of which one of the other three rebelling influencers has ignored the written warning I will have sent them.

There is going to be a lot of bloodshed today, but it could all have been avoided if they had just listened to me and followed the rules.

Out of all the problems I've been given today, the one that surprises me the most is Mason. She was my first influencer and although bosses shouldn't have favourites, much like parents shouldn't have a preferred child, she was definitely the one I was fondest of.

She was the guinea pig in my experiment and the first real test to show that what I had planned could actually be pulled off. When I'd started out with her, I had thought that a million followers would be ambitious. Now she has over 150 million, and she's one of the most famous people on the planet. A far cry from the shy, insecure girl that I met back in Sevenoaks five years ago.

I made her into what she is today. And this is how she pays me back. But I can't afford to show her any favouritism now. She deserves the same treatment that my other employees got. Rachel Barber. Laura Lissandro. Shay Parker. Ashleigh King. Sasha Spencer. Ivy Lane.

Now Mason Manor.

They all end up in the same place in the end.

They all end up six feet underground.

They all broke the rules and just like if you break the rules at any organisation, your employment is terminated. Okay so I go a little further than that, but the threat of death is the only way to keep the rest of them in line. Otherwise, it would be anarchy. And that's not a word that fits in my business plan.

Now where the hell is this hotel employee to take me out the back exit?

I look out of my hotel door peephole but can't see anybody outside in the corridor. Maybe I'll just find it myself. It can't be that difficult to find a fire escape or the tradesman's entrance. But just as I open the door, I see a sweating, frantic bellboy coming towards me.

'Sir, I apologise, but some of the women have got past reception and are on their way up here to your room right now,' he tells me, with a grimace of a man that is fearing for his job right now.

'What the hell do you mean they're on their way up here?' I snarl at him, looking down the empty corridor behind him that will soon be filled with desperate wannabe influencers all begging me to give them a chance at the life Emily Bennett has.

'Sir, I'm sorry. Our usual security guard is off sick today, and his replacement is, well, not quite as on the ball as he usually is. But we will get the matter sorted. I have called the police, and they are on their way to clear the crowds.'

'The police?'

This is getting out of hand. Never mind sending Colt to kill Emily's mum, I'll do it myself if that damn girl holds up my day any longer.

'There's no need for the police,' I tell the bellboy, who almost looks as worried as me about it all.

'I'm afraid there is, sir. There is quite the crowd outside the hotel now. All the entrances are covered. It seems there are a lot of people that want to meet you.'

My hand squeezes the strap on my suitcase, and I feel like tearing it off and throwing my luggage against the wall. Emily must have known what she was doing when she gave out my location on the podcast. She must have known there were hundreds of listeners right here in Manchester who would try and get to me before I checked out. She practically told them to come here and ask me to make them the next *PhoGlo* star.

The stupid bitch.

I hear noises at the end of the corridor, just around the corner where the lifts are. Then several young girls appear from behind the wall, looking at the room numbers on the doors, and I know they are looking for my room. The bellboy knows it too.

'Sir, I think it's best if you wait in your room,' he tells me, and I'm inclined to agree with him.

I drag my suitcase back inside and slam the door to my room as I hear the loud, excited cries of the girls on the other side of it.

'Sebastian! We want to meet you! Sebastian, we love you!'

Damn Emily.

As soon as I'm out of this room, then I'm going to kill her myself.

#NoGoingBackNow

Emily Bennett

I tell the driver to hurry. I don't know how much time I've got or how serious the damage is that I've done to myself and so I can't afford to waste precious seconds.

I feel bad for having to cut short my appearance on *The Florence Lee Show,* but she seemed to understand when I told her that something had come up and I had to leave abruptly. But I also have the feeling that even though my time on her podcast was brief, I've given her more than enough material to keep her avid listeners happy until the next show.

Saying Sebastian's name out loud for the millions of fans tuning in felt good, I'm not going to lie. I know how important it is for him to remain elusive and faceless. Unlike the influencers he employs, he is someone that craves anonymity. It's easier to get away with the things that he does when nobody outside his company knows who he is.

But now they know his name. Now millions of people will be googling him and talking about him in forums and message boards, on social media and especially in *PhoGlo* comments. Not only that but for those listeners lucky enough to be in Manchester city centre today then they might even get to meet the man of the hour in person if they go to the address that I gave them.

Giving up his hotel room was a stroke of genius on my part, and I know the chaos that will be causing for him right now. I even saw some of it for myself just to make sure.

When I left Florence's studio, I told the taxi driver to pass by mine and Sebastian's hotel, and sure enough, there was already a sizeable group of young women trying to get inside to where they had been told there was a man staying who had the power to change all their lives.

I know he will have tried to leave as soon as he saw me say his name into the camera. But hopefully, he didn't make it out in time. I can just imagine him now, stuck in his hotel room, cursing under his breath and wishing me dead. But I'm just one of many. From what I can tell, I'm not the only one of his influencers that has gone off-script today.

I know he's already sending someone to deal with Mason. I hope she will be alright, but she's a big girl, she can handle things herself. I have to focus on myself right now. Everything is going to plan so far, but there's no guarantee any of this is going to work.

I take a long gulp from the bottle of water Florence gave me before I left her studio, but I doubt it will do me much good. I need something stronger than this.

'How far?' I ask the driver, and I see his eyes looking at me sitting on his back seat in his rear-view mirror.

'Couple of minutes,' he tells me.

I could have called for an ambulance to get me from the studio, but I didn't want to risk Sebastian seeing it and getting suspicious. It was unlikely he would have done, what with him being stuck in the hotel trying to evade the hundreds of desperate girls outside but there's no point taking chances.

I've taken enough risks so far.

Taking another might be one too many.

I've been planning for this day ever since Mason told me it was coming six months ago. As soon as she warned me that Sebastian would arrange a meeting and tell me that I was going to kill someone for him, I had been preparing and planning for this as best as I could.

Of course, for most of that time, I had no idea about many of the details my plan would involve. I had no way of knowing where Sebastian would want to meet me, and I had no clue who it would be that he would want me to kill. But I could get everything else in place.

I saw Mason two months ago at a party in Dubai and asked her if she was happy with her situation. I had to approach the subject gently in case she wasn't on board with my plan and tipped off Sebastian that he had trouble in his ranks. But after several drinks, she confessed to me that she wasn't.

She said she felt trapped. Scared of Sebastian. And alone, even with millions of followers to her name. If there was any way to get out from under his control, then she was willing to give it a try. And so I had told her I might just have that way.

Because Mason was Sebastian's oldest employee, I knew that she would have the names of the other influencers currently working for him and sure enough she had been able to help. She knew them because Sebastian always wheeled her out for a meeting with them on their first day, just like he had done for me.

While he had been using Mason's allure to impress his new employees and make them fall further under his spell, he had also been giving Mason knowledge that would eventually come back to haunt him.

She told me the names of the other six influencers out there in the world who were also doing his dirty work for him and who were just as trapped and lonely as we were. Then I asked for the names of the three influencers most likely to want to get involved in the plan I was putting together.

She had given me them. Rochelle Turner. Harriet Harper. And Trey Squire, a rare male in his stable of mostly female influencers. Mason told me they would help me with my plan. They were just as desperate to get away from Sebastian as we were. All I needed to do was get in touch with them and let them know what I wanted them to do.

But that was easier said than done. We suspected that Sebastian used his team of hackers to monitor our social media accounts and even keep an eye on the kind of websites we were looking at on our personal mobiles. If he was capable of hacking into the algorithms of some of the biggest websites in the world, then he was definitely capable of getting into our phones.

But he wasn't watching us in person all the time. He was too busy for that, and he didn't have enough henchmen to do it for him. So that gave us an opportunity. But we would have to do things off-line. The old-fashioned way. No DM's. No emails. No video calls.

It's actually harder than you think trying to get in touch with someone in the world without any of those things. But our parents managed it somehow, so it had to be possible. In the end, it had been quite enjoyable.

Most people call it 'snail mail' and while there's no doubt sending a message by post takes more time than firing off a text message, the end result is still the same. I'd sent a short letter to the three influencers and recruited them for my plan. I'd done so by taking a look at their profile pages to see which luxury hotel they were staying in at that particular time and then sent an express courier package right to the reception desk with their name on it.

I'd kept the letter vague enough in case one of them was to show it to Sebastian but detailed enough to let them know that if they wanted to change their current situation, then it was possible. Thankfully all of them had responded in a positive manner.

I'd told them that if they were in on my plan, then they simply had to reply to one of the comments in their most recent *PhoGlo* post and use the Devil emoji somewhere in their message. That was the signal to tell me they were going to help me. I used that particular emoji because I couldn't think of a better one to describe Sebastian. It was either that or the poo emoji, but I thought that would be a little childish.

It was slightly tedious communicating with my newly recruited team of rebel through our comments section considering that all of us got hundreds of comments a day. That's a lot of scrolling just to find the hidden message. But it was worth it. And there was no way Sebastian and his team of computer wizards were bothering to do the same.

Eventually, the plan was set, and all it needed was a date. As soon as Sebastian summoned me to his hotel room in Manchester and gave me my orders, then I had it. I replied to one of my comments with the previously agreed message. 'Fridays are lit' followed by three fire emoji's in a row. That told them Friday was the day for them to do what I had told them to do. I chose that particular emoji because it was time for Sebastian to burn in hell.

Creative huh?

'We're here,' the taxi driver says, and I look up to see the entrance to the Accident and Emergency department of Manchester Hospital.

'You're a star,' I tell the driver as I jump out of the taxi and race inside hoping that I've made it here in time to see the rest of my plan come to fruition but well aware that I might already be too late.

#ThisBetterWork

Mason Manor

I hope Emily's okay. What she's done is crazy. Crazier than what I've done. But the risks are the same. We're both going to end up dead if this plan doesn't work. I can't spend too much time worrying about her right now. I need to get ready for the arrival of the man that is on his way to kill me.

I ignored the first of Sebastian's messages yesterday. Instead of uploading a post to my *PhoGlo* account talking about how using a company called InvestPlus would give you great profits and change your life I instead posted a photo of Centre Court at Wimbledon from my view on the front row.

He wasn't happy about that of course and so had sent me a written warning message about halfway through the second set of the match I was enjoying. In response, I posted a selfie of myself with the famous green grass court behind me with the hashtag #CatchMeIfYouCan.

For my millions of followers looking at my post, they would have thought it was just some cheeky message about my travelling lifestyle and the fact that I'm always on the move in this crazy world. But Sebastian would have taken a different message from it. He would have recognised that I am taunting him and daring him to send his man to come and put me back in line.

Now it had been almost twenty-four hours since my selfie on Centre, and I had spent this new day giving my followers a tour of the luxury room I was staying in at a five-star hotel in Chelsea. I had uploaded several videos to my *PhoGlo* account, and none of them were about the thing that Sebastian wanted me to post about today.

I was flying solo now, doing my own thing and treating his messages just like I treated the messages from the hundreds of men that slid into my DM's every day offering me a night I would never forget.

Delete.

But I wasn't completely forgetting about my former employer. I was on the lookout for the physical warning, which would be my final cue to tell me to go back to following orders before more drastic measures are taken. I hadn't been given it yet, but it was only a matter of time.

I knew that Sebastian's man would be in London by now and no doubt on the way to Chelsea, if he wasn't here already. Because I knew how it all worked. Two warnings before they make it look like suicide. They've done it to six of my colleagues already. I will become the seventh unless I fall back into line immediately.

But I have no intention of obeying any more of his orders. Nor do I have any intention of becoming the seventh influencer to die on Sebastian's command. If all goes to plan, the next person to die will be the man coming to get me.

Followed shortly by Sebastian himself.

It's an ambitious plan. It's possibly an unrealistic one. But ambition and unrealistic goals are the bread and butter of any good influencer. What do they say? Reach for the moon, and if you miss then at least you'll be amongst the stars?

Cute, but I have no intention of missing today.

I reach for the remote control and turn on the plasma TV that is fixed to the wall opposite my enormous bed. I'm dressed in one of the satin robes that the hotel kindly leaves out for each of their guests and I'm feeling refreshed after taking a shower in the huge bathroom that makes up part of my suite.

This is the life. This is the reason why so many people want to be rich. Because when you're rich, you get to stay in hotel rooms like this one. And when you're rich, you don't have to have a boss anymore. I was rich, but I had a boss. Until yesterday when I stopped following the rules. Now I'm free and all there is to do now is enjoy the fruits of my labour.

I scroll through the hundreds of channels that the TV has, but nothing grabs my fancy, so I hit the button on the remote that will take me onto the internet and onto Florence Lee's website.

When it opens, it is already displaying the video that I want to watch. It's the same video that I spent most of this morning watching. I watched it when it was recorded live, and I've watched it at least a dozen times since.

It's the video from her latest show and today's guest was none other than my good friend Emily Bennett. It's already had over five million views, and it's going to have one more now because I'm going to press play on it again.

I skip through the first half an hour because while it was entertaining, it wasn't anything compared to what came a few minutes after that. I find the spot in the video that I want, and then I hit the play button again.

Sinking back into one of the four goose feather pillows that lie at the head of my bed I turn up the volume and see Emily and Florence on the screen, and the sound of their voices coming into my room is a nice change in the otherwise silent suite.

'I'd like to say hi to my mum, Liz,' I watch Emily say. 'I know she's at home now watching in Billericay. If she's figured out how to find the video. Love you mum.'

She's such a nice girl. And she looks great in that Parakee dress. I'll have to ask her where she got it from when I see her next.

'Aww that's great,' Florence says. 'Anybody else watching? You must have loads of family and friends tuning in too. I can see that we have over seven million people watching right now. Is there anybody else you'd like to say hi to? Maybe a boyfriend perhaps?'

I sit up on my bed because I know the best bit is coming next. The bit that caused me to let out a loud yelp and fist pump at the screen when I first saw it happen a few hours ago.

'A boyfriend?' Emily says, playing the innocent, shy girl next door role to perfection.

'Or just somebody special?'

I notice again as I did before how Emily sits up straighter right after Florence says this part. She was getting herself ready for what she was about to say next. She was trying to stay calm. She must have had so much adrenaline running through her body at that moment.

'Well there is one guy,' Emily says. 'But he's very shy. Doesn't really like the attention.'

'You can say that again!' I say out loud to myself. I wish I had some popcorn for this. I could always have room service bring me some up. Maybe I'll do that for the next time I watch this video.

'Interesting,' Florence says. 'Could you give us a name?'

Hell yeah, my girl Emily can give us a name.

'Yes I can,' Emily says. 'His name is Sebastian Sawyer, and he is staying in Room 1507 at the HillBridge Hotel just around the corner from here. In fact, he's in his room right now watching the show.'

I feel my heart rate speeding up again as she says it. Not quite as fast as the first time I heard it but quick, nonetheless. Then I hit the volume button again for the last part of Emily's show-stopping display.

'Hi, Sebastian. I hope you're not mad at me for telling everybody about you. I'm just grateful for you giving me the chance to be an influencer. And I know you are willing to help so many other young women just like me if only they ask you nicely. Maybe they can come and ask you right now?'

Boom!

Wait for it...

I watch Emily blow a kiss straight down the camera, and I let out another cheer. *What a bad bitch.* I love it.

I'm going to watch this again. *Rewind.*

As I scroll back to the part I want, I remember I'm hungry, and so I reach for the telephone by my bed. I'm waiting for room service to pick up and tell me which flavour of popcorn they can send me when I hear footsteps outside my suite door.

I freeze. Hit the mute button on the TV. Leave the receptionist at the other end of the call hanging.

Is it him? Is he here?

Then I hear something being slid under my door.

I wait a couple of minutes until the footsteps are no longer audible, and then I get up off the bed and peer around the wall of my suite to see what has been delivered to me.

There's a white card lying on the plush beige carpet.

I creep towards it and check that the coast is clear through the door's peephole before I bend down and pick it up. I turn the card over and then I see it.

The symbol.

A circle with four dots in the middle.

I've just been given my second warning.

Now I know that the next time that man comes to my room, *he will be coming to kill me.*

#SickOfThisShit

Colt Miller

Another day, another goddamn influencer to try and keep in check. You'd think these kids would be grateful to have such a good job, never mind the fact they're all stinking rich and idolised by millions. But no. Apparently, that isn't enough for some people. Apparently, they want more than that. They want freedom too.

Well, be careful what you wish for kids.

I've just paid a visit to the hotel room of Miss Mason Manor and left my calling card on her doorstep. Hopefully, that will be the end of it. Hopefully, I won't be seeing her later tonight. Hopefully, I can get back to my goddamn vacation.

But I know there's not much chance of that. Even if Mason heeds the warning that I just gave her and smartly goes back to doing what Sebastian wants there are still three other idiots out there that have chosen the exact same moment to go the same way.

That's three more plane rides I need to make. Three more hotel rooms I need to visit. Potentially three more people that I need to wipe off the face of the planet.

I've told Sebastian numerous times that we need another guy, if not two. I can't be expected to keep on top of several people in several different places at the same time. I've just about managed it so far, but then all the other times he's needed me I have only been responding to one callout.

Now there's four on the same day. Rochelle in Casablanca. Harriet in Milan. Trey in Reykjavik. And Mason right here in London.

You only need a basic understanding of a map to know that all those cities are in completely different directions to each other. And I'm supposed to get around them all in twenty-four hours.

Good luck with that Colt.

I've warned Sebastian about a situation like this ever since he hired me five years ago. I told him that while I was happy to be on standby and drop whatever it was I was doing at the time to jump on a plane and fly to the location of whichever influencer was pissing him off, there was nothing I could do if several influencers started acting out on the same day.

I told him he needed more guys like me. He told me he would take my concerns on board and act on them as he saw fit. Unfortunately for me, that meant he had completely ignored my comments and stuck to his plan of just using one guy.

Lucky old me.

Sebastian didn't believe that it was possible for several of his influencers to start disobeying him all at the same time. He went to great lengths to keep them all separate from each other, and he paid people to monitor their communications over the phone and the internet. The only one he really trusted was Mason. He allowed her to meet the other influencers, only one at a time, because she was his golden girl.

His first.

He hadn't appreciated it when I'd told him that just because he trusted someone, it still didn't mean they could let him down. But now I was being proven right. Mason had started acting out. Going her own way. Doing her own thing. Just like the others had done before her. And coincidentally, three others had started doing the same thing at exactly the same time.

Sebastian had called me as soon as I had landed at Heathrow. I expected it to be an update on Mason, telling me she had made a mistake yesterday and the first warning had been enough to set her straight and make her fall back in line. I had been half expecting to just turn back around and get on the next flight out of London.

But then he had given me the news. Told me about the three other influencers who were now receiving a written warning. That meant that unless they apologised and went back to following orders that I would have to visit them in the next twenty-four hours too.

I told them it couldn't be a coincidence. The odds were too large of that being the case. What were the chances of three people who had never met each other all deciding to break the rules on the same day that Mason had inexplicably done the same?

I'd say there was more chance of me spending a night with the cheerleading squad of my beloved Arizona Cardinals Football team than this being one big coincidence.

But Sebastian had sounded harassed. Not just pissed off, which of course he was entitled to be. But overwhelmed. Almost out of control. Like he was losing grip on the carefully constructed business he had spent so many years making work.

He didn't tell me the full picture, but I'm known him long enough to recognise when he is holding something back from me. Something else was going on. Something other than the problem with Mason, and Rochelle, and Harriet, and Trey.

He had told me he'd call me back. I was still waiting.

I stroll out of the side entrance I used to gain access to Mason's hotel and pull the packet of cigarettes out of my jacket pocket. It's hot today, and London is one of the worst cities to be in when the weather's like this.

The place has never heard of air-con.

I light up and walk down the alley at the back of the hotel, and within seconds I'm back out onto the busy streets of Mayfair. Everyone is rushing around carrying shopping bags and looking at their phones. All buying whatever shit the adverts told them to buy. All checking their social media to see what their favourite celebrity has just been spotted doing.

For someone who feels contempt for advertising agencies and the internet, I know it's ironic that I'm an employee of a man that hires influencers to advertise to their followers over the internet. But morals and righteousness don't pay the bills. Rich businessmen do.

Sebastian pays me well, which is the minimum I expect for the things he has me doing for him. And the job has its perks. I get to see the world. I don't have to worry about what my retirement will look like. And I never have to go back to the same town that my ex-wife lives in again.

Most of the time, I'm sitting in a chair somewhere warm, sipping from a glass of Merlot and reading a crime novel. If the influencers behave, then there is no need for me to get up from my chair. And they nearly always behave, for the most part.

But when the time comes that one of them goes rogue, or four of them in today's case, then Sebastian picks up the phone and interrupts my reading and my drinking to tell me to pack my bags and head to the airport. And I always do.

As soon as I've finished my chapter.

But I have a feeling it's going to be a long time until I enjoy another glass of wine again or find out what happens to the characters in my book. Something doesn't feel right about all this. I have a feeling that Sebastian's employees have somehow managed to mobilise, and now they are fighting back.

I'm going to have to take extra precautions. Because if the shit hits the fan, then I have no doubts that Sebastian will pick up the phone and call another man just like me. And then he'll tell him to kill me before the police can get to me first.

I know too much about his operation.

I know every single person that he has ordered to be killed. *Because I'm the one that does it for him.*

#Think

Sebastian Sawyer

Two hours. That's how long I've been stuck in my hotel room waiting for the incompetent staff to let me know that the coast is clear from all the screaming wannabes outside and I can leave the building without risk of being seen.

The last update from the receptionist said that while they had cleared the reception area and the corridors on my floor, there was still a sizeable crowd all around the perimeter of the hotel. Unless I wanted to leave with a jacket over my head to avoid the cameras, then I was best to stay put.

There was no way I was leaving my room looking like a criminal getting put into the back of a police van, so I had chosen to stay here. And the longer this went on, the more I was thinking about booking another night's accommodation.

I overdid it on the whiskey last night. Three-quarters of a bottle was consumed by me, and even I know that a lot and I'm a man who enjoys a drink. Now I'm suffering for it. The hangover is lingering; no doubt made much worse by the situation I find myself in. But I've drunk all the fluids in the mini-bar and several glasses of tap water, and I can still feel the dehydration and the headache taunting me from my insides.

The thought of flying to Los Angeles now is completely out of the question. I wouldn't make it to the airport in time even if I wanted to. Which I don't because all I want to do right now is lie on the bed and get some sleep. Being cooped up in here all day, with the stresses of my employee's stupidity and the aftereffects of too much alcohol weighing me down, has left me feeling drowsy.

I really need some fresh air, but the windows are all sealed. It's for the best considering I'm on the sixteenth floor, but it isn't helping me much right now.

I'm pissed off and growing more so by the second. I'm too busy for shit like this. I don't have time to just sit idle in a hotel room. I have places to go, people to see and eight influencers to keep in line. But I have to make the best of a bad situation, so I pick up my laptop again and log back in to the secure network portal for my company.

From the dashboard on my screen, I can see the same things I could see if I was at my office back in LA. There are the live results for each influencer. Their likes, comments, follower count. I was right. Emily's appearance on *The Florence Lee Show* was enough to get her over the 1 million followers mark.

Normally I would want to celebrate such a milestone, and I would usually call the influencer to congratulate them whilst telling them this is only the beginning and that even better days are ahead. But there will be no such call with Emily today. I won't be congratulating her for giving out my name on one of the most listened to Podcasts in the UK. And I certainly won't be telling her that this is the beginning, because it isn't for her.

After what she has done to me today, it is the end for Emily Bennett.

I'd already asked my team of hackers to give me her current location, and I'm told she is on a train headed down south. I presume she is making her way back home, to Billericay, to where her mother lives. The poor woman has no idea the danger her daughter has just put her in.

But I'll let Emily continue on her way for now. As soon as Colt has taken care of Mason, then he will visit Billericay too.

Mason.

I feel so betrayed by her actions, hers more so than the rest of them. I don't understand it. I can't see why she would want to give up the incredible life I have given her. She knows what's going to happen to her. She knows the clock is running down on her life unless she messages me to apologise and instantly uploads the post that she was supposed to do in the first place.

But I keep checking my phone, and there is no message. No apology.

So I can't call Colt off.

I've considered calling her and trying to talk some sense into my oldest influencer. I would never usually entertain such an idea. I didn't call any of the others before they were killed. I just waited for Colt to tell me it was done. But I'm wondering if Mason deserves an exception. This is so unlike her. Five years of perfect obedience.

Until today.

I think again about what Colt said to me a few hours ago when he landed in London. About all the events of today not being a coincidence. About the possibility of the influencers working together.

I dismissed the idea. They don't know each other. They are scattered all over the world. My hackers are tracking their communications. There's no way they can be working together without me knowing it.

But after Emily's little stunt this morning I'm beginning to worry that too much is happening at once. This could be the perfect storm. Several influencers all going rogue at the same time. The fact that Mason is one of them is what concerns me the most.

I pick up my phone and call her. It's against my rules, but everybody else is breaking them today so to hell if the boss isn't going to break a couple as well.

Two rings.

Three.

Four.

After seven unanswered rings, I hang up. Now I'm more concerned. Mason is never far from her phone. It's how she makes her living after all. Not answering my call is a bad sign. It either means she is dead set on going it alone and is cutting all contact with me. Or she is angry at me about something.

Either way, it's bad news for me and all the work I have put into my company so far.

If I lose her, then I lose the 150 million people that follow her. That's 150 million people that I can influence and persuade. 150 million people who can be brainwashed.

150 million that I need to replace.

It's possible to replace her. Of course it is. Maybe that's what I need to do. Turn this whole situation around. Make a positive out of whatever plan Emily and Mason and the rest of them have been cooking up.

I pick up the telephone by my bed and call down to reception. When I hear Sally's voice on the other end, I ask her how many people are still waiting for me outside.

She estimates there are at least 200.

'Great', I say. 'I want you to pick the best looking one for me and send them up to my room.'

#PickMe

Amber Williams

I have to get inside that hotel. I have to get to that room. *I have to meet Sebastian and show him that I am willing to do anything to be his next influencer.*

I've already sacrificed a lot, and I haven't even got into the reception area yet. When I heard Emily say that her boss was staying here on *The Florence Lee Show,* I instantly got up from my desk at work and ran down here. My office is ten minutes away, and I thought I'd be one of the first to get here. Yet somehow dozens of other girls had made it here before me and by the time I arrived the front doors to the hotel had been closed.

Not to be deterred I had run around the back and looked for another way in. Then I'd seen several girls running through a fire escape, and I was on my way in to follow them when a strong hand had gripped my shoulder and yanked me back. It was a security guard, and he was there to close the fire escape before anyone else got in. He had told me to go home, but there was no way I was going to do that.

Not if there was the slightest chance of my life being changed today.

But now I'm just stuck with the rest of the nameless, faceless wannabes all trying to spot anyone that we think might be Sebastian and all wanting to beg him to make us the next big social media star just like Emily.

But the chances of that are getting slimmer by the minute. It's been two hours now, and they still aren't letting anyone inside. Even the girls that I saw run through the fire escape earlier have since been led out through reception by security and an extremely stressed out looking bellboy.

Now we are just one big crowd, standing at the front of the hotel and staring at the doors wondering if Sebastian will make an appearance.

Occasionally we break into chanting 'Let us in! Let us in!' or the more defiant 'we shall not, we shall not be moved.'

But mainly it's just sporadic cries of 'SEBASTIAN!'

This reminds me of the time I queued up for an open audition for a reality TV show. Me and my best friend camped out all night just to get a good spot in the line, and even then, there was still a thousand people in front of us. Just like now, I believed that if only I could get inside and put myself in front of the decision-makers then I could make them see that I was exactly what they were looking for.

But I hadn't been able to get that far that day. There had been too many other people ahead of me. My dream had been dashed. And now I am worried that the same thing is going to happen again.

I know I took a big gamble coming here. I should still be at work right now, sitting at the desk that I was manning before I heard Emily say that there was a man in town that could change your life if only you asked him nicely enough.

I'm not supposed to listen to podcasts or music while I'm at work, but I find it so boring that I need to do something to get me through the day. Data entry jobs are the dullest of the dull. Listening to *The Florence Lee Show* while I'm inputting mindless numbers into spreadsheets is the only way I can do it without wanting to throw myself out of the window by lunchtime.

The job is boring and so is the money. It doesn't pay me anywhere near enough the kind of income that I require to live the life I want. More vacations. More clothes. More shoes. Better parties. I can't get those things in data entry.

Even just thinking the words "data entry" makes me want to sleep.

I'm twenty-four-years-old. I'm a good-looking brunette with a winning personality. I'm in the prime of my life. I shouldn't be spending it typing insignificant words into a computer on the fourth floor of some insurance company.

I should be out there in the world, seeing all the amazing places like Palm Island in Dubai or the Vegas Strip, and not just the same four walls of my office for forty-eight weeks of the year.

I should be going to all the best parties, like at a club in Ibiza or a rooftop bar in Miami, not just the cheap Christmas ones that my boss throws for me and my middle-aged colleagues.

And I should be on first name terms with some of the most famous celebrities in the world, like

Rihanna, or Kim, or Kylie, or Mason, not just Derek in accounts or Sue on reception.

I deserve it. I'm not different from someone like Emily. The only difference is she got in front of Sebastian, and I haven't. Not yet, anyway. If I could just get inside.

If I could just make him see my potential.

Suddenly the front doors to the hotel open and I see the blonde-haired receptionist walking out. I saw her earlier while I was trying to get inside. She was on the other side of the glass doors and looked a little startled as she stood behind her reception desk looking out at all the frenzied women trying to get in.

But now she was coming out to us all, and she seemed to be looking for someone in particular.

I felt the people around me rushing forward towards her, sensing an opportunity, and so I made sure to do the same, fighting my way closer, desperately trying to get her attention just like everybody else.

It was probably pointless. A futile task. *I am just a needle in a haystack.*

But then I see her looking at me.

Then pointing at me.

Then sending a security guard to come and get me.

Suddenly I'm being led out of the crowd and taken towards the front door of the hotel. I can hear the screaming and the shouting from the desperate women behind me. They want to know what is happening. They want to know where I am going.

So do I to be honest.

Now I'm inside the hotel, and the screaming and shouting gets quieter as the doors are closed behind me. I look at the security guard for answers, but he just shrugs. Then I look at the receptionist who looks flustered by what she has just done. Then she forces a smile on her face and says the best five words I have ever heard in my life.

'Sebastian will see you now.'

#OneBornEveryMinute

Sebastian Sawyer

I answer the knocking at my hotel room door and open it to see two people standing on the other side. One of them is the stressed-out bellboy from earlier. And the other is an attractive brunette woman smiling widely and pushing her chest out.

Perfect.

'Did you get the pills I asked for?' I say to the hotel employee, without taking my eyes off the woman beside him.

'Certainly sir,' he replies and hands me a variety of packets. 'I got you different ones, just to make sure.'

I nod at him and take pills. My hangover is getting worse. If these don't shift my headache then maybe I'm coming down with the flu. *That's all I need right now.*

'And you are?' I ask the young woman stood patiently in the corridor alongside the man in uniform.

'Amber Williams,' she says, fluttering her eyelashes and tucking a strand of her dark hair behind her left ear.

'Nice to meet you, Amber. Please, come in.'

I step aside and allow her to enter my room. Then I close the door, leaving the bellboy outside alone.

I tell Amber to take a seat on my bed as I put several of the pills into my hand then tip them into my mouth and wash them all down with the glass of whiskey I had poured just before they arrived.

'It's an honour to meet you, Sebastian. I mean, Mr Sawyer,' Amber says as I feel the soothing alcohol disappear down my throat.

A good drink always makes things seem better. Then I turn to the eager woman looking up at me and force a smile.

'Likewise. And Sebastian is fine.'

'Great, thanks Sebastian,' she says as I lower myself into the chair in the corner of the room. My joints are definitely aching a little now. Maybe it is the flu. Oh well, it's not as if I'm going anywhere now.

'Amber, do you know why I've called you up here?' I ask.

She shakes her head. She really is attractive. Sally did a good job picking her. Maybe I'll give her a tip when I check out, but only if Amber does what I am about to ask her to do.

'Do you have a *PhoGlo* account?' I enquire, keeping my eyes focused on her.

'Of course! Do you want to see it?' she says, pulling her phone out of her handbag and unlocking it for me.

'That's okay. I just need you to post something for me.'

'Sure, whatever you want,' she says, and I can tell this is going to be as easy as I'd assumed it would. 'But I don't have that many followers. Only eight hundred and seventy-two.'

'That's okay,' I assure her. 'You will have a lot more than that by the end of the day.'

She laughs nervously before asking 'What do you want me to post?'

I sit forward and hold out my hand towards her. 'Can I have your phone?'

'Sure,' she says, handing it over.

I open the camera then raise the phone in front of me.

'I'm going to take a picture of you. Just act natural okay?'

'Erm, okay,' she says, quickly arranging her hair and sitting in an extremely unnatural position.

'Natural,' I say again, and this time she does a better job of sitting comfortably.

I take the photo then smile. 'Perfect,' I tell her, and she smiles at my approval.

Then I hand the phone back to her and tell her what words I want to accompany the picture.

'Type this, exactly as I say it. My name is Amber Williams. I am currently sitting in the hotel room of Sebastian Sawyer. Emily Bennett was right. He is the man that can make anybody a social media star. But he is also the man that can ruin a social media star. Someone like Mason Manor. She is old news now. Follow me and unfollow her. Mason Manor is cancelled.'

It feels strange saying those words. But also good. I wish I could be in her hotel room to see her reaction to the news. But my hotel room will have to do.

'One more thing,' I say and take Amber's phone again, before typing out the series of hashtags that I have committed to memory. They are the ones that my team of hackers say are the best suited to get the most engagement with your posts. And that's what I need for this.

Maximum engagement.

Amber's eight hundred and whatever followers is nowhere near enough. This needs to be read by Mason's 150 million.

'All set,' I say and hand the phone back to her. 'Hit share whenever you want.'

Amber looks at her phone then back at me nervously. Like she needs further instruction.

'Trust me,' I tell her.

And she does. She shares the post. In a moment I'll contact my team back at the office and get them to work their magic on Amber's follower count, while also making Masons magically disappear.

God it feels good to be the boss.

'I just need to send a message then we can chat, okay?' I tell her, and she nods her head and obeys me because she is new and she will obey every single one of my commands at this stage, just like Mason used to when she was new.

I pick up my mobile from beside the whiskey bottle and type a message to Mason. If she isn't going to answer my calls, then she will at least read my messages. If she tries to forward it on to anybody, then my team will block it. And besides Colt will delete it from her phone right after he has killed her, which will be very soon if she doesn't get her act together.

'Mason, as you will see, I have a potential new influencer in my hotel room. What happens to this young woman is up to you. If you fall back in line and

do as I say, then she will leave this room with five thousand pounds and a cool story to tell. But if you continue to disobey me, then she will leave this room in a body bag. Just like the one you will be leaving your room in very shortly. It's entirely up to you'

I hit send then put my phone down and smile at the grateful woman on my bed.

'So, Amber. Tell me about yourself.'

#TimesUp

Mason Manor

That evil man. *That rotten evil man.*

It's one thing to threaten my life. But to threaten a complete stranger? Some poor girl that has no idea what she's gotten herself into? It's despicable. But then again, I should expect nothing less from a man like Sebastian. This is exactly why Emily and I are trying to bring him down after all.

I wish I could speak to Emily now. Just check in and confirm that everything is okay. But I can't do that for a couple of reasons. One, it's too risky if Sebastian has someone intercept the call or read the messages. And two, I doubt Emily is in any state to talk right now anyway. Such a brave girl. But I'm brave too, and it's time for me to accelerate the plan.

After calming myself down after reading Sebastian's message, I know he is only threatening that poor girl's life as a last resort to get me to keep working for him. I'm his most valuable asset. I control the spending habits and voting patterns of millions of people. He doesn't want to see that just go down the drain. But he will kill me if I give him no other choice. It's business, after all.

But I know he won't harm the young girl in his room. This Amber Williams person. He's evil, but he's not stupid. Emily told everyone where he was staying. If a woman goes into that room and doesn't come back out again, then it's going to be pretty obvious who did the killing. And Sebastian won't risk going to prison, especially not for some random stranger he's just pulled off the streets.

So I feel confident enough to keep going with Emily's plan. I pick up my phone again and reply to Sebastian. I tell him that he should send his man up to see me now because I'm not going anywhere and I'm not doing anything he tells me to do anymore.

With that show of defiance sent, I open up the *PhoGlo* app for what I hope won't be the last time and take a selfie of myself. No makeup, hair all over the place, tear-stained eyes.

Perfect.

Then I type the caption to go with it. A simple one-line message to my 150 million followers and anyone else that happens to read it after finding my post amongst the hashtags I'm going to use.

I can't do this anymore

#scared #alone #theresnofilterforfear

Then I share the post to my account before taking a deep breath and getting ready for it all to be over.

#GoToWork

Colt Miller

I've snuck back into the five-star hotel in London that has the security system that is no match for someone like me, and now I am heading up the fire exit staircase on my way to Mason Manor's suite. I didn't expect to get the call to proceed for another few hours at least, but Sebastian has given the orders, and I'm paid to carry them out so here I am.

I've already been to the room once today to drop the warning under her door, and so I know exactly where I'm going, but I still move cautiously. Discretion is my middle name. Plus, I like it better than the real one my parents gave me.

I reach Mason's floor and move quicker now, not wanting to be interrupted by another guest leaving their rooms and seeing me walking past. It wouldn't be too much of a problem if they did. They would just presume I was another guest after all. But still, I'd prefer not to be seen just before I murder someone, even if I will make it look like a suicide.

I reach the door to Mason's suite and remove the black card that I carry everywhere with me. The one that gets me into any door that I need it to. Sebastian's hackers really are quite talented.

I raise the card towards the access panel on the suite door while keeping my other hand on the chloroform-soaked cloth in my trouser pocket. I believe Mason is expecting me and so there might be some shouting before I subdue her.

But this will put her to sleep quickly.

The light turns green on the panel, and I hear the suite door unlock. I walk in quickly and expect to see the occupant of the room either coming at me with some kind of makeshift hotel room weapon or cowering in the corner begging me not to hurt her. But I see neither.

The suite is clear.

I check the bathroom door, thinking that maybe she has locked herself in and that maybe I'm going to have to get creative in order to get inside, but it is unlocked. No sign of her in the bathroom either.

This is strange. She's definitely not here. The suite is big, but it's not that big. But according to Sebastian, who has been tracking her mobile phone, she was in her room just a few moments ago.

I do another quick sweep to make sure. Behind the expensive curtains. Under the king-size bed. Behind the screen of the marble shower and bathtub. But still no sign of her.

Nothing except the empty bowl of popcorn on the bed.

I'm just about to call Sebastian and get him to do another check on the location of Mason's mobile phone when I notice it.

The door beside the wardrobe. The one that leads to the next room and is sometimes used when two parties are staying in neighbouring suites to each other. It should be locked. If it's open, then I think I can guess where Mason is hiding.

I grip the handle quietly and bring the cloth out of my pocket.

Then I turn it. It unlocks.

Now I know where she is hiding.

So I open the door...

#SoLongOldFriend

Sebastian Sawyer

I'm halfway through listening to Amber telling me about her childhood when I notice a message flash up on my mobile.

I let her continue talking as I pick it up and read the words on the screen.

Done. Where next?

I feel a slight sense of loss for my oldest and dearest employee. Mason was a good influencer. She helped me grow my business into what it is today. But time moves on. Amber will take her place now.

I type out a reply to Colt but make sure to look up a couple of times at Amber to let her know that I'm still listening. But really, I am focusing on the set of instructions I am writing to my hitman.

Billericay. Emily's mum. I'll send you the address when you're on the way.

Then I put my phone back on the table and smile at Amber, showing her that she has my undivided attention again. She's chatty and has a quirky sense of humour. With her good looks and friendly personality, I can see that I am going to make quite the star out of her. Maybe not to the level of Mason Manor. But then again, why limit my ambition? Maybe Amber can be even bigger than Mason ever was.

The news of Mason's suicide won't start leaking out until tomorrow when a poor maid enters her suite and finds the body of the social media icon bobbing in the blood-stained waters of her bath, both wrists slashed and her eyes staring lifelessly open.

That will probably be around the same time that Emily lets her followers know that her beloved mother suffered a fall while she was home alone and broke her neck.

#RIPMrsBennett.

The news of those two tragic and untimely deaths will be enough to get my other three influencers to come to their senses and stop disobeying me. And Amber will already be way beyond her first ten thousand followers and ready to take up the mantle that Mason has left behind.

That will also be the same day that Florence Lee is admitted to hospital complaining of a fever, stomach pains and sickness but the doctors will have no idea to look for what's really causing her symptoms, so she will slip away too, leaving her millions of fans in mourning and unable to hear her daily urgings about voting for my rival candidate in the upcoming election.

Considering how badly the day started, things are looking like they are going to be just fine after all. Even Emily's little stunt has been turned on its head, and I've made something positive out of it. I've found my next influencer, and she was literally delivered to me on a plate.

'I feel like celebrating,' I say to Amber before she can get into her next story. 'Would you like a drink?'

I stand and pick up the bottle of whiskey and pour the dwindling contents of it into my glass. 'I can have room service bring you something up if you would like?'

Amber smiles and thinks about it for a second.

'How about champagne?' she asks, and then it's my turn to smile.

'Champagne sounds perfect,' I say, even though another bottle of whisky would be better.

As I empty the last of the bottle into my glass, I barely even notice that my headache still hasn't shifted despite all the pills. Nor do I notice too much the aching of my limbs and the small but growing pain in my stomach. I'm sure it's nothing a few more drinks and a roll around on the bed with Amber won't fix.

As I raise the glass to my newest employee and toast to an exciting future, I also make an internal toast to Mason, the original influencer in my company and still the best at the time of her death.

To Mason.

May she rest in peace.

#TriggerHappy

Mason Manor

I'm Mason Manor. I have black hair and brown eyes. I have 150 million followers on *PhoGlo*. And I have a dead man in my hotel suite.

His limbs are sprawled out in an unnatural position. His blood is staining the expensive carpet. And his eyes are still open, which is disturbing me a little. I'll be happier when he's been taken out of here, but unfortunately, this isn't just something room service can help me with.

I need the police for this one.

I shot him as soon as he came through the door to my second suite. He never saw it coming. Probably didn't even know what hit him.

It was a bullet from the handgun I carried in my handbag. The one I purchased in Rome and brought back on the private jet owned by a rich Italian businessman. There are many great things about flying on private planes, but the best one has to be the lack of security checks at either end.

Taking out the adjoining suite in a different name allowed me the element of surprise. I'm not sure why this dead guy or Sebastian thought I would just sit on my bed and wait for them to kill me, but clearly, they weren't anticipating what I had planned.

Of course, Sebastian doesn't know what has happened yet. He thinks I am dead and the man lying on the floor in front of me is on his way to Billericay to kill Emily's mum. But what he doesn't know can't hurt him.

There have been many benefits from working for Sebastian for so long. The money, the fame, the lifestyle. But top of that list has to be how much I ended up learning about his whole operation.

None of the other influencers ever got to spend much time with him once they were hired, other than a quick meeting after six months where he would instruct to kill for him.

But I saw him more often than that. I know I was his favourite because not only did he tell me once or twice after a couple of strong drinks but he actually proved it by inviting me to multiple parties that he was also attending and even letting me see his office once. And so, because of his friendliness, I learnt all about his business.

There's the team of 4 people he employs to hack into social media sites and improve our results online. From that, I was able to gather those same people were more than likely also hacking our phones and tracking our locations and so that was a useful thing to keep in mind for the future.

I also learnt about the army veteran he pays to visit any influencer who starts to disobey his orders. I presume that is the same army veteran that is now lying dead in front of me. I guess he told me about this man because he never thought he would have to send him after me.

I was always such a model employee. Sebastian never thought that I would never disobey him. *Until suddenly I did.*

I also learnt about why he does what he does. The business interests he has. The political figures he has helped get into power. The vast fortune he has amassed.

And then there was the fact that he allowed me to meet the other influencers and spend a little time with them. That was the most important thing of all. None of the influencers ever got to be in the same place together. But I was allowed to welcome them into the company when they joined.

Sebastian loved to hold me up as the shining example of what could be achieved with a little hard work and dedication. He would make me attend a meeting with them on their first day. That was how I met Emily.

He even let me attend the same parties as these influencers from time to time, just to check in on them and report back that everything was okay.

That was how Emily was able to tell me her plan.

Thank god for Emily. If it hadn't been for her courage and her desire to help us all then perhaps I would have been stuck working for Sebastian forever. But she had an idea, and that was all it took to get the ball rolling on Operation Freedom.

Or #SayByeToSawyer as I liked to think of it.

It was Emily that had helped me to feel so good about the future, but it was also Emily that was causing the knot of anxiety in my stomach right now. Because while I had executed my part of the plan perfectly, I still wasn't sure if she had been able to do the same at her end.

All I had to do was stop posting what Sebastian wanted me to yesterday and wait for the warnings to come. When it was time for my third and final one, I knew that a man was coming for me and so I had been prepared. Obviously, in a straight fight, I would have been no match for an army veteran, so I needed to catch him off guard. Leading him to an empty suite only to surprise him when he walked into the one next door was my way of doing that.

But how do I explain a dead body and a smoking gun in my bedroom?

I'd already sown the seeds for today's event several times over the past few weeks. I'd confided in a few friends at the various parties that I'd attended recently that I'd noticed a strange man following me. I'd told them that while nothing had happened to me yet, I was very concerned about what this person might do. I told them how I thought he was a crazy fan or obsessive supporter.

Basically, I told everybody that I had a stalker.

My social media post earlier today told everybody that "I can't do this anymore" and that I'm #scared and #alone and that there is #nofilterforfear.

To Sebastian, it would have just seemed like I was fearing for my life and trying to make him feel bad for sending a man to kill me. But to my friends at the parties who knew about my "stalker," it would have made perfect sense.

It will make sense that I bought a gun for protection and ultimately killed a man who had broken into my hotel suite to get to me. And the cherry on top was the last part of the plan, which had been to hide a camera in my original suite that would record when the man came in to kill me.

It would be a great piece of evidence to show the police and do the talking for me.

'Look, here was my stalker trying to get me. The guy broke into my hotel room with knives and chloroform cloth. What a freak. Thank god I was in my second suite when he arrived, and thank god that I was able to shoot him with the gun that I had bought for my own protection ever since I had first noticed him following me.'

And the best actress award goes to moi.

That was my part of the plan done. But that was only half of it. Emily had the other half, and her portion was even riskier than mine.

After a few moments, I hear a knock on the door. The police make themselves known to me, so I put my hands in the air. The gun is already a safe distance away from me on the other side of the suite. I've been crying fake tears for long enough to show how distressed I am. They step over the dead body as they enter the room. They tell me to put my hands behind my back. But then they ask me if I'm okay and I know they already think it was an act of self-defence. Those suspicions will be confirmed when they find what the man was carrying on him and watch the secret video footage of him creeping around my room.

As I'm led out of my suite and into the corridor, passing by dozens of startled guests who all heard the gunshot and are peering out of their rooms to try and get the gossip, I imagine what the headlines will be from today.

Social Media Star In Stalker Shoot out

PhoGlo Influencer Involved In Scary Suite Self-Defence

Mason Manor Murders Maniac Man

I'll get plenty of new fans after this. That's not really the point, but it doesn't hurt. Just because I don't work for Sebastian anymore doesn't mean I'm not a powerful influencer.

200 million followers here I come.

And there's nothing Sebastian can do about it now.

#WhatJustHappened

Amber Williams

When I found out I was being taken up to Sebastian Sawyer's hotel room, I was hoping for just one chance to show him that I could be his next influencer.

When he poured me the champagne and sat next to me on the bed, I was kind of hoping he would kiss me and tell me how beautiful I was.

And when we started having sex, I was hoping for it to be absolutely incredible, the kind of sex you read about in steamy books or perhaps watch in certain videos when you have the house to yourself.

What I hadn't been hoping for was to see him suddenly start struggling to breathe and fall onto the floor, clutching his stomach. I also hadn't been hoping to have to call reception and get them to send an ambulance to his room as quickly as possible. And I definitely hadn't been hoping for several paramedics and police officers to take over the room and seal it off as a potential crime scene.

'I don't know what happened,' I tell the policeman over and over again.

'Was it a heart attack?' I ask the paramedics over and over again.

And most of all, what does this mean for my influencing career?

I'm not getting any answers as I sit feeling fragile on the edge of the bed where Sebastian and I were lying together only an hour earlier. All I can do is look at the crazy scene around me.

I see the mixture of clothing on the floor, discarded randomly amidst the throes of a desperate passion.

I see the empty bottle of whiskey beside the almost empty bottle of champagne on the table.

And I see the paramedic zipping up the bag that contains the body of the man that was supposed to change my life.

#RememberMe

Emily Bennett

'You're not allowed to have your phone on in here. It messes with the machines.'

My mum laughs at me as she puts her mobile back in her pocket. It's not often that I'm the one telling someone to get off their phone, but rules are rules.

'I'm sure you've been sneaking a look at yours,' she says to me as she pulls her chair a little closer to my bed and tidies away one of the magazines that had fallen on to the floor.

'I've not actually. Well maybe a little bit,' I reply, smiling at her and taking another sip from my water bottle.

It's true. I've hardly been on my phone these past few days. Mainly because as I just told my dear old mother, it's against hospital rules to use them on the wards. But also because I haven't actually wanted to look at it. It's been quite nice to have a break from messaging and calling people. And it's definitely been nice to have a break from social media.

'How are you feeling?' my mum asks me for the sixth time since visiting hours started today.

'I'm fine,' I reply, even if that's not strictly true. I still feel rough from what my body has been through over the past twenty-four hours. But it's hardly surprising. There's a good reason that human beings aren't supposed to ingest antifreeze.

I wonder if I'm one of the first people to ever do it willingly.

Of course, I was never going to give Florence the poisoned can. She didn't deserve to die just so Sebastian could benefit. But I knew he had been watching on the live camera and if I wanted to make everything seem as real as possible, then one of us had to drink it. Rather me than her. At least I knew what I was getting myself into.

As soon as I'd given up Sebastian's address I'd left the show early and taken a taxi straight to the nearest hospital, where I immediately told them what I'd taken and that they had to act fast if they were going to save my life. I'd only taken a sip, but it was still enough to be deadly.

Nobody enjoys having their stomach pumped. I thought it only happened to youngsters who drank too much alcohol. But now I know it's also what they do for getting poison out of your body as quickly as possible.

Thankfully it had worked, and while I had a sore throat and a headache from a lack of sleep last night, I was going to be alright.

Which was more than could be said for Sebastian.

Unlike me, he hadn't known that he had been poisoned. That meant that by the time he was starting to show symptoms, it was already too late.

I believe his body was removed from his hotel room around 5 pm yesterday.

But bearing in mind how much of the tainted whiskey he had drunk, I was surprised he hadn't died sooner. I'd seen for myself how much he liked to drink when I'd first met him and so as soon as Mason had forewarned me about a meeting in six months' time in which he would give me instructions to murder someone then I had been preparing to be in his company again.

While I had expected the meeting to be in a public place, it had made it a lot easier when it turned out to be in his private hotel room. All I had to do was send Sebastian to get me a glass of water from the bathroom while I put four drops of my own supply of antifreeze into his whiskey bottle, and the damage was done.

I knew he'd have at least one glass while he watched me live on *The Florence Lee Show*, no doubt toasting to what he thought would be her imminent demise. But it was only while I was sitting there in the studio that I had the idea to give out his room number to all the people listening.

I thought there might be one or two people in the area that would try and get to see him if I told them he could make them rich and famous like me and so I hoped he might end up getting stuck in his room a little while longer and take to drinking some more of the hazardous spirit.

But I had never envisioned the sheer numbers of people that had turned up at his hotel and tried to get to him. In the end, he had been practically forced to barricade himself in, and I imagine most of the bottle was consumed while he did so.

One thing I hadn't accounted for was him sending a stranger up to his room and trying to use her as a ploy in his bid to get Mason to follow his orders. That was unpredictable, and I'm just relieved that the poor girl didn't drink any of the poison herself. Then again, the chances of a young woman drinking neat whiskey in the middle of the afternoon are pretty small, I guess.

Especially when the bottle belonged to an alcoholic who doesn't share much.

With Sebastian out of the picture in Manchester, and Mason taking care of his hitman down in London, me, her, and the six other influencers that had been living under a cloud of fear for so long were now suddenly free.

What about Sebastian's merry band of computer hackers? Well, they were stopped in their tracks as soon as Mason told the LAPD the location of Sebastian's office. That meant no more reading our personal messages. No more monitoring employee locations. And no more super hashtags that were guaranteed to make your profile grow at the speed of light, which was okay because we knew what they were already.

Now that me and the other influencers were free, we could use our powers for good. That meant only advertising products and businesses that were genuinely beneficial to audiences. It meant only campaigning for the release of prisoners that had actually suffered a miscarriage of justice. And it also meant only backing the honest, respectable politicians that really deserved to win their election campaigns. *So far, we haven't come across any of them yet.*

There was one more rule, and it was perhaps the most important one. There would be no be killing. There'd been too much of that already.

Now I can spend more time raising funds for my dad's charity instead of keeping Sebastian satisfied. Mason is able to spend more time back in England with her family and get some use out of her frankly ridiculous mansion. And my mum's life isn't at risk anymore.

Not that I've told her it ever was.

'Do you feel up to a walk?' she asks me as if she somehow knew I was thinking about her.

'You know what? I think I do,' I say, pushing myself up off the bed and sliding my feet into the pair of slippers that I've had for years but still fit me just as well as ever.

As we pass through the ward and outside into the gardens of the hospital, I see how beautiful a day it actually is and think it might be a good time to update my *PhoGlo* account for the first time in a while.

I take my phone out of my dressing gown and snap a photo of the stunning sycamore tree with the blue skies of Manchester in the background.

I caption it **New beginnings** and add a couple of generic hashtags like #summer #cooltree #getwellsoon.

Then I'm just about to share it when I remember that I could also use the powerful, top-secret hashtags that me and the other influencers at Sebastian's company were told to use for so long. Of course, I had memorised them all, and it wouldn't do my follower count any harm that's for sure. I have over 1.5 million now, but a girl can always use more.

I add the hashtags to my message then it's finally ready to go. This post is going to be great. The photo is stunning. The caption is motivational. And the hashtags are incredible.

What are these hashtags I hear you ask?

I could tell you.

But then I'd have to kill you.

#Epilogue

Ivan Ilghiz

Sebastian Sawyer was always clear with the instructions he gave me.

He told me where to move his money and when. He told me which markets he wanted to move into and how much of his wealth to have invested at any one time. And he told me if anything should ever happen to him at the hands of an enemy than I should avenge his death and murder those who murdered him. Unfortunately for him, his employees became his enemies.

But I will follow his instructions as always, so his death will be avenged.

Emily Bennett and Mason Manor will pay for killing my boss.

Emily and Mason are going to die.

INFLUENCER

Part two of the Influencing Trilogy...

Haters. Trolls. *Murderers.*

Emily Bennett is living the dream. Now a fully-fledged social media superstar, and free from Sebastian's clutches, she is finally able to do all the things she fantasised about before she was famous. Pay off her mum's mortgage. Start a charity in memory of her dad. And travel the world partying with her idols. Life couldn't be any better.

But while Emily has it all, one of Sebastian's former business associates is watching her. Following the orders of his dead business partner, Ivan Ilghiz now wants revenge. And he's hired just the right person to get it, someone that loves to kill just as much as Emily loves to update her PhoGlo account. Emily doesn't know it yet, but if she is going to stay alive, then she is going to have to become the one thing that every celebrity fears...
Anonymous.

We all have our haters.
But not all of them are as deadly as this.

Influencer is available now on Amazon in paperback and in Kindle Unlimited

Or turn the page for the first chapter...

Your Presence Is Requested At The Social Media Event Of The Year!

Dear Emily Bennett

You are cordially invited to the 21st birthday celebrations of social media star Zack Reynolds on the 1st August 2020.

The party will be an all-day event, onboard Zack's luxurious yacht, The Social Star.

Setting sail from Miami, the party will begin as the yacht glides through the Straits of Florida towards Bimini, a tropical island in The Bahamas.

As you arrive on shore, you will be greeted with a champagne reception and entertainment courtesy of several natives of the island, who will dance with you as you join them on the golden sands.

A sizzling BBQ will be served while the sun sets, and as the night falls in paradise, you will be witness to a spectacular fireworks display.

From there, the party will continue back aboard the yacht, and as you sail back to Miami, you will be treated to a live set from one of the world's premier DJ's.

As you can tell, it is going to be the must-attend social event of the year. Anybody who is anybody is going to be there, and I hope you will be there too.

RSVP to my agent Tommy ASAP at Tommy#TurnItUp@gmail.com

Bring your best hashtags, filters and selfie faces because this event is going to break the internet!

#PartyOfTheYear #Zacks21 #YachtLife

See you onboard,

Zack

#Boom

Anna Akari

It's easy to see why so many people think The Bahama's are the most beautiful islands in the world. There's the sand that is so white you could almost mistake it for snow if it wasn't for the fact that it was burning hot from the scorching sun overhead. There's the sea that is so clear that anyone who swims in it can see everything that is moving through the water beneath them. And there's the array of palm trees here, their curved trunks and bright green branches leaning over the beaches as if they are watching over all the sunbathers basking on the shores beneath them.

It's paradise. It's picture-perfect.

But to me, it's *borrrring.*

I'm not here to swim, or snorkel, or sunbathe. I don't care about pretty palm trees or beautiful blue skies. I hate tourists, I despise hotels and most of all I really can't stand the heat.

So what am I doing here on a tropical island surrounded by tourists, hotels and sea turtles?

I'm here on business. I wouldn't set foot in a place like this if I weren't being paid for it. But $3million is enough to get me to come here. I can always make an exception for that kind of money.

Although I still can't wait to get out of here.

Thankfully I don't have much longer to wait. In about five minutes' time, I will be boarding the private plane that will take me off this godforsaken patch of land in the middle of the ocean and fly me back home to my native Japan. But before I can do that, I need to finish the task that I came here to do and so with that in mind, I take my mobile phone out of my pocket and open up my favourite app.

But I'm not checking my notifications or updating my status. Unlike the large group of people who were partying on this island a few moments ago, I am not addicted to *PhoGlo*. In fact, I don't have any social media accounts. I'm in that rare group of people on the planet of whom you still can't find a photo online. Nobody knows who I am these days.

Not even the woman who gave birth to me.

As the app opens on my phone, I look out at the sea and notice how the moonlight is shimmering across its waves. For many tourists, this would be a good place to have a nightcap and enjoy the peace and quiet before retiring to their hotel rooms and sleeping in their overpriced, air-conditioned beds. But like I said, I'm not a tourist, so I'm not sitting here for a pleasant view or simply for somewhere to enjoy a beverage or two.

I'm sitting here so I can watch 200 people die in one minute's time.

I look back down to my phone and at the information on my screen. It tells me that the device I planted is currently 700ft away from me, just off the coast of the island I am sitting on. But I already know this because I can see the yacht from here and I watched it depart a few moments ago.

I'm still close enough to it that I can hear the loud dance music pumping out from inside, although thankfully I'm far enough away to not be injured when it explodes into a million pieces in forty-five seconds' time.

The app is open, and my phone screen gives me the option of pressing either a red or green button. If I press the red button, then the device on the yacht that is slowly moving away from me will be disabled, and everyone currently onboard will get to live. But if I press the green button, then the device will detonate, and every single person onboard will die in a blazing inferno.

It's the green button that I will be pressing in thirty seconds' time.

And I can't wait.

It almost annoys me that there is a red button on the app at all. It's not as if I'm going to change my mind at the last second and suddenly decide to let all these people live. That's not what I'm being paid for.

That won't help me get $3million in my bank account by the end of the day.

I'm a ruthless assassin. Pressing the green button is how I make money. The red button is only for quitters who shouldn't be in this business in the first place.

And they are the ones who end up dead themselves because they didn't complete their task.

But I always complete my tasks. I have a 100% success rate. It's why I'm so in demand.

I've killed 241 people so far in my career, and while I don't usually do bulk assignments, I will be adding another 200 people to that list in just fifteen' seconds time.

My sterling reputation is the reason why my current employer hired me and offered me the huge bounty. He is a Russian man, and even though he didn't tell me his name when he made contact with me, I have my ways of finding it.

He is called Ivan Ilghiz, and for some reason, he wants eight social media influencers dead. He gave me a list of their names.

Mason Manor.

Rochelle Turner.

Stella Robinson.

Harriet Harper.

Trey Squire.

Nikkie Morris.

Molly Chan.

Emily Bennett.

Of course, I hadn't heard of a single one of them, but I was more than happy to kill them, especially when he told me how much he was willing to pay me.

Armed with the list of names, I had begun to make my plans to assassinate each of them individually. It would have been a little time consuming to traverse the globe on the trail of that many different influencers, but it was something I was willing to do for millions of dollars.

But when I had started looking into each of the targets on my list, which annoyingly meant I had to download a stupid app called *PhoGlo*, I had noticed that every single one of them was planning on attending the exact same birthday party on the exact same day.

The party was on a yacht that was scheduled to sail between Miami and Bimini, and every single person on my list would be onboard at the same time. So then I got creative and told Ivan that not only would I be able to kill every single one of the people he wanted me to, but that I could do it for him in one fell swoop.

It's hard to tell how excited somebody is when you are only talking to them via encrypted online messages, but I got the distinct impression that he rather enjoyed my little plan. Not only would it result in the death of every person on his list, but the fact that so many other people would die along with them would mean that nobody would be able to pick out any one person as the specific target.

With the go-ahead from Ivan, I put my scheme into action. Stage one consisted of getting myself on board the yacht disguised as a waitress and leaving my bomb in a box that was disguised as a present for the birthday-boy yacht owner.

I made sure that everybody on my hit list was onboard when the yacht left Miami this morning, and I checked again when the same yacht left The Bahamas a few minutes ago.

All the people who Ivan wants dead are on board. Okay so there are also several other 'innocent' people on the yacht that weren't on his list but sometimes that is just the price of doing business.

And speaking of business, it's almost time.

There was a large firework display on this beach about half an hour ago, but I have a feeling that the light show I am about to witness will be a lot more spectacular than that.

Five...

Four...

Three...

Two...

One...

My finger taps the green button, just as easily as if it were liking a cat video or sharing a selfie.

And just like that, the mega yacht gliding through the smooth seas in front of me is obliterated.

I see the fireball erupting into the dark sky out at sea first. The glow from the flames briefly illuminates the shore, and I can spot several tourists who were lying on the sand and enjoying a romantic evening suddenly jump to their feet and begin shouting for help.

Then I hear the loud boom that accompanies the explosion and feel a tingling sensation deep within my soul as the shockwaves from the blast rush over me.

I close the app and put my phone away. My work here is done. Everybody on the list is dead.

PhoGlo has just lost all of its stars.

As I take a long refreshing sip of my dry martini and watch the yacht burning on the sea, I suddenly see what all the fuss is about regarding this part of the world.

It actually is a nice place to visit after all.

Free Influence Prequel

If you would like to read *Influence Me,* a short prequel story about the day that Sebastian discovered Mason on *PhoGlo* then click the link below:

https://dl.bookfunnel.com/sw8mx7dtyx

Also By Daniel Hurst

The bestselling psychological thriller:

TIL DEATH DO US PART

What if your husband was your worst enemy?

Megan thinks that she has the perfect husband and the perfect life. Craig works all day so that she doesn't have to, leaving her free to relax in their beautiful and secluded country home. But when she starts to long for friends and purpose again, Megan applies for a job in London, much to her husband's disappointment. She thinks he is upset because she is unhappy. But she has no idea.

When Megan secretly attends an interview and meets a recruiter for a drink, Craig decides it is time to act. Locking her away in their home, Megan realises that her husband never had her best interests at heart. Worse, they didn't meet by accident. Craig has been planning it all from the start.

As Megan is kept shut away from the world with only somebody else's diary for company, she starts to uncover the lies, the secrets, and the fact that she isn't actually Craig's first wife after all...

Available now on Amazon in paperback and in Kindle Unlimited

Read on for the first two chapters...

1

MEGAN

The thought of getting out of bed to do nothing all day might appeal to some people, but it's not all it's cracked up to be. I've never considered myself to be a lazy person, yet that seems to be what I've become. How did this happen?

Three words.

I got married.

I don't regret saying 'I Do' to my husband, Craig, but I do regret saying 'I quit' to the only boss I've ever had before. That's because while I have a sparkling ring on my finger, a large home in the country and a loving husband who earns a fortune in the city, I don't have much else.

No children. No friends. No job.

The no children situation is okay because both Craig and I agreed not to have kids before we married. He said he'd never wanted them, and I was happy to say the same, having always doubted I'd be able to pull off motherhood without going insane. My lack of friends is a shame but is unfortunately just what happens when you buy a house at the opposite end of the country from where you were born. But the job situation...

Now that is something that I would like to change.

Craig is the General Manager at the London Branch of a Swiss bank, so money is not an issue for us. His base salary is staggering enough before you factor in the end of year bonuses, which are frankly obscene, but are still gratefully accepted. But the financial security that my husband's job has given us has meant that it was deemed unnecessary for me to work as soon as we were married. Being told at the age of twenty-nine that you could retire and put your feet up might sound like a dream come true to most people, and it certainly was to me when I heard Craig say it, but now I'm thirty-two, and I'm not so sure.

Yes, I have money, but it's my husband's money, not mine. I haven't earned a penny of it, and while he is happy for me to spend a chunk of it each month on nice things for myself and the house, even that's starting to grow old.

I want to make my own money.

I want to have a purpose and a profession.

Most of all, I want to have a reason to get out of bed in the morning.

The sound of Craig's electric toothbrush in our en-suite bathroom is like a buzz saw to my fuddled brain right now. But I'm not tired. I'm the opposite. I sleep too much. Through until noon some days. But not today.

Today I am determined to get up and make the most of all my free time.

Craig will leave the house in about twenty minutes when he has put on one of his expensive suits and chomped down a Granola bar. He will close the front door behind him at 6:10 am before getting in his Porsche and driving to our nearest train station, which is fifteen minutes away, or ten if he opens up the engine on the quiet country roads. I've told him he's not to speed, but boys will be boys. Besides, it's not as if there is ever anybody else out on the road at this time.

We really are in the middle of nowhere.

With Craig out of the house all day, I will be alone again. But instead of browsing retail websites and filling my virtual shopping basket with things that I don't need, I am going to do something productive today.

I am going to look for a job.

It's hardly an earth-shattering thing to do, but I haven't worked for three years, and the thought of putting my CV out there is enough to give me butterflies. But that's not the only thing that I'm anxious about.

I'm not sure how Craig will take the news about me wanting to go back to work.

The toothbrush is turned off, the toilet is flushed, and finally, the bathroom door opens, and I get my first glimpse of my handsome husband today. He's always been a morning person, and his smart appearance is evidence of that. The clock beside the bed is showing 06:06, but my man is up and ready to take on the world, which is more than can be said for me, as I lie beneath the duvet suffering from a bad case of what can only be called 'bed-head.'

"Oh, you're awake," Craig says, obviously surprised to see my eyes open and watching him from across the spacious bedroom. "Sorry, I thought I was quiet."

"That's okay, I want to get an early start today," I tell him, knowing full well he will be intrigued enough to ask why I need such a thing, unless he presumes that there is a sale about to start on one of my favourite retail websites.

"What for?" he asks, putting on his tie and growing more dashing by the minute.

"I was thinking about seeing if there are any good jobs available," I say, nervous to see what the response will be. It's not that he wouldn't want me to work. It's just that he might not understand why I would feel the need to.

"A job?" he replies, pausing as he pulls on his suit jacket. I'd expected him to be surprised. Maybe it's a silly idea.

"I didn't know you wanted to get back into work," he says, now fully dressed and ready to leave. "I thought you were happy not having to go to an office every day."

"I was. I mean, I am. It's just..."

I pause, not wanting to get into it just before he's about to walk out the door. I don't want to make him late. Then he definitely will be speeding.

"It was just an idea," I say, downplaying it a little. "We can talk about it tonight."

Craig smiles and moves towards the bed, leaning over me and kissing me on my forehead. "Whatever you want, darling."

Then he heads for the door, leaving my heart aching a little at the thought of not seeing him until he returns this evening.

"Have a good day!" I call after him as he leaves, his footsteps thudding down the staircase before I hear the rattling of his car keys from the hallway below.

"See you tonight, love," he calls up, before opening the door.

For a second, I can hear the sounds of the birds singing in the trees outside, the fields around our home filled with the sounds of nature as another day dawns in our rural retreat.

Then the door slams and there is nothing but silence.

Home alone.

As per usual.

2

CRAIG

I can't believe Megan is thinking about getting a job. I thought she was happy with our arrangement. I make the money, so she doesn't have to. I'm the breadwinner, and she keeps the home fires burning. I go to work. She stays in the house.

That's how it's always been since we got married. It's how I want it and I thought it was how she wanted it too. But I guess I was wrong. Something has changed, and now she is talking about getting a job.

We'll see about that.

Opening the driver's side door on the black Porsche parked outside the house, I hop inside my expensive vehicle and feel the familiar thrill of knowing that I will soon be powering it through the quiet country lanes towards the train station. As I fire up the engine and put the car into reverse, I don't even need to glance at the time on the dashboard because I know exactly what it will be. 06:15. On the dot. I leave at the same time every day, and I arrive home at the same time every day. I like my life to have structure and routine and as few surprises as possible, which is why Megan's admission this morning has me so riled up.

Pushing my foot down on the accelerator pedal, I guide the beast at my fingertips down the quiet road, past the farmer's field opposite my house and in the direction of the small train station where I will catch the 06:32 service into Central London. But my mind isn't on the twists and turns of the route ahead. It's on Megan and her desire to find herself back in gainful employment again.

Most women would be happy if their husband earned a fortune that allowed them to not have to commute every day to a job they loathed. How many people can say they got to retire at the age of twenty-nine because they had somebody willing to take care of them and allow them to enjoy their life, instead of having to spend the best years of it toiling away behind a desk or standing over a photocopier?

I know all about hard work, having left university with a first-class degree and gone into the working world, beginning as a Teller on the cashier desk in a branch of a Swiss bank in Manchester. With my dedication to the role and my willingness to learn, it didn't take me long to become the Head Teller, and after some time spent working abroad in Head Office, I was on the fast-track to the senior level. I was Head of Retail by my late-twenties and head-hunted by the London branch to become the UK General Manager before thirty.

Fast forward three years, and here I am, just thirty-two and already at the top of the food chain in my place of work. Not only that, but I am also the proud owner of a seven-figure home in the Berkshire countryside and a breath-taking black supercar that makes me purr almost as much as the engine does. I have loyal friendships, made in both my childhood and adult life, as well as many hobbies, including football, badminton and squash. And to top it all off, I am married to Megan, the beautiful brunette who caught my eye on a night out in Manchester.

The only thing an outside observer would think I was missing would be children, but that's where they would be wrong. I don't want kids, and I made sure my future wife didn't want them too. Megan is an easy woman to persuade and regardless of whether she did want them or not, I was able to sway her to my viewpoint, and now she believes that children are as unnecessary for a happy life as I do. That means that there isn't anything that I want right now. I have it all, and everything is how I planned it to be.

Until Megan told me she was going to look for a job.

It's not that I don't appreciate my wife's desire to earn her keep and do something more productive with her days than blow a big chunk of my wages on shoes, handbags or another awful cushion for the sofa. It's just that I like to apply the same structure and routine in my life to that of my darling wife and that means knowing exactly where she is and what she is doing at all times of the day.

There's a good reason why I made sure to buy a house in the middle of nowhere, a long way from anybody, never mind anybody that Megan might have known before meeting me. It's because I want to keep her at home, not under lock and key, but far enough from anyone else to prevent them from threatening the perfect control I have over my spouse's life.

Megan thinks I told her to retire because I love her and want her to enjoy her life. In truth, it was because she is easier to manage when she is stuck at home all day and utterly dependent on me. But the fact that she wants a job threatens not just the routine I have put in place for her but also the large degree of reliance she has on me.

Her own job would mean her own wage and her own disposable income. It would mean new people in her life and new social events in her diary. Most of all, it would mean she isn't totally and utterly under my thumb.

Not that Megan realises that. She thinks I'm the perfect husband and that she still exercises her own free will in our relationship. How cute. She has no idea.

That is the way that I will keep it.

But the unexpected development this morning means I have some thinking to do as I speed on towards the train station, going much faster than I should be on these roads. Megan would hate it if she knew I was going this fast. Then again, she would hate a lot of things about me if she knew them.

But she doesn't.

I intend to keep it that way.

About The Author

Daniel Hurst has his online home at
www.danielhurstbooks.com

You can connect with Daniel on Facebook at
www.facebook.com/danielhurstbooks and on Instagram
at @danielhurstbooks

He is always happy to receive emails from readers at
daniel@danielhurstbooks.com

Books By Daniel Hurst

THE 20 MINUTES SERIES (in order)

20 MINUTES ON THE TUBE
20 MINUTES LATER
20 MINUTES IN THE PARK
20 MINUTES ON HOLIDAY
20 MINUTES BY THE THAMES
20 MINUTES AT HALLOWEEN
20 MINUTES AROUND THE BONFIRE
20 MINUTES BEFORE CHRISTMAS

THE INFLUENCING TRILOGY (in order)

INFLUENCE
INFLUENCER
INFLUENCED

STANDALONE PSYCHOLOGICAL THRILLERS

TIL DEATH DO US PART

Made in the USA
Las Vegas, NV
06 February 2025